Deadly Sting:

A Deacon Bishop Mystery

Michael Paulson

BooksForABuck.com

June 2009

Deadly Sting: A Deacon Bishop Mystery

Michael Paulson

BooksForABuck.com

June 2009

ISBN: 978-1-60215-100-0

ONE

"I've been trying to phone you for two goddamn days, Bishop!"

I knew him as Peterson Barrows—recently a judge with Travis County Court. It was Saturday afternoon and we were in my office. I was leaning back in my desk chair, wishing I was anywhere else. He was leaning over the desk, railing as if God Almighty had called him to signify.

"I got your messages, Mr. Barrows," I said, when he paused to take a breath. "And if you will check with your secretary she will confirm that I did return your call."

For nearly two decades, Barrows spent most of his time on the Bench either accepting bribes, or offering them. However recent events changed his fortunes. Apparently some vindictive P. I. who shall remain nameless (me), instigated a corruption investigation against Judge Barrows. This resulted in his resignation to avoid facing the public humiliation of impeachment.

"Jesus Christ, Bishop!" He flapped both flabby arms. "If you're going to be in business, get a Goddamn receptionist!"

As a judge, Barrows had been just as pretentious. In fact during his tenure he insisted that all who addressed to him did so by his title, rather than simply his name. Peterson Barrows liked to give the impression that he was the only living judge in all of Texas.

I made a mock beseeching gesture. "I can't find one who'll work for love, Mr. Barrows."

"I had to cancel appointments to come downtown," he continued to bluster. "My clients are important people, Bishop. Time is money for them."

The pompous former-judge stood about five feet three inches tall, and looked nearly as wide. To give his baldness that gently carpeted appearance he combed his greasy, gray mop forward from the last point of growth, near the back of his oddly peaked head. On the plus side, his blue suit looked expensive, as did the crimson bow-tie embracing the goiterous flesh between his silk shirt's collar-points. He wore a new, black belt, its buckle glinting like real gold. The creases in his trousers stood up like machete-blades sharp enough to cut a swathe through any jungle. Barrows's shoes were shiny and black. They were the expensive, handmade kind men in my income-bracket can only dream about. Both of his socks matched, albeit in red argyle. I gave him seven out of ten points for his choice in apparel. I docked two points for the argyles, and one for his open zipper.

"Time is money for me, too, Mr. Barrows." My patience had faded.

I got up and opened the window behind my desk. A honeybee flew in as I settled back into my chair. It buzzed the top of Barrows's head as if the sweet stink anointing the lawyer's mop might be suitable for honey-making.

Irritated by the insect's impudence, the lawyer took a swing at it.

The bee was not impressed and dodged Barrows's attack with little effort.

Then, after making another buzzing circle, it casually flew up to the ceiling and perched.

Peterson Barrows's fist crashed on the desktop with a resounding thwack. "I'm talking *real* money, Bishop!"

His ongoing pretentiousness irritated me to the point that I blew smoke at Barrows, when he tilted closer. I was hoping he would take the hint and leave. Instead, *'The Judge'* remained seated, coughing and fanning the air between us with one pink paw as if I was someone from whose company he could not bear to depart.

"Can't you put that filthy thing out?" he sputtered.

I blew more smoke into his face before chipping, "Peterson Barrows, Esquire. How you must've hated leaving the Bench for a career chasing ambulances, and grieving widows. What happened? Did somebody catch you with your hands full of mob-money, and tell the news-services?"

He thrust an accusing finger at me. "I don't have to take unfounded accusations from the likes of you!"

"In my office you take what I dish out, Barrows." I enjoyed my success at bringing a purplish glow to his sallow jowls. "Don't let my bad manners keep you from appointments elsewhere."

His fat jaws snapped shut with a resounding crack, like a bulldog's on a newfound-bone. Then with a guttural roar he sprang his great bulk from the chair like a fat monkey leaping from a limb.

I simply stared at him and, after a moment of indecision, Barrows settled back into the chair he overflowed, growling, and cursing under his breath.

"You should see a doctor," I suggested. "Maybe he can do something about your blood pressure. Right now your face matches your tie."

"Dammit, Bishop! I'm not asking you to investigate the disappearance of Jimmy Hoffa."

"That's the problem, Mr. Barrows," I snorted. "If you were, I'd be interested. I'm pretty sure I know where the bastard is buried."

The lawyer flushed to the ears. Spittle dribbled from one corner of his wide mouth as he choked for control. "It's an easy goddamn job! It requires three simple tasks. First, you meet flight 267 at Austin airport. It arrives at eleven o'clock, this Friday. Second, you follow one of its passengers until she stops for the night. Third, you telephone my office and leave a message as to where that passenger is staying." His stubby arms splayed, then. "That's it. How much simpler does it have to get, for Christ's sake?"

I gave him more smoke. "I'm still not interested. But I'll be happy to recommend somebody."

He slapped one fat palm upon the desktop with an echoing crack. "Dammit! I want you to do it!"

"I'm already dancing, Mr. Barrows."

The lawyer jerked upright, his thick, gray brows crowding the bridge of his big nose. "What in hell does that mean?"

"You picked a bad time to cut in."

"Jesus Christ, Bishop! Talk English!" Barrows's lips pinched together with impatient irritation.

"I've got a case, Mr. Barrows. You'll have to find someone else." I was low on cash and unaccompanied by prospects. But who am I to pass up a chance to tell a small lie in order to irritate a man I grossly disliked?

Peterson Barrows slumped against the back of the chair. "Jesus Christ on a fucking crutch! We're talking about one goddamn night's work! It requires that you only…"

"No need to rehash that point, Mr. Barrows," I interrupted. "It changes nothing."

"I don't have time to check out another man, Bishop!" Barrows eyed me like a hungry Bass pursuing a retreating Perch. "Look. I'll pay double your rate."

I quickly snuffed out my cigarette in the ashtray on the desk, and grinned at him. Never let it be said that Deacon Bishop allowed greed to become an uncommon consort during dealings with clients of low repute. Particularly, if those consorts are foolish enough to pay twice what the job is worth.

"Sounds like we can do business, Mr. Barrows." I dragged a yellow notepad from the desk's center drawer and took out a pen. "What's the subject's name?"

He withdrew a brown banker's envelope from inside his expensive suit, and tossed it onto the desktop. Then he pulled out a fat black wallet and snared five one-hundred-dollar bills from its glutted interior.

"Everything you need to know is in that," he declared regally, dropping the cash on top of the envelope. "I want two things clear, Bishop: She's not to know she's being followed. And nobody—and I mean nobody—is to know you're working for me."

"As far as the latter is concerned nothing would please me more."

I set aside the cash and opened the envelope. It contained a check made out to me in the amount of $500 and a snapshot of a redhead—the type of woman dirty old men like me dream about on cold, rainy nights. She was about twenty-five, possibly a model. She had a high freckled forehead, playful green eyes, prominent cheekbones, delicate nostrils, and a provocative mouth. I let my lusty imagination run rampant for a moment, considering the possibilities of her lipstick getting smeared on my favorite body-part.

He returned the wallet to its keep. "She already suspects she's being watched, so stay sharp."

"After seeing her I have to admit I lied about what pleases me most, Mr. Barrows. I'll take an eight-by-ten glossy of her on a bearskin rung with several hundred wallet-sized in a variety of naughty poses. I'll use the little ones to paper the ceiling above my bed."

A flash of malevolent fury twisted the former judge's countenance. "Get your mind out of the gutter, and turn it over."

Reluctantly, I did so. A handwritten description glared back at me: height, weight, hair-color, skin-tone, hobbies, education (which included mention of a Ph.D. in Entomology and an M.D.), food preferences—everything except her name.

"I'd never have pegged her for an egghead who likes bugs and gives shots." I looked up at him.

"Just follow her, dammit!" He squared his shoulders with renewed contempt.

I picked up the cash and fondled it, trying to control my temper with homespun common sense. When that failed, I did a mental toss of the dice. Heads, I would reach across the table and slam-shut his lights. Tails, I would keep the money. Lucky for Barrows I got tails—which promptly refocused me on her and that mouth of hers.

"A name would help, Mr. Barrows."

He stood up sharply. "What in hell for?"

"If nothing else, I'll have to call her something when we communicate," I casually replied.

The lawyer's gimlet eyes shrank to pinpoints. "Just refer to her as Miss X."

I had an impulse to grab Barrows by his fat neck and make him eat the photo. But a second toss of the mystical dice gave me tails again—and more fantasies about her. So I pasted a grin upon my puss and pocketed the cash.

"How can I reach you?" I asked

He took a business card from his vest pocket and tossed it upon the desk.

I picked it up. The card was ivory in color, imprinted with his name, office-address, and telephone number. The typeface was some sort of fancy script. The ink was gold-colored. The paper smelled of chocolate.

"My secretary's name is Natalie Parker," he declared. "If you need anything contact her."

"In case something unexpected happens, Mr. Barrows…"

Between their curtains of fat, Barrows's eyes quivered with disdain, as if they beheld me as a pornographic photo in a silver frame. "Look! It's a simple Goddamn job…"

His voice caught in his throat as the honeybee dropped from the ceiling with a vengeance. This time it buzzed directly to the end of the lawyer's bulbous proboscis, and buried its stinger.

Barrows let out a scream. Then he slapped his throbbing nose with both hands, trying to drive the bee away. The bee hit the floor amidst an outflow of blood from both of Barrows's nostrils, the crimson flood spewing across his face and clothing.

"I'll be in touch regarding Miss X, Mr. Barrows," I told him, smiling at the lawyer's misery. "But were I you, I'd do something about your blood pressure. You damn near exploded just now."

I went home, fixed a tuna sandwich for supper, and then went to bed. I was not tired—I intended to spend the night in a dream where I chased a redhead who wasn't supposed to know she was being followed.

TWO

Late Friday evening, I changed into my powder-blue pinstripe, carefully selected my cleanest paisley tie, put on my least-wrinkled shirt, stepped into my favorite black brogues and went out to the Buick.

By 11:15 I was at Austin International Airport. I was also being questioned by Airport-Security concerning the Mauser holstered beneath my arm. I had attempted to pass through their metal detector on my way to the passenger de-embarkation area without disclosing my favorite ornament. As gritty as the questioning pair tried to get about the penalties for violating Federal rules and regulations concerning handguns, I managed to retain my weapon-of-choice as well as my freedom. I merely gave them a peek at my gun-permit, P.I. license, social security card and driving license—followed by a short spiel concerning my being the bodyguard of an arriving Washington dignitary whose name I could not divulge.

After a brief discussion, where they speculated as to whom that dignitary might be, I was waved past the checkpoint. By then I was late for Flight 267's arrival.

I hurriedly followed the signs until I reached the area where the plane was scheduled to arrive. Much to my relief, the flight was also late. Its point of appearance was a secluded spot at the very end of the air terminal. In fact it was the farthest point one could get without leaving the terminal building. While this rarely used location offered few amenities, but it did provide a view of the main runway. So I went over to the row of windows overlooking the blue lights marking the moonlit landing strip. There I entertained myself by making faces in the glass while concocting methods whereby I could smoke without being seen.

Thirty minutes later, the tires of a massive jet hit the tarmac with a smoking screech. A droning male voice officially announced Flight 267's delayed arrival. I remained at my point of vigilance until I saw the jet taxi up to the exit ramp. Then I strode into one of the alcoves that provide seating for passengers intending to board the next departing flight. There I clipped fingernails, adjusted belt, tied and retied shoes while pretending to ignore the disembarking passengers.

The redhead was as easy to spot as a priest offering to demonstrate safe-sex practices in a nunnery. Her hair was the shade of red that glints in the sunlight with gold strands. There were a few more freckles on her finely chiseled nose than the photo had disclosed—but they did little to discredit her beauty. She wore a denim shirt, tight jeans and western boots, each item new. A dark, leather handbag hung from one of her shoulders. It also looked new. A thin, gold necklace bearing an equally thin cross dangled from around her neck. She stood about five feet seven inches tall and was fully equipped with all the accessories a dirty old man like me preferred.

The blue cloth covering her lower limbs was skintight. This augmented the visual appeal of her full hips and meaty thighs. The latter were the kind that locked out all sounds when a man was hard at work with his favorite form of yodeling.

The redhead's walk was also alluring. Her buttocks shifted back and forth like a pair of well-oiled pistons. From the way her muscles flexed within their denim casing, I knew she would be worth talking to bed. There was, however, some doubt in my mind as to whether I would survive such an experience.

Her breasts were full and firm. They bounced slightly with each movement, like a pair of ripe Cuban pineapples bumping against the confines of a plastic grocery-bag. I tried not to drool as she swayed past. But the way the synchronized interaction of her upper and lower regions kept dragging my tongue from my mouth made that not only impossible, I had all I could do to keep from tripping on it.

A few dozen passengers back, I fell into line. Even at that distance, my dirty mind ran amuck. Each jiggle and jump of her swaying buttocks made me feel very, very young and increasingly ready to prove it. I tried to control my wanton mood, but without success. Whoever she was, she was doubtlessly worth any price a man had to pay.

Ten minutes later, we were moving past the luggage carousels. Her stride did not even slow at the bang and screech of suitcases being offloaded onto conveyers. I assumed the redhead either traveled without baggage or her suitcases never made it on the plane from the last point of departure. In any event, she left the terminal and quickened her steps toward the line of taxies at the curb.

I followed, blissfully dreaming of silk sheets, passionate gasps mingled with the scent of rose-oil and the clink of handcuffs. All it would take for me to make my fantasy come true was my special tact with the opposite sex coupled by lots, and lots of money.

As the redhead made for the first taxi in line, I lagged back, meandering casually toward the second. But in mid-stride she stopped and pulled out a cellular phone. I came to an immediate halt, squatting and pretending to address a loose shoelace.

After punching numbers on the phone she spoke with someone, briefly. Then she rang off, turned and quickly reentered the terminal. I did a lazy about-face, mimicking a man searching his pockets. Then I gave her some distance before resuming my study of the invigorating effects feminine attributes on a dirty old man's libido.

The redhead went into a magazine shop and thumbed through several display racks. Eventually, she selected a publication of the photo-glutted gossip genre. It had a pretty male face on the cover and a banner promoting weight-loss through sex. She paid for it, then went out to the rows of chairs near one of the baggage carousels.

As the redhead sat down, she glanced around for a clock. Spotting it on a distant wall, she compared what she saw to the plastic ticker wrapped around her wrist. Then with an impatient face, she slumped into one of the chairs.

I tried to picture her standing in front of a classroom full of bored teenagers explaining the complex lives of six-legged vermin. Somehow, she did not fit the image. I then tried to put her into a physician's office, inoculating some guy's backside. That did not work either, mostly because my aversion to anything that punctures kept the guy from being me. From my point of view the redhead was far more suitable as a model for a painter who specialized in naughty nudes.

The redhead got comfortable, crossed her legs, opened the magazine and began to read.

I strolled over and settled onto something preformed and plastic a few rows behind her. As I watched magazine pages swish, I kept wishing *I* could shed a few pounds through sex. The tough part would be finding something female with my uniquely perverse inclinations. The handcuffs, camera and rubbing oil would be an easy match. Finding a woman who shared my delight in cold pizza for breakfast invariably resulted in a stumbling-block.

Again, the redhead checked her watch. I assumed from her agitation that she was waiting for someone—her lover, most likely. That would explain the interest in the magazine and her perception of time passing with agonizing slowness. I tried to think back to the last time I had been emotionally involved with anyone. But that just made me feel very, very old.

She abruptly rose, abandoning the magazine.

I got up, pretending that coincidence had casually lured me in the same direction.

At this time of night, staying invisible in an airport was not easy. Very few other people moved about. Those who did offered little cover because they were all pressed for time.

The woman stopped and glanced back.

I pretended to take an interest in satisfying an itch.

She continued on without any obvious worries. Either she did not find me suspicious, or she had no concerns about my presence—either possibility conflicted with what Barrows had claimed about her being suspicious.

With each stride the redhead glanced about as if purposely taking note of the people she met, and the shops she passed. Her walk was as steady as when she left the plane. But now her gait was less determined. Coming down the ramp with the other passengers, she had a destination. She had a purpose. Now the redhead showed a lack of enthusiasm. It was as if she was uneasy about her future, as if she had suddenly made an unpleasant change of plans.

I stuffed hands into trousers and kept my distance, wishing the no-smoking signs were intended to curb the Texas tradition of impromptu barbeques.

A quarter of an hour later, the redhead developed an interest in fast food. At the food court, she paused in front of several cafés to read the menu. Each time she decided against the offerings. Turning abruptly, she headed back to the magazine shop. There she roosted at the paperback racks, seemingly engrossed by every publication on display.

I faded into the background, scratched and waited.

Ten minutes later the redhead came out empty-handed. Her face looked grim, almost gray with agitation. I had not been able to catch her movements in the shop. Consequently, I did not know if she had made another call, or had received one. Either way, something had changed. Instead of an aura of impatience, she now displayed obvious dread.

Again, she checked her watch against the nearest clock. Again, she strode off, this time keeping her chin tilted down and forcing her arms to keep cadence, with each stride. From her stiff walk and clenched fists it looked like she was weighing options and not liking the alternatives.

I followed, getting breathless keeping her in sight. At the place where she left the magazine, the redhead stopped long enough to retrieve it. Then she hurried back to the food-court.

At a joint offering vegetarian fare she spent a great deal of time perusing a menu taped to the glass, near the entrance. I could not tell if she was using the glass as a mirror to see if I was still playing shadow, or if the magazine had inspired a burning desire for calorie-counting. I turned away slightly, as if checking the droop of my waistline. That seemed to be her cue to enter the café.

On a table near the front, the redhead dropped the magazine. Then she strode over to the counter and placed an order.

I took up a position where I could watch without being any more obvious than the swollen bee-sting on the end of Barrows's nose.

After receiving her food, the redhead paid, took it to the table she had previously dressed with the magazine, and sat. She set her purse on the floor by her feet and began eating.

My stomach started to growl as I watched her gulp a lot of green, red and gray. I tried to console it with the reminder that her meal went against all the rules of nature. Each bite lacked the fat, cholesterol, and calories any unhealthy feeding-frenzy should provide. My noisy stomach did not buy it.

Thirty minutes later, she was still seated in the restaurant, her food consumed, the wrapping paper and cup tossed to the trash, the magazine sitting unopened in front of her. I was praying for nicotine and a pepperoni pizza, but my guardian angel did his usual job of ignoring every plea.

Then from behind me, I heard the rapid clip-clop of approaching male shoes.

I turned to see a well-heeled, thirtyish man in a new gray suit trotting toward the vegetarian café. He was dark, with a muscular six-foot frame and a tanned, smug face. His tie was electric blue, and looked crisply new. A matching bit of starched cloth jutted from the suit's breast pocket. I had no idea who he was or what his intentions might be, but I immediately disliked him—perhaps, because he represented all I could never be to a beautiful woman.

When the man reached the restaurant, he rushed inside, going directly over to the redhead.

Without remark, he settled across the table from her and showed a lot of bleached teeth.

She looked up with a start, but did not smile back. Whoever Toothy was, he was not who she was expecting. Whoever Toothy was, she knew him and was not happy about him being there.

I had an urge to walk in, buy a cup of coffee and dump it into his lap. But I fought off the impulse. There was something insidiously wrong with buying coffee and not being able to enjoy it with a cigarette—dumping, or not.

Toothy began talking, making cocky hand movements.

Red tilted away leaning hard against the back of the chair like he had a terminal case of bad-breath. I decided her lack of interest in his repartee was because she preferred older, more experienced men. Particularly those with private detective leanings, wrinkled suits, stained ties and mismatched socks.

He suddenly fell silent, his smile dying like the bloom of a flower dowsed with acid. The redhead said something and wagged her head.

He leaned across the table and resumed talking, one forefinger thumping the tabletop for emphasis. The look on his face had become menacing.

There was more head-shaking from her.

In response, one of his hands shot out and gripped her forearm. She jerked free of the intrusive mitt, like a mouse fleeing a raptor's clutching talons.

I wanted to go over and meld his face with the tabletop. But I fought off that impulse, as well.

He ceased talking and leaned back in his chair, crossing his arms in defiance. That was when she said something short and probably not very sweet.

Toothy shrugged and stood. Then he stepped over to where she sat and ran a fingertip against the slope of her neck.

The redhead repelled away, giving the toying hand a sharp slap.

His palms went to his hips and he glanced about with embarrassment.

She said something without looking at him.

That was when he pulled out his wallet. From within, he withdrew a folded piece of paper. With wallet palmed, he peeled open the paper between thumbs and fingers and set it upon the tabletop, directly in front of her.

Her eyes dipped to the table and held fast on the paper. From the way the redhead's shoulders sagged as she read, it was clear she was hoping what lay before her would turn to dust. Her right hand moved and the forefinger flicked the paper off the table.

He said something, while grimacing with discontent. Then Toothy bent down and picked up the offending offering. Afterwards, with more words from him, he returned paper to wallet and it to his suit.

She wagged her head, resolutely.

He tilted down and said something, his mouth close to her ear.

The redhead sat in silence a moment before giving a feeble nod.

Toothy eased erect, grinning. She took what looked to be her plane-ticket from the purse, and handed it to him.

With a cocky smirk, Toothy left.

She remained where she was, her face white, her teeth chewing her lower lip, her body rigid.

I was too far away to see anything but neatly printed, short lines on the first piece of paper, the kind so often representing a newspaper-clipping. I assumed either she or someone she cared for was mentioned in the writing. I also concluded that the writing's content represented information she found distressing.

My commitment to Barrows meant I could not interact with her, directly. But that did not mean I would have to forgo giving Toothy a discrete lesson in the subtle aspects of sexual conquest. I rubbed my knuckles and grinned. Whatever her unpleasant visitor had planned, there was going to be an abrupt and painfully disappointing change on his future.

The redhead reached down to the floor by her feet, grabbed her handbag, and set it upon her lap. From inside it she took out a stick of gum, and a pen. She unwrapped the gum and plopped it into her mouth. While quickly masticating the rubbery substance, she wrote something on the unprinted side of the wrapper. Afterwards she took the gum from her mouth, smeared it against the printed side of the wrapper, and then pressed the marriage of gum and paper against the table's underside. It was not a classy act. It was also not something I would expect from a woman of her education. But the intent was obvious. Whoever she had arranged to meet must have been told where she intended to sit and would get the message after she left with Toothy.

The redhead dropped the pen back into her handbag and returned the latter to the floor.

Her shoulders suddenly arched as if a pain had shot along her spine. My stomach suspected it was a nervous tick due to the lack of fried-meat in her diet. From the look on her face, it was more likely the result of having come to a difficult decision, one she did not relish pursuing.

The redhead glanced about like she was worried someone watching might have read her mind. Then she simply sat and stared at the table, as if awaiting instructions from the great god of all Formica.

A few moments later Toothy returned, carrying two cheap, mismatched, vinyl suitcases. She glanced at her watch, put her handbag on the table, opened it and took out a handkerchief. She blew her nose. As she put the handkerchief away, one of her hands slipped deftly beneath the table and gave the gummed wrapper another good pressing. After that, she glanced at her unwanted admirer, offering a look not unlike the condemned to the executioner just before the noose was drawn tight. They briefly exchanged words, him grinning like had had just won the lottery, her face bitter. Then she grabbed her purse and stood. Toothy cockily headed off with her luggage, not even glancing behind.

She followed like a kicked dog, leaving the magazine on the table.

After they passed my point of observation, I moved to the restaurant as fast as my old legs and wheezing lungs could manage. At her table, I sat down and pretended an interest in the magazine while I retrieved the wrapper. It read,

'Complications. Romero sent Rodney Terrance. Rancho Relajar. Get there quick!'

I pressed the gummed wrapper back to its place of concealment. Then I trotted after them as quickly as I could without alarming airport security or doing permanent damage to my creaking joints.

I spotted Toothy in the parking ramp as he unlocked the trunk of a new, lemon-colored Cadillac. Without waiting for him, the redhead got into the car on the passenger side. I waited until he was dumping the second suitcases into the trunk. Then I quickly moved up behind him, offering my best lost-tourist plea.

He slammed the trunk closed, ignoring me, then headed for the driver's door. I followed, waiting for the right moment to garner his cooperation.

Just as he pulled the door open, my left fist, carrying all my weight, caught his left kidney.

He turned, his body crumpling.

I let my right fist test the strength of his jaw.

There was a distinctive cracking sound, followed by a low whimper of pain. When he hit the concrete the toe of my right shoe addressed his expectant gonads several times in rapid, sharp succession. Then I redirected my foot-attack toward his liver.

Between Toothy's shrieks of pain and bodily contortions, I decided the interlude he'd planned for her would be postponed—indefinitely.

Then with a parting kick to his face, I turned, lit a cigarette and casually strolled away. There is something immensely exhilarating about starting a long-overdue exercise regimen. The fact was, one bout and my knuckles felt ten years younger.

At the terminal building's taxi stand I jumped into the first cab in line. Then I told the driver, a clean-cut Hispanic-type, to lead-foot it out of there.

"Where's the fire, amigo?" he asked as he put the hack into gear.

"You know a place called the *Rancho Relajar*?" I asked.

He leaned back in the seat giving the rearview mirror a look of astonishment. "Yes, indeed-dum. A motel for the sex-crowd—usually two or more to a room. Sometimes there's standing-room only."

I passed him a fifty. "Stand on it like your sister just checked in there with Jack-the-Ripper."

The tires squealed as we roared off. "My sister wouldn't be caught dead in that flea-trap," he remarked, over one shoulder. "But that bitch ex-wife of mine... Now, there's another story."

"Sounds like we married the same woman. Redhead?"

He let go a laughing howl. "In all the right places!"

"How far to *Rancho Relajar*?"

"Twenty miles, give or take." He gave me a curious glance before adding, "You're the first guy I've ever taken there on his own."

"I'm a sucker for rooms with a view."

He nodded, "You'll get that from the overhead mirror—plenty. But I can tell you from personal experience it won't be as much fun, alone."

"That's okay. I need the practice."

THREE

The taxi shuddered against buffeting winds as we flew onto State Highway 183. When we passed the access road from the airport parking ramp I looked over in time to see Toothy's Cadillac crawl away from one of the pay-kiosks and merge into traffic. It was going in the same direction.

Toothy was driving. But the way he was hunched over the steering wheel, I suspected he was not enjoying the luxurious interior or the comfortable ride as much as he used to.

I leaned forward to peek over the cab driver's shoulder. The speedometer needle was hovering just above the speed limit. "Are you driving with the brake on?" I taunted.

His foot thumped on the accelerator. "Ah, you've got one waiting for you, amigo." He gave me a grin in the mirror. "That's the way to do it, man. Get her to pay for the room. Why not? You'll be doing most of the work once the sheets get warmed. Hey! If you've got a threesome going, I'm reliably informed by my wife's attorney there's a discount on the video-equipment rental. That way you can memorialize the fun and games."

I settled back and lit a cigarette. "Sounds like I've been missing out."

He laughed. "Get it while you can—which at your age, means anytime its available."

"Busy place, I take it?"

"Hell, yes, man! Mirrors on the ceiling. Vibrating beds. Video cameras. You can even buy appliances to help out in cases of equipment shortage—or for satisfying those hard to please urges. That's where I caught my ex, the last time. She had all options stuffed and both hands grabbing for more plug-ins."

Recalling the content of the redhead's note I said, "I've heard rumors linking a guy named Romero to that place."

He nodded. "Jesus Romero. An *hombre* from my old neighborhood. He owns the dump."

His last statement took my by surprise. "What gang does he run with?"

"None, man, not no more." His head shook as if to emphasize his reply. "Jesus is a big-time gambler, now. Lots of money. Lots of women." His hands briefly left the steering wheel in a spread. "Who needs a gang with that kind of action?"

"Was Romero one of those you caught with your wife?"

He laughed. "No way, man. Those guys were blind, desperate and insane. Jesus is a class act. He beds only the very best."

"I've been known to make a wager on the dice. But I've never heard of Jesus Romero. Where does he work the tables?"

"He catches the action all across town, no special place." His shoulders jumped. "But lately I hear he's been hanging out at the Hole in One. You're meeting him at *Rancho Relajar*?"

"No," I said, scratching my chin. "Just considering a future business connection. What's he like to deal with?"

"Tough, man." He tugged at one fat earlobe. "And he's got hired help if it's needed. A guy by the name of Rodney Terrance is his main muscle. I wouldn't get tight with those guys unless you're ready for some heavy-duty risk."

"I've had dealings with Rodney—not much more than show, when it comes to him. An old lady with a heavy handbag could kick his ass."

The driver's eyes found me in the rearview mirror. They were big with disbelief. "I don't think we're talking about the same guy, man."

I leaned forward and peered over his shoulder. The speedometer needle dangled at eighty. "Let's see if this thing can fly, huh?"

His right foot kicked the accelerator to the floorboards. "Damn! She must be one hot fox!"

The needle climbed past ninety and I eased back.

He said, "You pay the speeding ticket if we get stopped, man."

"I'll even cover the cop's usual tip."

The cab took the first Round Rock exit and hung a screeching left, running a light. The cabbie hit the brakes to dodge a truck going upstream. Then he punched the accelerator and we were airborne, again.

"The fifty's on top of the fare, right?" he asked, over one shoulder.

I leaned forward and saw the speedometer needle again creeping past ninety. "As long as we land upright."

At Sam Bass Road, the cabbie stomped the brakes and then punched the throttle, sending the cab dancing around a snake curve. When we hit the straightaway, he let go a howl and jammed the accelerator back to the floorboards.

Seconds later the cab started to shimmy.

I asked, "How good are the tires?"

"Fair to putrid in a dead run," the driver cackled. "Relax, man! We're almost there."

Two minutes later we careened around another curve on two shivering tires. Then, with renewed determination, the cabbie caught a dirt side-road and let the engine unwind. That was when he put the high-beams on and suggested I grab hold of the panic-bar.

I leaned forward and checked the speedometer. He had buried the needle.

The taxi barreled past a blur of brush and trees. Then we slid around another sharp curve that intersected with an asphalt stretch. He did it with both hands on the wheel and a salsa-song on his lips.

A few seconds later, his hands did a quick clap over his head. "Get ready to eject, man!"

We shimmied past a long row of tired-looking businesses, surrounded by high hurricane fences topped with razor-wire. The fences would not keep intruders out. They would slow them down while hauling goods out.

"Start the count-down!" he shouted, as the road narrowed to residential area asphalt. With that, he slammed on the brakes, quickly dropping the speedometer back to thirty. "We can coast the rest of the way, man."

Less than a quarter of a mile ahead I saw purple neon blinking, *Rancho Relajar.*

"Back exit, man," he confided. "Less conspicuous, or so my ex told the divorce-judge. I think he was screwing her, too."

"Was his name Peterson Barrows?"

He glanced back nodding. "You know that bastard?"

"Not in a friendly way."

Both his hands locked onto the steering wheel and flexed, angrily. "I have to pay that bitch alimony for the next twenty fucking years!" Then he flicked off the headlights and nosed the cap into the parking lot. "You want me to come back in the morning?"

"I'll need you to wait."

He glanced back, his brow furrowed in disappointment. "Hurry to get here. Hurry to leave. Don't you believe in foreplay, man?"

I gave him a friendly pat on the shoulder. "I had that in the airport parking-ramp."

"I can dig it," he sighed. "That's where my ex usually started an evening."

"*¡Lequel part votre et m'essayant d'attraper en haut!*" I laughed.

He turned his head and grinned. "*¡Le plus rapide l'améliorer, amigo!*"

I handed him another fifty and got out of the cab. Then through the side window I told him, "Keep the motor running. I'll be as quick as I can."

"Don't disappoint the lady, man!" he scolded. "And don't throw your back out trying to get the job done, quickly. My sister's husband did that. It was three years ago. And he ain't worked since. I know… they moved in with me."

I strolled to the motel's front lot and looked around. Parked in a spot near the entrance was an old pickup, with a flat tire. I went over to it, leaned against one of its front fenders and lit a cigarette. I could see headlights approaching about a quarter mile away. Minutes later, I realized the approaching vehicle was not the lemon-yellow Cadillac. I puffed on the cigarette wondering if something unpleasant had delayed the redhead.

Two cigarettes later, the Cadillac rolled in. It had barely stopped in front of the motel entrance when the redhead jumped out. The shirt-seam at one of her shoulders was split and her lipstick was smeared. Despite my efforts to curb his impulses Toothy had apparently sampled her cooperation.

The trunk-lid popped open. Then he crawled out looking worse than when I left him for the experience. In addition to the bruise I had given his jaw, there were scratches and blood smeared in all directions across his face. Whatever had passed between them, it had not been to his liking.

She went around to the trunk without giving him any heed, and grabbed her suitcases. Then she hurried into the motel's office.

He hobbled to the back of the car, slammed down the trunk and then made a painful return to the driver's door. After letting go a series of curses while crawling back into the caddy, he made a quick u-turn, and roared away in the direction from which he had come.

I dropped my cigarette and raced back to the cab. The note she left behind strongly suggested that Peterson Barrows had not been completely honest with me. This was more than a simple tail-job.

"Let's go!" I told the cabbie, as I jumped into the back seat. "Out the front way!"

He frowned into the mirror. "What did you do man? Bend her over, knock and then ask for a rain-check? You ain't been gone but half an hour."

I pointed at the Cadillac's receding taillights. "Get it going and in high gear."

We careened out of the front lot on two wheels. Ahead I could just make out the Cadillac's silhouette.

"Shit, man! What happened?" His eyes were again in the mirror. "Short fuse? Or, no fuse at all?"

"Delayed connection."

He resumed watching the roadway ahead with a sympathetic nod. "I had that once, man. But chasing her down won't do any good. Take it from me, man. Once they go off the boil, it's over."

"Just get close enough to keep it in sight. But stay back far enough so as not to worry him."

The driver gave me a confused over-the-shoulder glance. "Him? Him who?"

"Him, in the Cadillac."

He slammed the steering wheel with the palm of one hand. "Damn! I never figured you for one of those, man!"

I choked back a laugh. "Relax, hombre. I'm a straight-arrow all the way."

He tapped the windshield with one fingernail. "Then what's the action with that Caddy?"

"He was with the lady."

The cabbie half turned in the seat to look at me, wild-eyed. "You ain't carrying a gun, are you?"

I pulled my coat aside to show the holstered Mauser.

"You ain't gonna' kill him are you?" he whimpered, still looking back at me.

"Not tonight."

He returned his attention to the windshield, the taxi slowing down. "You ain't gonna' kill me, are you?"

"And face Father Drapula at confession? Not a chance, amigo. You and I are brothers at arms in the battle of the sexes."

"Damn, I'm grateful for that priest!"

We tailed the Cadillac to the Shar-Pei Apartments on Hawkshaw Street, in Austin. Toothy got out and hobbled inside like a man with two bowling balls between his legs.

"Man," the cabbie said, his voice dipping with pity. "From the way that guy moves she fucked the eyes right out of him."

I chuckled, "And you were wondering why I wanted to get there, early."

"No offense, man," he counseled, "but at your age you should pick one who's a little less rough. If a quickie did that to him, a night with her would kill you."

I waited until Toothy got inside. Then I took out my cell-phone and dialed Peterson Barrows's office. I left a message that Miss X was staying at *Rancho Relajar*, thus completing my obligation to my ne're-do-well client. Now I was on my own time and there were still questions in need of answers. Tomorrow would be soon enough to take another flier at Rodney Terrance. But I was too curious about the recipient of her note to call it a night. I eased back in the seat and told the Cabbie to make the return trip to the airport so I could retrieve the Buick.

The cabbie put the car into gear and we eased out of the parking lot. "How long have you known that broad, man?"

"Not long."

He glanced back. "How much longer you planning on knowing her?"

"Just long enough to get the job done."

The driver nodded, returning his eyes to the business of driving. "From the way that guy walked, man, getting the job done with her won't be easy."

FOUR

An hour later, I was resting my elbows on top of the *Rancho Relajar* reception-desk. There was a good-looking blond kid behind the counter wearing green chinos, and a gold shirt complimented by a Pooh-bear necktie. He was grinning. I was not.

"Need information," I told him, in my best imitation of the forlorn husband.

The young guy stared past me at the Buick parked out front. "Prices vary by the room," he droned.

"A redhead checked in about an hour ago," I told him. "Is she still here?"

The happy face faded. "Fridays mean lots of redheads, Mister—bottled and otherwise."

"Blue denims, shirt with a tear at one shoulder. Very nice, coming, and going."

His eyes went dreamy for a moment. "Oh, that one. I remember her."

"My wife." I forced an angry twist to my mouth.

He blinked several times and then his lower lip started to twitch. "We don't check marriage licenses, Mister. What folks do here is there business—that's how we look at it."

"Is somebody with her?"

"Please, Mister…" He rested both palms on the desk, and tilted toward me. "We don't want any trouble. Did you have a fight with her? Is that the reason for the tear in her shirt?"

"Dammit, man! Is somebody with her?"

18

Deadly Sting

The desk-clerk paled, his Adams apple working overtime. "I don't rightly know, Mister. All I can tell you is she booked a room with a double-bed."

"What room number?"

"Look, Mister, I'm sympathetic to bad marriages." One of his fingers began a rat-a-tat, on the counter. "I got family with the same problem. My cousin married a real asshole—some Private Detective who spent all his time betting the ponies and dodging the Mayor. Take it from me, you busting in on them won't help."

"Tall, dark, and dreamy was the guy with her?"

The kid glanced about as if looking for a place to run. "I'm not saying anybody's *with* her. I'm just saying if there *is* a guy with her, doing the confrontation thing isn't smart. Why don't you go home and get some rest? I'm sure she'll turn up. These extramarital flings never last. My cousin had half a dozen before divorcing that guy."

I took a deep breath, and slowly let it out. "It's the kids I'm worried about," I declared, trying to make my throat quiver with emotion. "They don't belong in a place like this."

His mouth dropped in shock. "She never said nothin' 'bout no kids."

I gave a despairing shrug. "She wouldn't. She's that type. Look, I don't want trouble. I just want to know that my kids are okay." I fumbled with my lower lip, as if thinking. "I supposed I could call the cops... Might even be illegal for kids to be in a place like this... Could get this place shut down... You and the others arrested... But..."

"No cops!" The clerk's hands flailed the air between us. "Not that you don't have a right – considering the kids, and all. But..."

"I have to do something," I interrupted, with a placating spread of my hands. "A place like this could warp my kids' entire attitude about life, and love. I might even have to sue the pants off..."

"What say we work this out between ourselves?" the young guy interjected. "What say I go to her room and tell her you're here? She can bring the kids down to see you. And then..."

I shook my head. "She'd bolt." I reached up and pretended to wipe tears from my eyes. "You see, I've got a court order granting me custody of the kids, and she knows that. At least, I'll have it come morning. I'm afraid she'll take my boys and rabbit. Then what'll I do?"

"Ok. What about this..."

"With all those men she hangs out with..." I made a beseeching spread with my arms. "You'd understand if you had children of your own." Then I leaned toward him, thumping the countertop with a palm as I spoke. "Maybe I should get the child-protection people down here? They could take my boys and hold them until morning... Of course that would mean the news services... And what with the Mayor up for reelection, he'd want to make an example of this place—on account of you allowing children to watch what goes on. Can I use your phone?"

His eyes bugged as he screeched, "Let's not panic!"

"I suppose if I had the room next to hers I could sort of keep an eye on my kids, from a distance." I glanced around, tugging my belt, as if I was assessing legal recourse. "A place like this and a woman like that, God knows what could happen. Two, three or four of them goin' at her all the same time… My poor boys watching… I can't bear to think about it." Then I reached across the counter. "Give me that damn phone!"

One of his hands slammed down on the receiver protectively. "Did you say four men?"

I nodded. "I wouldn't have to talk to her, not until the court-order arrives. She wouldn't be any the wiser about me keeping an eye on things. I'd never let on that you helped me."

"Four?" he croaked, his neck turning purple. "In a double? In front of children? That is disgusting!"

I offered him my back. "The more I think about it, the more I think the cops should be here." I turned around to face him, offering my most malevolent glare. "You know the drill—sirens, lights the whole damn nine yards."

He tilted forward offering me a pleading look. "Sweet Jesus, Mister! If the cops show up and arrest me I'll probably get kicked out of law school."

I sent one hand across the counter, jerked his hand off the phone and lifted the receiver.

A split second later he slapped down a registration card.

"She's in 111," he declared, with a frantic trill in his voice. "You can have 109, next door. Just sign the card. All I ask is that you don't do anything until after seven tomorrow morning. That's when my shift ends. Dear lord, four in a double—in front of kids. I'll be disbarred before I'm even barred."

I filled out the card with the name Finnegan and an automobile plate-number from fantasy land. Then I handed him thirty dollars for the room-rental. As he gave me a key I grabbed his wrist, firmly.

"I want to see how she registered," I told him.

His head wagged. "Mister, that's against policy."

I gave his wrist a slight twist. "Better show it to me. I wouldn't want to go through all this if we're not talking about the same woman. Bloodbaths are so hard to explain, should the worst happen."

"Bloodbaths?" he whimpered. "Worst happen? Mary mother of God, what are you planning to do?"

I tilted my head so my eyes could peer toward the heavens. "Nothing any man with firm religious beliefs wouldn't do for his kids' salvation."

Quickly, the clerk reached beneath the counter with his free hand and dragged out a stack of cards. "Whatever you do, I don't want to know about and it can't happen until after seven, ok? Not until after seven."

I let go my hold and he quickly fumbled through the pile. Eventually he extracted a registration card and held it out to me. Scrawled across the top of the card, just above the registration fields, was *Jesus Romero*. A different hand had filled out the card with, 'Gwen Keith, Norman, OK'. I took the card and turned it over. On the back, in the same hand as the Jesus Romero notation was a date, a time, a price, and a code number.

"Is that her handwriting, Mister?" he asked, clearly hoping it was not.

I nodded. "At least she didn't dirty my name when she registered. Although Father Drapula will be disappointed. Gwen Keith is his mother's maiden name." Then I tapped the card and asked, "Why is a gambler like Jesus Romero noted here?"

The kid swallowed thickly. "So I'd know where to bill the room. He owns this place."

I made a loud sucking noise with my teeth, and dropped the card onto the counter. "I suppose I should be grateful he's picking up the tab. I mean if I'm not getting the dancing, why should I pay for the music?"

He nodded in frantic agreement. "Seven o'clock, remember? Please, please, please don't forget?"

"Mr. Romero picks up the tab a lot, around here?"

His head went into wag-mode. "I've worked here nearly two years. This is the first I've seen it."

"What's Romero look like?"

"I'm sure he's not with her, Mr. Finnegan."

"I asked what he looked like?"

He gulped, "About an inch or two shorter than you. Chunky. Gray hair, long. Look, Mister, I might be able to sneak out a few minutes early—say six-forty-five? Just don't do nothin' before then."

I made a point of pulling my suit coat to one side, as I scratched my ribs. The kid's eyeballs rolled back in his head after he spotted the holstered Mauser.

"Sweet Baby-Jesus!" he whimpered. "Five corpses in a double with two kids watching."

"Dresses nice, does Romero?"

The kid dragged one palm across the dots of perspiration forming upon his forehead, his worries clearly growing. "If Mr. Romero's with her it ain't his fault, Mister. I'm sure he don't know she's your wife. Killing him before payday…"

"Did I say he was at fault?" I let my coat fall back into place. "Did I say I was going to kill somebody?"

"No," the kid whimpered, retreating a step. "But from the look in your eyes… And that gun…"

"I just bought it along just to give it an airing."

He gave me a disbelieving look. "If you shoot Jesus before he signs the paychecks, I won't get paid. Mister, I'm overdue on a car payment. My girl wants a boob-job. No car means no way to get to my law classes. No boob-job means no girlfriend. See the fix that gun puts me in?"

I nodded sympathetically, raising my right hand. "I swear on a stack of bibles there will be no gunplay." Then I gave him my most threatening look as I added, "But if my wife should decide to sneak out, I'd be sorely disappointed if you didn't let me know."

"Mister, if I see her heading anywhere not only will I call your room, but I'll send up flares." Then he pointed to the lump under my coat. "Do you have a permit for that gun?"

"Does it matter?"

"Not if you don't take it out until after—shall we say, six-thirty, at the latest?" One of his hands began to stroke his throat. "I feel a cold coming on. I'm sure I'll be long-gone by then."

"Six thirty? You're sure?"

He nodded, giving me a wobbly grin. "I've already forgotten what you look like. In fact, I'm certain we never even spoke."

I gave the nervous kid a reassuring wink, and left.

After parking the Buick in the lot I strolled up the walkway to my room.

The fact that Jesus Romero was paying for the redhead's stay made me think there must be some sort of financial agreement between them. But what? From the looks of her luggage, she didn't have much in the way of cash. So that meant she was not someone he planned to gamble with. Was she entertainment for a forthcoming evening of card-play? She had the looks for it. But if that was the case, who did she leave the note for?

I unlocked the motel room's door and quietly crept into Number 109.

The room was surprisingly clean, but it was not my idea of a good night's rest. The place was decorated for those in search of an athletic love-life. The focal point of the main room was a king-sized bed with a bed-sized mirror glued to the ceiling directly above it. Several straight-backed chairs occupied wall-space, presumably to oblige audiences during Olympian exhibitions. There was a small walk-in closet with lots of hangers. The bathroom had the usual accommodations plus an oversized shower, for those desiring the ever-so-refreshing group-scrub.

The main room extended into a kitchenette. A Formica counter bedecked with a microwave, lubricant-warmer and a sink, occupied most of that area. Above the counter was a cartoon-window displaying a pastoral scene, framed by real curtains. On either side of the latter, were cupboards. Below the counter was a small refrigerator and rows of drawers.

I pulled open cupboards, jerked back drawers and investigated the refrigerator. The cupboards contained dishes and drink tumblers. The drawers held flatware and bug-corpses. The refrigerator contained an empty condom wrapper. Its freezer-compartment held two trays of ice within a thick shroud of frost.

I grabbed an ice-tray and a tumbler. Then I introduced the two. After returning the tray to its frost-encrusted chiller, I pulled a pint of Jack Daniels from my pocket and doused the ice. Then I sipped and weighed possibilities of food delivery. I had no sooner decided on pizza, than the steady squeak of bedsprings titillated my ears.

I cocked my head and determined that the sound was coming through the common wall between my accommodations, and Room 107. A few seconds later, the squeaking took on the accompaniment of dramatic moaning. Then both sounds escalated into a frantic, pounding, wail. It was like the legs of the bed were bouncing up and down upon someone's foot, much to the sufferer's delight. To this was added the femininely frantic cries of, 'Yes! Yes! Yes!'

Whoever they were, at least two of them were having a terrific time.

I set aside my envy and went over to the wall adjoining Room 111, and listened.

Most people do not talk to themselves. But there were sounds coming through the plasterboard. Mostly, it was pacing by small feet. I dragged over a chair and sat down to continue my eavesdropping. Apparently the redhead was still in wait-mode, and still nervous.

I was beginning to feel the same. From the git-go the job paid too much for what Peterson Barrows expected, in return. But I chalked up his desperation for my services to him being generally reviled by the entire P-I community. Now, however—considering Jesus Romero and Toothy—I suspected that Barrows had a personal interest in the redhead. Had love replaced greed in the former-judge's heart? Or was there something more sinister behind his interests?

I considered possibilities. A man in love hires a P.I. to tail the object of his affection only when he suspects that object of being unfaithful. So was Barrows having an affair with the redhead? If so, did he suspect her of infidelity with Romero? Considering her looks and his egocentric attitude, I doubted it.

How did Jesus Romero know she was at the airport? Had he been the reason she used her cell-phone on the way to the taxis? In any event, why had Romero sent Toothy to meet her at the airport? Clearly, Toothy had his own romantic ideas. Then there was the person she intended to receive the note. Was that person male or female? Was that person her significant other? Or a business connection?

My mind refocused upon Peterson Barrows. Since I was convinced that he lacked a romantic link to the redhead, it followed that one of his clients did. But why had that client hired Barrows to retain the services of a P.I.? Why not do so directly and save the price of Barrows's intervention? Was it possible that Barrows client was a well-known society figure? If so, why would a social climber want to involve Romero?

No, I was missing something.

I did a rethink. Was it possible she had ended a romantic affair and was being pursued by someone of an overly possessive nature? That could explain my being hired. It also suggested that the one wanting her followed had something other than a friendly reconciliation in mind.

What if ending that relationship included taking up with another man? That could explain the note's intended recipient. As for Romero, it was possible that she had hired him as a protector. That would fit with him arranging accommodations for her. But that still left Toothy as a loose cannon. That also did not explain the clipping Toothy had shown her. Whatever it contained had changed her from resistant to compliant, at least to the extent that she accompanied Toothy.

I lit a cigarette and sipped my drink. The sounds from Room 107 rose to a screeching crescendo, and then fell silent. I glanced over, still envious. Then I heard the thump-thump-thump of bare feet running across linoleum. This was followed by the rushing sounds of a shower, and contented female singing. She was not only loud, but clean.

A phone rang from within Room 111.

I pressed an ear against the wall and listened. When the ringing stopped, a woman's voice asked, "Where are you, Albert? No. I'll wait for you here."

It was a confident controlled voice, firmly pitched, and almost expressionless.

There was a brief pause. Then I heard the phone hit its cradle. Although it was possible that 'Albert' was being used as a woman's name, it was not likely. That meant at least four men knew the redhead. Barrows, Toothy, Romero and Albert, with Albert being the one she expected to meet at the airport.

A mushy tapping came through the wall, like fingertips pushing buttons. Then I heard the redhead saying, "Let me speak with Jesus Romero."

There were more tapping noises.

This time they were sharp and rattling, probably elicited from lacquered nail-tips impatiently hitting varnished wood.

Presently she said in an angry tone, "I'm where your boy dropped me. What's going on? I told you I'd get in touch as soon as I got settled in Austin. There was no need to send Rodney."

There was a pause.

"Albert didn't beat the shit out of Rodney."

Another pause.

"How in hell would I know who did it? Rodney's your flunky. He probably has enemies on every corner…. Damn right I clawed his face! Your boy tried to maul me on the way here. You listen to me, Romero, I don't care what Rodney told you. What he got from me, he had coming. Further you can tell Rodney that Albert will be looking him up to make sure I'm not bothered, again. I don't give a shit, Romero…"

At that moment, the noise from Room 107 began anew. This time the bed springs were chorused by at least two females screeching their lungs out. As entertaining as it might have been any other night, the sounds drowned out what was being said in Room 111.

I cursed, sipped and pressed my ear harder against the separating wall.

When the vocalizations from Room 107 once more subsided, I heard the redhead say, "This may be your idea of safety, but I'm not so sure he won't look for me here."

There was a brief pause. "Did you let my sister know I was in town? Okay, what about the DVD?"

There was another pause. "We made a deal, Romero. You agreed to get me that damn DVD no later than this Friday."

Still another pause. "I don't care what problems Wolf is having on Dyson Island. You were paid to get the DVD, not pass along his whining."

The clues were beginning to jell. Albert was her love-interest. She had a financial arrangement with Romero concerning a DVD that was in the hands of somebody named Wolf, who probably resided on Dyson Island. As for who she suspected might find her at *Rancho Relajar*, that individual was probably Peterson Barrows's client. So far, so good. But where in hell was Dyson Island?

"Dyson Island..." I muttered, over and over as my brain went into overdrive scanning memory cells.

My ear against the wall detected a repeat of the phone landing on its cradle. This was followed by silence. Then the voice beyond the wall said slowly and emptily, "Constance, you stupid bitch."

"Constance," I whispered.

I got up quietly still wondering about the island, the DVD and the players. Then I crept over to the bed like a thief. There I took off my suit-coat to lie down. The redhead—Constance—expected Albert to visit. If Romero was interested enough to set up this place as her hideout, it was likely that he would also pay a call.

I smiled. That could make things very interesting. Particularly, after Constance told Albert about Rodney's less than gentlemanly behavior.

"Rodney, Albert, Wolf, a redhead named Constance who registered under an assumed name, Dyson Island, a guy who was looking for Constance, and Romero," I muttered, as I sat down on the bed. "It doesn't sound like real-life. In fact it would make for a nice soap opera. But it was real. And all of it was somehow connected to Peterson Barrows."

Suddenly the confusion cleared as my alcohol-lubricated memory finally made the connections. The redhead was Constance Kirkland Dyson. The man she feared would find her here was none other than Jacob Dyson—her father-in-law. Jacob Dyson lived an island several hundred miles offshore from Galveston Beach. I had no idea the rock was called Dyson Island, but why not? Dyson had married Billionaires Annie Finch. They had leased the island from Venezuelan authorities. So they could call it what they wanted.

The Dyson's had a son named Phil. And Phil married a world-renown expert on honeybees, named Constance Kirkland. Constance had a Ph.D. in Entomology and an M.D. Early last year, Annie died. Shortly thereafter, Phil died. Constance and Jacob Dyson had a falling out over money he accused her of embezzling. Constance had been arrested as a result of Dyson's accusation. But the case had not been prosecuted due to lack of evidence. And recently, Jacob Dyson hired Dr. Edmund Wolf, as his chief research chemist, on Dyson Island. Wolf was also an expert on bees.

I felt I now knew the players—with Jacob Dyson being Peterson Barrows's client. But I was still confused about the game, and my role in its outcome.

One thing was obvious. Constance's arrival had not been the world's best-kept secret.

I took another sip of Jack Daniels. As best I could recall, the amount of the alleged embezzlement amounted to less than a million. A large amount for most people, it is true. But for a billionaire like Dyson, that amount was barely pocket-change. So why would he go to the trouble of hiring Barrows only to have Barrows hire me, to follow a woman how had robbed him? And why would Jacob Dyson stipulate that my job ended when Constance stopped for the night? If finding the embezzled money was Dyson's motivation, it made more sense to tail her to the reclamation-point. That suggested my efforts were merely a prelude for someone else's.

Barrows had stressed the importance of not being seen. But he must have realized that tailing anyone in an airport at that time of night without being noticed was impossible. Therefore, I would end my chase and someone else would pick it. Constance, having seen me would assume that she was no longer being tailed. That worked. Except, why go to all that bother if Constance was destined for a benign outcome? It was more likely that her pursuer had something murderous on the docket. After all, Jacob Dyson had publicly threatened to kill Constance Dyson.

Jacob Dyson had not given a reason for his death threat. It was assumed he felt betrayed by the alleged embezzlement and had overreacted when the last member of his family died. Based upon decades of police experience, those who make threats rarely follow through. Words are spoken in the heat of anger and then forgotten as emotions cool. In this instance, Constance Dyson had been adamant about her innocence. The authorities finally had to agree when they could find no trace of evidence. Perhaps there was no theft? Perhaps something had angered Jacob Dyson to a point that he wanted revenge of any kind. Even if he had to perjure himself to get her arrested.

I drained my glass and set it on the bedside table. The events surrounding Constance Dyson's arrest went back to just after Phil Dyson's untimely demise. During a visit to Austin's Ainslie Park, the young man had been stung thousands of time by swarming honeybees. Although Phil Dyson had no known sensitivity to bee-venom there had been enough stings to put his heart into sleep mode, and Constance into widow's weeds.

Local experts admitted that they had never heard of so massive an attack. All were confounded by the circumstances. A search of the area found no evidence that honeybees ever nested in Ainslie Park.

When pressed for an explanation as to why the bees attacked in such force, none of the experts could offer an explanation. This, of course, created a minor panic among residents living near the park, which prompted Austin's Mayor to extract a probability estimate of a future attack from the head of the university's entomology department. The odds of such a reoccurrence were described as being, 'one in ten million'. Of course losing against the odds had been a common factor in Texas life, through out its long and tumultuous history.

Curiously, at least from my personal prospective, Phil's death was similar to that of his mother's—Annie—who preceded him to the grave. But in Annie's case only a single sting had been necessary. Annie Dyson was known to have a severe allergy to bee-venom. Still, the possibility of two members of one family dying as a result of bee attacks was so slim, I could not help but wonder if there might be something sinister going on.

I snuffed out my cigarette in the ashtray-stand next to the bed, and let my back and heels put dents in the blanket. The question was what to do with what I knew and suspected? I was only assuming that Jacob Dyson was pursuing her. It could be someone else. And I had no evidence to support my supposition that there was something sinister behind her being followed. But what if I was right? What if Dyson was after her? What if he did make good on his threat? He was sitting hundreds of miles offshore, with an unbreakable alibi.

I had nothing pending. So I could stay around and keep an eye on Constance. The cash and check from Barrows would carry my efforts for a few more days. If something dangerous was in the works, I might be able to foil it. If nothing ominous occurred, then so much the better for her. In any event, it would be fun to gum up whatever game Barrows was playing.

I let the back of my head join the palms of both hands on the pillow. Then I began to weigh other possibilities. What if Peterson Barrows *had* no client? What if Barrows had something nasty planned for me, with Constance Dyson merely a convenient ruse? My coming here would be convenient for any hired talent Barrows had waiting outside.

As farfetched as the idea seemed, it was not impossible. I had made no secret about exposing Barrows's un-judge-like activities. And I was not shy about demanding his impeachment. For a man like Barrows, having to resign from an office that offered him god-like power must have been akin to castration. He would want revenge, not to hire me for an easy job. But if that was true, why use Constance Dyson as bait? Why not use somebody I knew? Someone I hated. Or, better yet, someone who hated me.

After deciding that paranoia was making me crazy, I shifted my thoughts to murderous methodologies. If Phil and Annie were murdered, why do in that fashion? Why not use the old standby of bath-drowning for Annie? Annie's bee-venom allergy might have been too tempting but young men are always getting killed in vehicle accidents. That would certainly be easier than training a bunch of bees to attack. Based upon my limited experience with buzzing creatures in striped fuzzy suits, they were not particularly cooperative with respect to human intervention. Although the one that had stung Barrows in my office had used excellent judgment. But as a horse-player, I could not help but wonder.

I closed my eyes, considering ways to sic a hive of bees on Peterson Barrows's fat behind, without getting my own stung.

FIVE

I must have drifted off.

The next thing I heard was a knocking sound.

I jumped off the bed and hurried over to the window. From behind the curtain, I peered outside. All I could make out was the silhouette of a man's dark suit standing in front of Room 111.

I tiptoed over to the adjoining wall, sat down in the chair, and pressed my ear to the plaster. I heard the door open, followed by a man's entering footsteps. Then there was the sound of the door closing.

It was easy to imagine the grin on the guy's puss as he said, "Hello, Red."

"Don't call me 'Red', Romero," Constance said, dryly.

I heard her lighter footsteps, as she moved away.

"Albert should arrive anytime."

Jesus Romero chuckled. "You don't need him with me around."

I didn't like his voice. It was high and rasping, like a guy with a habit of whispering dirty jokes in church. My right hand began to throb. I looked down and realized I had knotted it into a tight, angry club. I let my fingers go limp and continued to eavesdrop.

"I don't need your kind of protection," Constance declared, confidently. "Your boy, Rodney, must've told you that."

"He told me plenty." Romero let go a nervous chuckle. "After talking to you I decided to have another chat with Rodney. So I rang his place. Only, I got no answer. Could be he was out. But I'd told him to stay put, until I called back." There was a purposeful pause. "Could be something bad's happened to Rodney. Could be he's dead, like George Lipton."

"What are you implying?" she demanded. "That I killed George?"

"George died the day he made a play for you. See why I'm worried about Rodney?"

"George was stung to death by Jacob's bees. I doubt anything like that would happen to your flunky."

There was another purposeful pause. "You didn't object when Harris suggested feeding George's body to the sharks."

I could not place Harris. But the implication was that he worked for Dyson.

"I didn't like George," she said. "Why should I care what Harris did? As I recall you kept silent as well, Romero."

"I was just visiting," he protested. "What goes on out there is none of my business."

"You were visiting because Jacob Dyson sent for you. If not to kill George, then for what?"

"Business."

"Sure, Romero." She laughed sarcastically. "Killing business."

The toilet in Room 107 flushed, rattling the pipes. For many seconds I heard only muffled voices and the water. As the pipes fell silent, I heard Romero suggest, "Maybe Dyson hired that guy who tailed you?"

"So he could beat Rodney up? I doubt it. Jacob wants *me* dead, not Rodney."

"You keep sayin' Dyson wants you dead," pressed Romero. "But I don't see the percentage. What does killing you get Dyson?"

"That crazy bastard doesn't need a reason."

There was another pause. Then Romero suggested, "Maybe Dyson found out about Wolf's DVD? Is that DVD worth killing for?"

"Jacob would kill to keep me from getting it." Another round of pacing, but light footsteps, this time. As she moved Constance asked, "Did you get in touch with Wolf?"

"Got him on the radio just after I talked to you. Wolf's doing a rethink on this whole deal. Sorry, Red."

She stopped, her voice rising. "Bullshit! That damn lawyer swore we had a bargain!"

His footsteps moved. Hers retreated.

"I've had enough pawing, damn you!" she cried.

"Relax, Red."

"Get away from me!" Constance's voice broke with frustration. "You may be hot stuff in the barrio. But you don't do shit for me."

I heard his feet trundle away. Then he stopped. "You should remember who your friends are."

"I do," she said, once more in control. "I also remember what happened to Annie."

"That was an accident."

"Like hell it was. Everybody on the island knows you killed her."

"I had no reason to," he protested.

"Didn't you? She'd ordered Jacob to cut you off the payroll."

Silence fell between then. Then I heard more moving about.

"Maybe Annie and me did have words," he admitted. "But she saw sense after I explained everything. I wasn't the one leading Phil down the garden path on those investments."

"Is that why you told Harris it would take only one bee in Annie's bedroom to get her out of everybody's hair?"

"So maybe Harris did it," said Romero, defensively. "Or maybe Phil. Phil was gettin' real tired of that old woman ragging on him."

"Phil wasn't on the island the day Annie died. But you were there, Romero."

"So was Harris! So was you!" His voice was sharp, and threatening.

"But, you were with Annie just minutes before it happened. What did you do? Load a syringe with venom and inject her?"

I heard him make several heavy strides before stopping. "Shut your big mouth before I shut it for you."

"Am I hitting too close to home, Romero? Rodney told me how interested you were in pheromones. He told me how you'd spent a lot of time in Ainslie Park just before Phil's death. What were you doing there, Romero? Looking for hives? Or maybe looking for a spot to leave some?"

"You start spouting that around and I'll kill you!"

She laughed. "I'll mention that to Albert."

"All right," Romero said in a placating tone. "I got out of line with that. But Phil's death was an accident. He was at the wrong place at the wrong time."

"Like hell, he was. Jacob had you set it up because of Harris."

"Why? Because Phil complained that Harris was a cranky Russian who drank too much?"

"No. Phil and I figured out that Harris was a Chechnyan Islamist. One of those terrorists who killed all those Russian kids in that school."

A cold chill ran down my back, then. If Constance was correct and Harris was a member of the Chechnyan Separatists, Harris and his people would not want her telling the world about their business with Dyson.

"Okay, Red," scoffed Romero. "If you think I killed Phil, how did I do it? How in hell did I tell ten thousand bees to sting him? Tell me that."

Her voice was low and even. "Pheromones, as you damn well know."

"I don't know shit about no damn pheromones!"

From the tenor of his denial, I did not believe Romero.

"Bullshit," she spat. "Jacob clued you in quick enough on how to use it. With two thousand hives and an unlimited supply of pheromone, you had plenty to practice with. Then Jacob met your price for killing Phil."

"If it was Dyson's setup job, then it had to be with his girlfriend, not me."

"Girlfriend?" Constance echoed, in abrupt surprise.

"Didn't Albert tell you?" His voice echoed genuine surprise.

"No."

"She hooked up with Dyson right after Lipton died." Then his voice rose, again, in protest. "So if bees can be set up to kill it was Dyson and her, not me."

Constance Dyson's voice suddenly went soft as if she believed him. "Did Albert tell you who this woman is?"

"No," he snorted. "Albert said I wouldn't believe it if he did tell me… like it's a big joke. Maybe it is a big joke. But get it through your head. I had nothing to do with any killings—not there, not anywhere."

There was a gap of silence for many seconds. Then she said, "I need that DVD, Romero. There must be some way to get Wolf to deliver."

"Wolf claims he no longer has it. That it's in Austin." Romero's voice took on a conciliatory tone. "But he can't come here to collect and I ain't goin' there. No payment. No DVD."

"I thought you were the brave warrior."

"Those two Russians are crazy. Especially Little. That moron shot my hat off my head, last trip to the island. He thought it was real funny. I didn't. So if you want that damn DVD, you'll have to wait for Wolf to get clear of Dyson."

"I can't wait!"

His voice went deep and curious. "What's on it, Red?"

I heard her moving, again. "Wolf told me it holds the proof about Annie's death. Who did it. How they did it. Everything."

"Who'd he say did it?" The question came out like a dry choke.

"Wolf wouldn't give the name." She hesitated. "But he did say that Jacob was behind it. He also said the DVD would prove it. That's all I care about. Once and for all, I'm going to nail Jacob for what he did to me and Phil."

"Sounds to me like Dyson killed Annie."

She stopped. "No. Wolf was clear about that. Dyson didn't do the actual killing. But he was behind it."

"Must be Dyson was in Annie's room—with the killer. Must be he was there to make sure nothing went wrong."

"I wouldn't be surprised," she said.

"How'd Wolf get something like that?"

"He found the DVD recorders Annie used to monitor what went on in her room when Wolf was snooping through her things, after she died. Wolf took the DVD's to his room and checked them out. He saw Annie's killing and contacted me."

There was a lengthy pause. Then Romero said, "Forget that DVD, Red. What do you care, now? Phil's dead. Nailing Dyson for killing Annie won't change anything."

"Like hell, I'll forget!" she railed. "You get hold of Wolf. You tell him to get his ass here if he wants his money."

"I'll tell him. But I don't think it'll do any good. Wolf says Dyson's gotten real spooky. Nobody leaves the island without permission. Wolf says Dyson's worried about not finishing the project."

"Then tell Wolf to get sick. Tell him to get so sick that he needs a doctor. Dyson will let him come to Austin then."

"Dyson'll get a doctor to come out there. Wolf thinks Dyson no longer trusts him. I'd forget the whole thing, Red."

"I can't! I have to get it!" she wailed, in a frustrated voice. "If you don't have the balls for the job, I'll get Albert to go back there."

"Relax, Red. I'll think of something."

"I don't need thinking. I need action."

"You'll get it. Just give me a couple of days to work out the details. What say you and me go somewhere and get a bite to eat? You'll feel better, then."

"I've already eaten." Her steps padded off, presumably away from him.

"Albert's a mistake, Red. You can't trust him."

She gave out a bitter laugh. "Says you."

"Who but you and Albert knew where you'd be stopping on your way to Austin? Not me. But Dyson caught up with you, just the same. Otherwise you wouldn't have been followed at the airport. So who tipped him, if not Albert?"

There was more silence as if she were toying with the accusation.

Romero's steps shuffled, then stopped. "Give Albert the shove. Forget this DVD business. You and me can run this town, Red."

"Run this town? You? Romero, you couldn't carve a plug for a dog's ass."

"I cover my turf."

Her voice became shrill. "Your turf is what Salvator Portello let's you keep."

"Salvator Portello don't mess with me. He knows better." There was another pause. Then Romero cooed, "This fighting ain't doin' either of us any good, Red."

There was more silence. In my mind's eye I could see them staring at each, his eyes beginning to burn, hers cold and repulsing. As disjointed as their relationship obviously was, why had she involved Romero in her plans? Why hadn't she interacted directly with Wolf?

"Maybe you'd like it better if I backed out of this deal," Romero speculated.

"Fine. Give me the jewelry and be on your way."

"Maybe I'll keep the whole package—as a souvenir.

"Just try it, you bastard! I'll have Salvator Portello cut you into chunks and feed you to the fishes. How's that for souvenirs?"

Anything was possible. But Salvator Portello doing a hit at the behest of a beautiful woman, was about as probable as Santa Clause delivering presents in July… to me. Had Sal gotten romantically involved with Constance? If so, it would be a first in his history. But she had just arrived in town. So, when had it happened? Salvator had been traveling for several weeks, a month or so back. Maybe… But if she had something going with Sal, why not have him go to Dyson Island and get the DVD?

Romero laughed in a hollow tone that failed to belie his sudden nervousness. "Salvator Portello? You may be letting him dip his wick, Red. But no way is he going to make a move against me. Not over you."

Her voice jeered. "How 'bout I call him right now, Romero? How 'bout we test your theory?"

"Relax. I'll keep my word, Red." Again, he was placating. But this time it was out of fear, not a desire for intimacy. Romero was moving as he said, "Let's put this all behind us."

She shouted, "I told you I wasn't interested!"

There were the sounds of a brief struggle. "I'll kill you before I let you touch me again!"

"You didn't complain before!"

"Then, I was getting even with Phil. You don't think I enjoyed it, do you?"

There was the sound of a slap.

She let go a startled cry.

Then I heard his steps moving toward the door.

"I'm big-time in this town, Red," he declared, in a frustrated tone. "I don't need some lame bitch giving me shit!"

Constance Dyson didn't respond. Then I heard her in the kitchen running water and making ice-tray sounds. After which, her steps padded back.

She said, "If you hit me again, I'll have Salvator box you in cement."

"Maybe I got out of line, with the love-tap. Let me make it up to you. I know this new place. Exclusive. Good food. Dancing. It's called the *Hole in One*. Maybe I've been going about this Wolf thing all wrong. Maybe what needs to be done is for me and Rodney to go to Dyson Island, and shake things up. We'll deliver Wolf right to your door."

"When?" There was desperation in her voice.

"I'll head for Rodney's place right now. I'll call you tonight and give you the timetable. In the meantime, just sit tight."

"I won't be here. When Albert arrives I'm checking out. This place gives me the creeps."

"To where?"

"That's between Albert, and me."

There was a clunking sound like something moderately heavy being dropped on wood. Then he said, "You'll probably need this. Just in case the lies I've been tellin' you about Albert are truths. See you at the Hole in One, Red."

SIX

I heard the door open. After which, Romero muttered something I could not understand.

The door shut.

She cursed.

I did a hurried tiptoe to the window and peered out from behind the curtains. The light over my door gave me a view of Jesus Romero's face and clothes, as he hurried away.

The kid at the desk was right. Jesus was a sharp dresser—right out of an old gangster movie. His tailored black seersucker would have made a good down payment on a new Buick. Complementing it were black shoes, a black shirt, and a shiny white tie. His face had the polished brown finish of a wooden statue. His hair was grayish-black and shoulder-length. His stubby fingers were decorated with golden rings.

I crept back to the wall.

For many seconds I heard nothing. Then there were the sounds of fast footsteps, back and forth. These were accompanied by drawers being pulled open and then shoved shut. Finally there was the faint snap of a latch.

Constance Dyson was packing to leave.

I slipped on my coat and headed for the door. I could go out to the Buick and await her exit, then follow. Or I could try to gain her confidence and perhaps a small bit of gratitude along with a whole lot of information.

It had been along time since I had benefited from a woman's gratitude, a very long time. I adjusted my tie, grabbed the doorknob and gave it a turn.

It was a simple situation for a man of my extensive romantic experience. I would speak. Constance Dyson would listen in awe. In the end, nature would take its course. The only resistance I would have to overcome was her feminine wiles, virtue, intelligence, fear, foreboding and possibly nausea. If all went well, she would be forever at my beck and call.

With my optimism at its usual peak—somewhere around my ankles—I took those two steps from Room 109 to Room 111 while practicing my come-hither smile. There, I gave my friendliest shave-and-a-haircut tap on the door.

A number of seconds passed during which I heard nothing from within Room 111. Then I detected the sound of soft footsteps followed by the click of a lock being released. After which the door opened a couple of inches and a nicely-chiseled, freckled nose came into view.

"What do you want?" she asked.

"Could I borrow some ice?" I hoped the darkness would hide most of my physical defects and the general decay of my out-of-date clothing. "I thought the two of us might have a drink."

"Get lost."

"How about a little mercurochrome for Rodney Terrance? I gave him the manners-lesson at the airport. You finished his instruction on the way, here. I suspect he'll never view life and love in the same light."

She stared in silence. Then the door opened a bit more and the rest of her beautiful face edged into the opening.

Her mouth was crudely outlined in fresh lipstick, which I guessed she had put on in preparation of Albert's arrival. She had changed blouses from torn, blue denim to silky white. The light from the room's lamp adjacent to her cast a yellow hue obliquely across her eyes. It gave the illusion that each green iris contained glistening spots of bubbling gold.

"Why are you following me?" she said. "Did Jacob Dyson hire you?"

I introduced myself and my profession.

Her head cocked slightly, casting shadows down the soft slope of her long, supple neck. "That doesn't explain why a P.I. is following me."

"I was hired to keep an eye on you. What about the ice?"

"Who hired you?"

"A local attorney. Did you hear what I said about the ice?"

The door started to close. "Tell your boss I'm not interested."

"As Romero suggested, don't forget your friends, Mrs. Dyson. I could be a big help. Or, I could be a big hindrance. It all depends on you."

The swing of the door stopped. But she did not move. Her eyes were white moons within a black sky as they studied me. The door opened a bit more. Her face darted into the opening, her eyes turning upward to lock upon mine, her mouth parting slightly.

I liked the effect. It gave her a wanton, hungry look.

While I waited for a verbal response I pulled a pack of cigarettes from inside my coat, and sloughed one out.

"I don't have any money," she eventually murmured.

"I'm not expecting any."

"If you don't want money, what do you want—as if I can't guess?"

"Not that, either. You see, when I took this job it was misrepresented. Consequently, I've terminated my association with my employer. This, of course, means I'm available to assist when and where I'm needed."

After stuffing the filter between my lips, I put away the pack and dragged out the Zippo. A flick on the spark-wheel gave me yellow fire. I touched it to the end of the cigarette. In so doing, the flame's illumination smeared a bit of copper-gold light across the tip of her forehead, nose and chin.

She looked at me in silence for a minute. "What's in it for me?"

"Protection, for starters. I'm also very handy when it comes to retrievals. Romero, for example, has no plans to return what you gave him. He also has no plans to swap your jewelry for that DVD. In fact, I'd be surprised if he's even made contact with Wolf."

"You read his dirty mind, I suppose?"

"Figure it out for yourself. Romero says he's too scared to go to Dyson Island because of some clown named Little. Then he says he and Terrance will go there and bring Wolf to you. If I were a betting man, which I am, I'd say your pal Romero is the star of that DVD. As you said, he'd been with Annie just before she died."

The muscles in her jaws worked in silence.

I continued with, "I'll convince Romero to be a good boy and play by your rules. In exchange, I want information—only information."

"A private investigator with scruples? I find that very hard to believe."

"On rare occasions, I get a case of honesty. In this instance, the information I get from you will help me resolve another problem."

Her face pulled back. "I don't think so, Mr. Bishop."

"What have you got to lose, Mrs. Dyson?"

She fell silent, again.

"What about this?" I pressed. "I get your jewels from Romero and return them to you. Then I bring Wolf to you. You two complete your deal. Then you fill me on what I want to know."

Constance drew in a shuddering breath. It came out as, "And in return for all this effort you just want information?"

I took a drag on the cigarette and nodded.

"Romero was to get a cut of the jewelry for his trouble," she said. Her voice was low and resentful. "Roughly fifty thousand."

"My offer stands."

Her body leaned heavily against the doorjamb. "Romero won't like you butting in."

"I bust his types for exercise when I'm bored."

The door opened wider and she leaned one cheek against its edge, still watching me with the misgivings of maturity. "Maybe you do, at that. You handled Rodney easily enough."

"Do we deal?"

She asked with a suspicious tenor in her voice, "Why not go back to your boss and get explanations from him?"

"He lies. But, then, all lawyers do. It's a requirement of the profession. That way, when they become politicians, their tongues won't accidentally touch a truth."

I blew smoke to the star-dotted, black sky. "I've got a pint of Jack Daniels in my pocket. Why don't we have a drink and get down to details? If I don't like what I hear or you don't trust me afterwards, I'll move on."

Constance eased erect, placing one hand on a cocked hip. "How did you know about my flight?"

"Somebody talked. Romero suspected Albert—I'm inclined to agree."

She hesitated a moment. Then Constance backed away, swinging the door wide.

I entered confidently.

She continued to retreat over to the suitcase on the bed.

I glanced around the room. It was a twin to the one I had rented. Her other suitcase rested near the entrance to the kitchenette. Her purse lay open on the floor near the bed. The air smelled of perfume—*Shalimar.*

"Who's Albert to Jacob Dyson?" I shut the door.

"Albert Rothfield." She suddenly looked like a naughty little girl who was trying to decide whether or not to play a mean trick. "My father-in-law's chauffeur, or was."

"By father-in-law, you mean Jacob Dyson?"

She nodded. "He's the only one I've ever had."

"I've had three. They all wanted to kill me. I think it had to do with their daughters returning to them after divorcing me."

I returned my eyes to Constance. That was when I noticed her right hand was concealed behind her back. From decades of police-experience with overwrought individuals, a hidden hand was not a good sign of things to come —unless I was feeling suicidal. I unbuttoned my coat and wished I had gone home.

"I don't like surprises," she remarked.

"Then we agree on something." I still wondering what she held in her hidden hand.

"Maybe we can do business. Maybe we can't. Lay it out for me, Bishop, so I can decide. All the dirty details."

"You tell me how to get to Dyson Island. I'll get your jewels from Romero and return them to you. Then I'll fly to Dyson Island and bring Wolf here. Up-front I want answers to a few of my questions. When I deliver on the DVD, you answer the rest."

Her brows arched. "Questions such as?"

"For starters, tell me your father-in-law's connection to a lawyer named Peterson Barrows."

Constance stiffened at the attorney's name, her right hand still out of sight. "Never heard of the man. Is he the one who hired you?"

I nodded. "And you know damn well who he is. Does Barrows work for Dyson?"

Her eyes flickered as she weighed my question. It was like that idea had not occurred to her. "What were you supposed to do once you found me?"

"What I did. Let Barrows know where you were."

An unpleasant sneer spread across her face. "So you're holding me up to give Barrows time to send people to kill me?"

"I expect my former client does have someone en route—but not at my urging and not under his instructions to kill. Barrows doesn't have the stomach for murder." I pulled my coat aside so she could see the holstered Mauser. "In any event, I don't need help when it comes to solving people-problems. I'll get you away from here to any place you name as part of our arrangement."

"Everybody's got a gun these days," she said, with a wilted sigh.

"But mine's bigger than most." I winked. "What makes you think Dyson would put a contract out on you? Death-threats are usually empty."

"In a town called Justice, somebody put a bomb in my motel room. I'd never been to Indiana, before. So it wasn't someone local with a grudge." Her voice had risen. She brought it under control and said more quietly, "I'm not sure how the maid who came to clean my room took it when she found herself blown to hell. But I expect she was disappointed. Since then I've been across three other States, buying time, and hoping. And in all three States I've dodged speeding cars, and flying bullets." She smiled without mirth. "I've developed quite a knack for it."

"Sounds like Albert's been keeping Dyson well-informed. Or did you share your travel-plans with a third party? Salvator Portello, maybe?"

Her brows arched in surprise. "You know Mr. Portello?"

I nodded. "Since we were kids. I used to kick Sal's ass around the block to entertain the neighbors."

Her eyes widened slightly. "I wondered why your name was so familiar. Mr. Portello mentioned it several times. He doesn't like you, Mr. Bishop."

"The feeling is mutual. I like his brother, Dominic, even less. Have you met Dom, yet?"

She nodded, her eyes still wide with surprise.

"Have you made any communication to Dom about your travels?" I asked. "Mailed notes? Phoned messages?"

"What are you implying?" Her voice was thin. "That Dominic Portello steered Jacob my way?"

"Somebody did. If not Albert, Dom would make a good second guess. He would sell you out for pocket-change."

Her green eyes lit with concern. "I did leave my itinerary with him to give to Salvator, as I planned to meet him along the way. But business kept him in Austin."

"It's an election year. Sal has to keep the bribes flying in the direction of the vote-counters so the right politicians stay in office. Does Dom have any connections to Dyson?"

"He knew Phil. I can't say whether Jacob knows Dominic."

"What about Wolf? Did Wolf know when you would arrive in Austin?"

"Dr. Wolf knew I was going to Indiana. That was where we were originally planning to meet."

"Whereupon, he or Albert or Dom informed Dyson," I remarked. "Have you been given any proof there actually is a DVD?"

Her eyes dipped. "No. But—"

"Recording a killing is an odds-off proposition, Mrs. Dyson. It happens. But with such rarity that those recordings are novelties of the first order."

Her eyes came back up. "I have no reason to doubt Wolf."

"Tell me about Harris and Little?"

"Jacob claims they're CIA. But I know different."

"What do Harris and Little have to say for themselves?"

"They would hardly admit to affiliation with a terrorist organization, if that's what you mean." Her mouth became a thin line.

"Is there anyone else on the island I should worry about, when I go there for Wolf?"

"Not that I know of. But it's possible that Harris has other people there. I haven't been to Dyson Island for several months."

"Why would the CIA or a foreign power take an interest in Jacob Dyson?"

"A project he's working on. I can't give you details, so don't ask. If Harris and Little are really CIA, doing so would land me back in jail."

"Did Wolf approach you directly with the offer of the DVD?"

Her head wagged. "A third party did."

"Who?"

Constance took an interest in her watch, avoiding my eyes. "That's my business."

"It was Barrows wasn't it?"

Her right hand came into view, then. It was a nice hand, milky-white, well-formed, with tiny dots of light brown from a spritsing of freckles. Her fingers were particularly appealing, delicately chiseled and exquisitely manicured. The nails were bright pink. I tend to notice little things like that in a woman. Especially when the object of my fascination clutches a small, chrome-plated automatic pointed at my chest.

Her voice was barely audible. "I've decided to manage without your assistance, Mr. Bishop."

Constance held the weapon gingerly, as if it might bite. Naturally, I was not the least bit worried. However, the hairs on the back of my neck stood straight up in absolute terror.

"Looks like you've got all you need in hand," I quipped, wishing I was anyplace else. My right forefinger pierced the air in the direction of the pistol as I asked, "Who gave you that shiny toy? Romero? Or did you take it from Rodney during the romantic interlude between clawing his face, and arriving here?"

A barrier of hostility was now between us, like an electrified fence carrying deadly voltage. "What difference does it make?"

"Something about Greeks bearing gifts comes to mind." I waggled my pointing finger. "If that gun was used in another killing, for example Rodney Terrance's...."

"What makes you think Rodney is dead?"

"It was Romero who suggested that," I countered. "Romero also suggested that you forget about that DVD. I think it was Romero who left you that gun. See my point? If your jewelry-holder did kill Annie Dyson, Romero could be setting you up for a murder-charge. In so doing, he's not only stopping you from getting that DVD but sending you to the death-house." I extended my hand. "Give the gun to me. I'll get rid of it."

Her hand flexed on the weapon as if it was suddenly hot. "You've got it all worked out, huh?"

I let my mitt drop. "Why should I lie?"

More flexing. However she remained silent, her stare deadpan, neither afraid nor angry.

"From what I heard through the wall, you had an affair with Romero," I remarked. "Did your husband know?"

She took aim at my head with the pistol. "You got big ears."

"Tell me about pheromones," I said, feeling like a fly with one foot stuck in a spider's web and another on a grease-spot. "As I recall, the police described your husband's death as a freak accident of nature. But you suggested that pheromones were used to incite the bees into killing your husband."

Her free hand went to her face, then to her hair and back down.

"How do pheromones make bees kill?" I pressed.

Her gun-hand began to tremble. Quickly, I said a small prayer to any being on the God-frequency, begging them to make certain the weapon's safety was on.

"It's not like in the movies when a man gets shot," I told her. "No staggering. No groaning out the meaning of life. The dead just drop like so much cooling meat. You can actually see the moment life departs. It's when the pupils blow wide. One second you're looking at an iris in a shiny eyeball. Then next, you're staring into blackness at the center of something dry, and withering."

"Shuttup!"

"You remember that sight the rest of your days. No matter how many times it happens, it seems to be a unique event. It's as if the finger of God reached down and touched each eyeball to blind the dead against seeing their killer through eternity. I know. I've killed many times. Each one I remember as if it was today, this moment. I recall what they looked like, what their voices sounded like, what they smelled like. It comes back to me again and again. Somebody I meet on the street, someone I overhear in a room, someone I smell in an elevator. The hairs on the back of my neck rise up each time and though I know it is impossible, I look over in expectation."

"Shuttup, shuttup, shuttup!"

I sidled over to the nearest chair, and sat. "Forgive me. There's nothing worse than being talked to death. We Texans are notorious for it." Then I indicated the gun with a tilt of my head. "Either put it away or pull the trigger. I'm tired, my feet hurt and I'm still out of ice."

She snorted faintly, before lowering the pistol and dropping it into her purse. "You don't scare easy. I'll give you that."

I took a drag on the cigarette and blew smoke toward the ceiling. "Nonsense. I'm in constant terror. You just didn't notice."

She slumped onto the bed next to the suitcase and clasped her hands between her knees. Her face was taut, the red hair framing it looked like tangled yarn made of coagulating blood.

"How long ago did you tell Barrows where I was?" she asked.

"Long enough." I checked my watch. "We could go out together, whereupon I would protect you against anybody waiting. Or, I could leave and you could move on with Albert. It's up to you."

She got to her feet and tugged at the belt on her jeans. "Do I get fully undressed? Or would you be satisfied if I just dropped my jeans, and bent over? All I need is for you to get me out of here and keep whoever's been sent busy for an hour. Surely a quick jump is worth that?"

"Don't bother undressing." I stood up and went into the kitchenette. There, I dropped my cigarette butt into the sink. I called to her, "I'm the kinky type. Just leave your clothes on. I'll do it all in my head while we drive. That way we don't have to worry about those confusing safe-sex issues." I returned to her and pointed to the open suitcase. "Anything else for it?"

She lifted her shoulders. "You're the strangest man I've ever met."

"I keep hearing that." I went over to the bed and closed up the suitcase. "Mostly from women. I think it has to do with my preferences for handcuffs, oil-rubs and video cameras. Do you want to leave a goodbye-note for Albert? I wouldn't recommend continuing to live with him."

Her eyes went wet as they stared into mine. "I'm not as cold as you think."

On impulse I caught her by the wrist, holding her fast.

Her free hand came up, its fingers curled and spread like manicured hooks ready to tear meat. She tried to claw my face. I grabbed her hand and pinned both her arms behind her back. I had no plans with respect to carnality. I just wanted to feel her against me.

She hissed, "I should have known!"

I jerked her tightly to my body.

Constance tried to knee me in the groin. But she was too close to do anything but scuff my thighs. I forced her hands behind her and using them at the small of her back, pinned her pelvis to mine. Her eyes closed in defeat. Then with a sigh of resignation she went limp, her head tilted back, her lips parted. I could feel her body warming mine. I had a sudden urge to carry her over to the bed. But the timing was all wrong. I had not taken my vitamins.

After a moment her lids raised in a questioning glare. "Either let go of me or get on with it."

I bent down and pressed my mouth to hers. She responded. A moment later I released her wrists and she wrapped her arms about my neck. Constance tasted salty and eager. I slid my hand beneath the back of her blouse and was just touching the clasp to her brassier when I heard the door open. Silly me. In my haste to charm the beautiful redhead, I had forgotten to set the lock. We broke apart and I turned. That's when I noticed seven feet of muscle-bound, dark-haired fury in a brown flannel suit watching me from the doorway.

"Sorry I took so long to get here," he growled, still studying me. "I couldn't shake a tail. The old man must've had us followed. Who's the tattered suit?"

"The one who paid for it," I told him. "Who buys your rags, slick? Her, or some other desperate woman?"

If I had succeeded in punching one of his buttons with my comeback, he did not let on. But, I set myself to be on the safe side.

The redhead grabbed up her purse and hurried away from me. "His name's Bishop, Albert. He's a P.I. Peterson Barrows hired him. Give you any ideas?"

Deadly Sting

"Sounds like we've been taken at both ends," Albert grumbled. "Did the creep get what he came for?"

"He got more than I'd planned on giving," she smirked.

He smiled comprehendingly at me. "Bad mistake."

The color in his face was rising. His eyes had taken on an eager glint. Then he said to her, "Go out to the parking lot, and wait. This won't take long."

She hurried past him continuing outside.

He made a noise in his throat and lunged forward, throwing a sharp punch, straight, very fast and well-practiced.

I stepped inside it quick, cool and cunning.

Unfortunately, he was a Southpaw and what I took for his power-swing was just a jab.

My right missed his jaw. His left didn't miss mine. It snapped my head back, sending me dancing.

By the time I had my legs under control, he was behind me, arms wrapped around my chest.

I jerked out the Mauser.

He started to lift me.

I managed to cock the pistol's hammer, intending to send a round into one of his feet. But the way he had hold of me I could not get it clear of my own body. There didn't seem to be any point in hanging onto the gun. So I released the hammer and let the pistol drop to the floor.

That's when I managed to get a grip on his wrists. They were thick and sweaty, hard to hang onto.

Albert jammed me to the floor using his weight.

My head bounced off the linoleum, momentarily stunning me. When I went limp from the impact, he grabbed my wrists and jerked them behind my back. Then he twisted fast and dropped a knee like a pile driver into the center of my spine. That accomplished, he pulled backward on my arms stretching the ligaments at my shoulders into thin strands of screaming pain.

I opened my mouth to give out a yell, but no sound came past my teeth. The words caught in my throat wouldn't allow me to breathe.

I squirmed for all I was worth and managed to get one hand free. I clawed behind me for his hair. But as soon as I got a hold, Albert twisted me sideways and shifted his legs so that one was beneath me and the other on top. A second later they formed a scissors-lock that crunched down hard enough to make my lower ribs creak.

I twisted within his hold, flailing at his face with both fists.

Before I could do any damage, his hands went to my throat and squeezed.

Red lights flashed in my head, a reflection of the glutted blood vessels at the back of my eyeballs. The room began to swim around me. I tilted backward trying to get as much distance between my forehead and his face as I could. Then I swung my skull forward into his face with all the force I could manage.

There was a loud crack as my forehead struck his nose. Instantly his hands and legs went slack.

I scrambled to my feet, looking around for the Mauser. But before I could get to it he was up and holding a chrome Beretta.

"They tend to jam." I rubbed one hand against the fresh bruises on my throat.

He batted at the blood running from his nostrils. "You're just being hopeful."

"You're damn quick for a big man," I remarked. "You must have spent time in the ring."

He nodded, flexing the gun in his hairy mitt.

"How much is Jacob Dyson paying you to keep him informed on her?" I asked.

"Enough," he told me with a waggle of the gun. His voice had sunk almost out of hearing. "I'll get even more for getting rid of her." He gave me a murky grin. "I figure I'll get a bonus for capping you."

His forefinger curled on the trigger but nothing happened.

I lunged across the distance separating us and caught Albert on the side of his skull with all my weight behind a right hook.

His jaw went limp, and I grabbed the Beretta.

He came back for more, sending something that felt like a freight train into my gut.

That's when I got real clever and swung the gun. It put a dent at his temple, which sprawled him across the linoleum. I sidled over to the Mauser and picked it up. Then I tossed the Beretta onto the bed.

Considering the age and weight difference, I was quite proud of myself. He was down and out. I had only a few bruised ribs and an abraded larynx for the experience.

I holstered the Mauser and backed toward the door. All I had to do, now, was find Constance Dyson. Then I would explain the stupidity of impulsive actions.

That was when my nose caught the scent of Shalimar and something hard hit the back of my skull.

The next thing I knew I was riding a bottle-rocket over black nothingness, its flames burning my skull. There was no need to find the beautiful redhead. There was no need to explain about the stupidity of impulsive actions. She knew all there was to know—after catching me with my back turned.

"Never trust a redhead!" I groaned to the emptiness.

With that, the rocket exploded into a fiery ball, scorching me from head to toe before dropping what remained of my being into a deep, dark, bottomless pit. Ah, Bishop. You are, indeed, a man to contend with. On any given day you can be suckered from twelve different directions.

SEVEN

When my eyes opened, the room was dark. My skull felt like it had spent the last six months pinned between competing pile-drivers.

I tried several times to get to my feet, but for reasons beyond my comprehension, my shoes could not find the floor.

I tried moving my head to see where I was. But that set my stomach rolling like a log floating down a fast-flowing river.

I tried to shift onto one side. However the slightest change in position resulted in a deafening rumble between my ears. I finally decided that either my brain had gotten loose and was banging around the room, or I was actually dealing with a serious health-issue. I closed my eyes and waited for my body to repair itself—or expire.

Some time later, I opened my eyes again. It was still dark. But this time when my feet tried to do their stuff, they found something solid.

I stood and staggered about, looking for the door. For some reason it had been moved. While I was unconscious some asshole had mounted in on the ceiling.

I made a jump, trying to grab the knob. But it dodged my hand and I fell flat on my face, against a wall covered in linoleum. Thinking I had been tripped by some jokester hiding in the dark, I got up and made a few wild roundhouses.

That was when a floor lamp went on the attack.

Fortunately, my fists were tougher than its shade. A couple of swings later, I cold-cocked the two-light bastard.

That must have sent a shiver of fear through the door. It immediately dropped down to where doors, belong.

I stumbled over to it cursing threats about deconstruction, destruction and detonation. But my bullying was unnecessary. When I tried to grab the doorknob this time, the brass handle reached out and meekly slipped into my mitt.

I turned it, the door automatically opened and I staggered outside.

The cool night air caused my eyeballs bug out of my head and dance down the lamp-lit, concrete walkway leading to the parking lot. My peepers stopped near a man leaning against the fender of a new red pickup. After looking him over, they bounced back with news that he was tall, lanky, longhaired, and wearing a checked sportcoat with light-colored slacks. Suspiciously, he was not wearing a tie and his white belt matched his shoes. However, there was some dispute about the fellow's facial features. One eyeball maintained that it had seen only shadows and lines between bleached-blond mop and scrawny neck. The other claimed that the same area contained nothing but dark lumps and a set of glasses with lenses thick enough to double as portholes in a diving bell.

I blinked each eye back into place. Then, I staggered on.

When I reached the door to Room 109, I gave another look in the direction of the parking lot. The fellow in the sportcoat was standing erect and staring intently in my direction. From the way he fish-eyed me I assumed the clown was either someone looking for a missing wife who had poor tastes in consorts, or he was a bill-collector looking to repossess the silver in my teeth. Either way I was not in the mood. I opened the door, wobbled into Room 109, and then shut the rest of the world out.

After making my meandering way into the kitchenette, I leaned over the sink, and turned on the tap.

After a moment, I gathered the strength to splash water on my face. That was when my stomach took another roll.

This time it gave a determined retch that acquainted my mouth with the bile that had been collecting during my respite in Room 111.

After vomiting green for what seemed like several lifetimes, my stomach got tired of turning itself inside out and went back into gurgle-mode.

I eased erect, jerked down one of the curtains framing the cartoon window over the sink, and used it to wipe my mouth and face. That was when my eyes focused upon the painted characters in the window-scene. Even if I was standing on my head, the sun shining on those purple daisies, flying bees and chirping sparrows made the view irresistible. So much so, I tried to crawl out of the room and into the cartoon.

When that failed I took my frustration out on the scene with a hard swing. But instead of busting glass, my fist punctured plasterboard. It also caused a stir with the bee trying to pollinate the sparrow.

As I rubbed my sore mitt, my brain cells began to reconnect. A few seconds later, I remembered Constance Dyson and Albert Rothfield. Then I began to recall more important things. Like my shoe-size, the length of my inseam and the price of dental floss. After that, my brain gave me an instant replay of the entire evening in the form of a flash-video on steroids.

That was when I realized how much trouble I had dumped Constance Dyson into by letting her take me by surprise.

Although Rothfield had confirmed Romero's suspicions that he was responsible for tipping Dyson to her movements, Constance assumed Romero had lied. Complicating matters was my suggestion to Dyson that Dominic Portello had been the source of information. Not only was Constance now with Albert, my suggestion would have laid to rest any suspicions she may have been harboring about his fidelity, with Dom the new focus of her worries.

Rothfield would point. Constance, thinking she was safe with him, would follow. At some point, considering Rothfield's remark about Dyson paying him to get rid of her, he would do so—permanently.

Legally, I had no obligation to Mrs. Dyson. Particularly after the blindsiding she had given me. But morally I felt Constance deserved to know the truth about Albert Rothfield. Unfortunately, my best chance to rehook with her was at the Hole in One—wherever that might be. This meant finding the joint and watching it during its operating hours, hoping for her to show up. Still there was a good chance Constance would go there—assuming Rothfield did not kill her, first. Romero's lack of effort to get the DVD and him having the jewels she intended for its purchase, meant that Constance would do all she could to maintain contact.

I turned intending to spend a few hours sleeping before driving home. That was when I was reminded of the old adage about keeping unwanted visitors out by locking doors. Standing in the main room was the sportcoat I had noticed by the pickup in the parking lot.

"Lost?" I asked, trying to blink my eyes into focus.

He shook his head, letting a long, blond forelock shift down across his face. "Constance Dyson. Where?"

Not only was his response pithy, his accent reeked of Russian heritage. I leaned back against the counter, still trying my best not to fall over. "No idea."

He moved closer. In so doing, one of his hands slipped inside his plaid sportcoat.

I tried to look casual as I dug for a cigarette. Up close I could see that he was gaunt, about mid-sized with thick glasses, large ears and big hands. The collar of his sportcoat was turned up. That let the cloth nestle into an overgrowth of dirty hair, like a snot-rag shoved into wet moustache."

"Where?" he repeated.

As thugs went, this clown was an amateur at the threat-game. Instead of taking out his weapon where it could do some psychological good, he kept his hand positioned inside his coat. To my mind that meant he was either unarmed and trying to bluff me into submission, or the gun he carried was a Berretta with its usual jamming potential. I could understand him not wanting to show a gun like that. It was far too embarrassing. I lit the cigarette and blew smoke at him.

"She go Albert?" he demanded, impatiently.

"Check with me tomorrow, Slick," I urged. "I might have some ideas, then."

He stopped and splayed his legs. His one hand was still hidden. The other was knotted into a fist. Tension visibly vibrated in his legs.

"Where go?" he demanded.

His stubbornness was beginning to irritate me. "Haul it someplace else, pal, before I lose my temper and punch your face into history."

The hidden hand came into view holding an old Lugar, its barrel affixed with a long silencer. From the grin spreading across his face my time was up.

"Constance where go, Bishop?" he grunted, waggling the gun proudly.

His knowing my name came as an interesting surprise. It could be explained if Peterson Barrows had discussed my hiring with him or his superiors. Or it was possible that Jacob Dyson had whispered the sweet nothings Barrows had shared as part of the directions to *Rancho Relajar*. Considering Barrows's exposure should Mrs. Dyson die an unnatural death while I was in his employ and following her, I doubted the guy with the Lugar was working on the lawyer's nickel. That left probabilities pointing to Dyson. In any event, I was in deeper trouble than I had planned.

"You deaf? Or just plain stupid?" I demanded. "Did you see her in her room? Do you see her here? How in hell would I know where she is? Obviously, she left. Obviously, I don't know where she went or I would be following her." Then I turned back to the sink and gave the tap a twist.

As I leaned over pretending to wash my face, I slipped the Mauser from its shoulder holster, cocked it and held the pistol against my chest. "Beat it before you make me mad."

I heard his footfalls approach. Then he stopped. This was followed by a thump as he fired a round into the cabinet next to my right leg. Whoever he was, he was about to get his last lesson in the art of gunplay.

In one motion I dropped to my knees, rotated towards him, aimed the Mauser and let it bark twice.

Both rounds found new homes in his chest.

That resulted in another thump as his finger clenched tightly on the Lugar's trigger, causing the weapon to fire one last time. The round hit the floor and then ricocheted into the ceiling.

He smiled, as if satisfied with his final effort. Then the fellow sagged to his knees and dropped over onto his face, like a manikin toppling from a display stand. I got up and wobbled toward him, sighting the Mauser on his skull.

"That desk-clerk is not going to like this," I muttered, giving my tongue a scolding cluck. I kicked the Lugar from the dead man's grasp. "I hope you and Barrows weren't pals, fella'. Because I haven't cashed his check, yet."

I squatted down and rummaged through his pockets. I found two hundred in cash, a scrap of paper with a telephone number scrawled upon it, and a wallet containing a Baltimore driving license bearing the name: *Edward Little*. What was the name Constance had mentioned as one of the men who worked for Dyson? Little?

I pocketed the money. Then I dragged out my handkerchief, wiped my prints from the wallet and put it back where I had found it.

As I stood up I muttered, "If you're CIA, I'm Sister Theresa. But Chechnyan, I'll buy."

I went around the room looking for the casings ejected by the Mauser. After retrieving both, I walked over to the phone and dialed the number on the paper from his pocket. It rang several times before a nasal, male voice answered at the other end of the line with, "512-772-3918."

"Who's this?" I asked.

"Wrong number," came the reply. Then, the line went dead.

I dialed back, but got no response.

I set down the phone, turned and faced the mess on the linoleum. A killing —whether accidental, self-defense or otherwise—means a homicide investigation. That promised me the rest of the night under a police grilling. I decided that submitting to such an ordeal with my head still buzzing and my eyes still seeing things that may or may not be real would not be in my best interests. However, that did not solve the problem of the corpse.

I considered covering him with a blanket and putting a 'Do Not Disturb' sign on the door before crawling into the bed. But motel maids are a quirky lot. They use passkeys on locked doors, notice corpses where there should not be any, and from time to even let the management know about P.I. types sleeping in a bed near a lake of red sticky-stuff.

I checked my watch. It was not quite sunrise. Then I cocked my ears for the sound of sirens.

I did not hear anything along those lines. Although, the screeching coming through the wall adjoining Room 107 was giving a good impression of one. Perhaps nobody heard the shots? Or, perhaps somebody did and chalked it up to repeated backfires or a malfunctioning sex-toy?

I took out my handkerchief and went around the room wiping off handles, drawer-pulls, counters, refrigerator and anything else I might've touched. Then, I staggered outside and went back into Room 111 where I did the same.

Five minutes later I was stumbling down the sidewalk to the parking lot. As a former police officer I knew it was wrong to leave the scene of a shooting. I also knew there was a good chance I could lose my P.I. license for making such a transgression. But my recollections were still scattered and my stomach was taking an interest in turning inside-out again. So I thought I could justify it on emergency medical grounds, should I be caught making my departure.

At the Buick I paused to listen, again. I did hear sirens, this time. Coming closer? I lit a cigarette and listened some more. Yes. The sound was definitely getting louder. Was it in response to a report of gunshots?

I checked my watch. It was not quite six-thirty, in the morning. Yes, that undoubtedly was the reason.

Still, I had signed the register as Finnegan. With a little overdue luck, the authorities would put out an all points bulletin for a psychotic Irishman with redheaded leanings. I got into the Buick, started the engine and nosed it toward home.

EIGHT

Late the next evening, I had breakfast-come-lunch-come-supper-come-snack at Hugo's Snake Pit. It is the only rib-joint in Austin that serves barbequed rattlesnake as its specialty. Then I followed the moon to the Shar-Pei Apartments.

Considering that Constance Dyson had accused Jesus Romero of killing Phil Dyson—which Romero had denied—there was a small possibility that Rodney Terrance might have insight into the hotly-debated issue.

My approach to the subject would be direct. I would ask questions. Terrance would answer—one way, or another. At the very least I would find out where to get my hands on Romero. I would then address the gambler in the same vein, adding a few quick questions concerning the whereabouts of Mrs. Dyson's jewels. Then after that knuckle-busting discussion, it would be Peterson Barrows's turn to make explanations.

Despite the burning in my belly from the Serrano's in the BBQ sauce, my fists itched with anticipation.

When I arrived at the Shar-Pei Apartments it looked like most of the tenants were making an exodus. Some were likely going to night-jobs. Others were probably headed for the shopping malls. The rest were almost certainly getting an early start on the ever so popular hobby of finding short-term romance before the night ended.

At a starlit spot in the lot near the front doors I parked the Buick, and got out. Then I hurried up to the building, and went inside.

There was only one Rodney Terrance listed amongst the mailboxes. He occupied apartment 311. I pushed the buttons under each box, hoping some desperate soul would press the electronic lock-release on the main door. Nobody had an interest in letting me in. In particular, I noticed that Rodney Terrance had not responded.

My memory went back to Romero's remark about Rodney not answering the phone after being instructed to remain at home. Had Albert, after reading the note Constance left at the café, driven directly to Terrance's apartment? Had Albert, upon arriving at the apartment and seeing the scratches on Tarrant's face, assumed the worst and finished what I had started at the airport? It was a grim possibility with disappointing overtones. Dead men tend to ignore questions.

I glanced around to make certain I was not being observed by security cameras, or passersby. Then, I took out a credit card and slipped the latch on the inner door. A tug later, I was inside the main apartment building.

From the plush feel of the brown carpeting beneath my treading shoes and the smell of fresh glue coming from behind the sparkling yellow wallpaper, the place was either new or newly renovated. I cocked my ears expectantly as I strolled toward the elevators, but I did not hear one sound. For an apartment building, the place was unusually quiet. No thumping music from the idiot who partied every night. No screaming children from the apartment occupied by the baby-maker. No arguing voices from the newlyweds. No veiled threats by the apartment manager to evict late-paying pensioners. Considering the overwhelming silence, the Shar-Pei apartments would be a nice place to live. Well, for anybody but me. I would miss the not so neighborly camaraderie, and its resulting pandemonium.

The elevator took me up to the third floor.

Minutes later I was knocking on apartment 311.

A few seconds after that, having gotten no response, I was slipping the door-lock. A quickstep later, and I was inside Terrance's apartment, shining my penlight down into Rodney's eyes. They were nice eyes. They were the kind of unblinking eyes that you find in a dead man.

I locked the door, switched on lights, put my penlight and credit card away, and then studied the death-scene. It was unusual, despite my many years experience investigating homicides. The quirkiness I saw had nothing to do with rampant butchery, as is sometimes the result of murder. Quite the contrary. In fact, Terrance looked blissfully comfortable, lying on his back upon the floor. He was fully dressed in tan slacks and shit. His hands were at his sides, crushing the blue carpet. His shoes were off but his white socks were on. One side of his face rested casually upon a yellow throw-pillow. The whites of his eyes reflected the overhead lamp and seemed to stare at the moon beaming in through the front-room windows.

Deadly Sting

Except for his unblinking stare and the several thousand dead bees on his corpse, Rodney Terrance looked like he was about to get up and shake my hand.

I squatted and touched his neck with my fingertips. I was not expecting to feel a pulse. Rather, I was interested in the temperature of his skin. It was quite warm. In fact, it felt nearly normal.

I then tried moving his head. It twisted on his neck like a well-oiled bearing on an axel. Rigor mortis occurs in stages, beginning with the face and neck. Since those muscles had not yet stiffened and his skin felt as warm as my own, Rodney Terrance had died less than an hour before my arrival.

I tilted his corpse onto its side and fumbled past the insect-bodies to his trouser pockets. I found loose change, a clean handkerchief, a ring of keys, a plastic container of dental floss and a new leather wallet.

I took out the wallet and handkerchief. Inside the leather was seven hundred in cash, half a dozen credit cards, an expired driving license and the slip of paper I had seen him show Constance Dyson.

After removing the paper I pocketed the cash. Then using his handkerchief I wiped my fingerprints from the wallet, and returned the expensive chunk of leather to its keep.

After that, I stuffed his handkerchief into my pocket, stood and unfolded the paper.

It was photocopy of a news clipping concerning the death of Phil Dyson. The article touted various theories for the bee-attack. The one that interested me was the possibility that Phil Dyson's death had been a homicide orchestrated by someone with a grudge against the Dyson family, using pheromones as a chemical motivator. The article went on to quote several bee-experts regarding that theory—including Dr. Edmund Wolf. Each expert agreed that a particular pheromone could bring bees into a stinging frenzy. But those same experts denied the feasibility of such a practice. To date, they claimed, no one had isolated the various pheromones generated by honeybees. Interestingly, pheromones were what Constance Dyson had accused Romero of using to bring about the swarm that killed her husband.

I stuffed the article into my pocket and then eased the body back to its original position. As I stood, I could not help but wonder why that article had so much impact on Constance? After reading it she had became passive to Terrance's demand that she accompany him. I also could not fathom why, if the information in the article was benign, a clown like Rodney Terrance would carry it around? Was it because the article substantiated the possibility that murder could be accomplished using bees? Assuming, of course, the controller had isolated the correct pheromone despite those expert opinions. Or was there more to it? Like one of the experts questioned being behind Phil Dyson's killing? Perhaps someone like Dr. Edmund Wolf? Or had Terrance used the article to remind Constance of what *she* had done to her husband?

I let my eyes drift over the piles of dead bees. What were the odds of a man being stung to death in his apartment? Granting that Terrance's death made that plausible, what were the odds that this same man would carry an article written about a previous death by bee-stings? Conceding all that because he had been, what were the odds that one woman who was an expert on honeybees could have three people in her life succumb to bee attacks?

Then, again, what were the odds of one billionaire named Jacob Dyson having a wife and son killed by bees? Dyson had his own resident bee-expert in the form of Dr. Edmund Wolf. Dyson also, according to Constance, had Jesus Romero on his payroll.

Had Romero killed Rodney Terrance in this bizarre fashion, because of what Constance had told him? Had he done it on his own? Or was Jacob Dyson behind it? According to Constance, Romero understood the pheromone responsible for starting a bee stinging attack. Further there had been enough time, since Romero left Room 111 at *Rancho Relajar*, for him to contact Dyson and for Dyson to fly a bunch of hives to Austin. It would take a pilot braver than me to spend hours trapped in a plane over an ocean with several thousand bees flying around the cockpit, but I assumed there was a way to do it without getting stung.

Constance had the expertise with bees to arrange something like this. She would know how to transport them. She would understand any limits with the pheromone agent. She also had a good motive for killing Terrance. But Constance was on the run. Did she have ready access to a bunch of hives?

Between her and Dyson, the latter using Romero as his orchestrator, the finger of suspicion had to point to Jacob Dyson. Regardless, one question kept racing back and forth across my brain: How in hell did all those bees get into a third floor apartment? It's not like they had elevator privileges.

I glanced around the room. The place was nicely furnished. Open drapes framed the two front windows like white pillars. The walls and ceilings were swirled beige plaster. The blue carpeting went from wall to wall. It looked like freshly-cut felt—except where the bees had collected in dark, smelly clumps. Ivory-colored leather covered a davenport, armchair and hassock. A few mismatched tables supported lamps, but that was to be expected in a bachelor's pad. Terrance had a large, flat-panel television hanging on one wall – also to be expected. On the other walls was a variety of shelving holding up knickknacks. These, in line with bachelorhood, were of the pornographic variety. To my right was a doorway leading to the kitchen. To my left was a passageway leading to what I presumed would be the bedroom and bath.

Outside a delivery truck rumbled past, focusing my attention back on the windows. Both stared across the rear of the apartment building's property towards a highway. I was about to begin my search of the apartment when I realized that the sound level of the truck's engine and tires had been much higher than normal. In a building with modern windows—designed to muffle outside noises—a passing vehicle would barely be noticed. But there was no ignoring that truck.

I went over to the windows. The locks on both were set. So how did the sound leak through so dramatically? On further examination, I noticed that one of the windows had a round hole about the size of a golf ball cut through the double-glazing. That explained the noise. It also brought about a few questions. For example, why did something dark and syrupy encircle the opening on both sides of the window? And why would someone put it there after cutting the hole? And who, among the possible suspects, had the expertise to cut that hole?

Considering that Rodney's apartment was three floors up, the window must have been removed from inside the apartment to cut the glass. That meant someone had gotten into the flat unnoticed or perhaps by invitation. That same person had spent about thirty minutes carefully cutting holes on both the inner and out panes. Then, he or she spent another bit of time daubing each side of the opening with the goop that still lingered there. Afterwards, the window had been returned to its place—all either without Rodney Terrance noticing or with his approval.

I was not much of a housekeeper. But even my lack of a dusting instinct made me doubt that Rodney Terrance had encouraged the hole. Regardless, why do it at all? Unless...

I pressed my face to the glass and looked out, and down. There, on the moonlit grass I spotted several white boxes. Those boxes were a dead match with my remembrances of beehives. Since the boxes were directly below the perforated window, I felt it was a safe bet that they were the source of the bees. I also felt the hole in the window was the passageway the bees had used to enter the apartment. But why would bees make the trip up to the hole? Had the goop lured them there? Not having seen the like before, I had no way to prove or disprove a connection between pheromones and the goop.

If Jacob Dyson had supplied the hives, he had been very foolish in not having whoever placed them into position return and haul the hives away for burning. If there was not a manufacturer's label on the hive, there would be fingerprints. Either could direct investigators to Dyson's front door.

Then there was the practicality of the murder-method to consider. Why not just come up here, knock on the door and shoot Terrance when he answered? It would be quicker, cleaner, less visible and a lot simpler. Admittedly, it would not be as much fun for the killer. Being enveloped by thousands of stinging insects would have been a horrific way to die. If meting out punishment was an intended part of the murder process, the perpetrator had succeeded.

I took a step back from the window, taking out Terrance's handkerchief and using it to wipe the point-of-contact my face had made with the glass. After that, I breezed through the living room using Terrance's handkerchief as protection against depositing fingerprints while lifting leather cushions and peering under tables.

Finding nothing of interest other than a couple of porn magazines, I went into the kitchen and made a similar rummage. This time, I dawdled through cabinet-shelves, drawers and the refrigerator. I found nothing, other than what was expected.

Leaving there, I moved across the living room and down the hallway.

In the bath I made an interesting discovery. The medicine-cabinet was open, and most of what had been within was piled in the sink. A foot powder tin had been emptied into the toilet, leaving talcum residue on the porcelain rim. The bottom of a toothpaste tube had been cut off and its contents squeezed-out that opening.

It was possible Rodney Terrance had been doing a cleanout just before he was killed and enjoyed the occasional debauching of containers before tossing them to the trash. But I felt it was more likely that his killer had been searching for something small enough to hide almost anywhere. Considering the amount of search-effort and the resulting time needed, I assumed that his killer had done this before the bees entered the apartment. So why had not Terrance noticed the mess? Or had he, too late to stop his killer from letting the bees in? Or had the bees attacked with such suffocating force as soon as Terrance entered his apartment that he could not flee?

I continued my search of the bathroom by removing the top of the toilet-tank and draining it by way of the flush-mechanism. At first inspection there was nothing in there that did not belong. Then I took out my penlight and shined it down the water-overflow pipe. There, dangling by a bit of thin, clear, plastic thread was a small tubular container.

I fished it out, expecting to find a stash of cocaine. A glance through the clear plastic suggested otherwise. Within was a dark, syrupy substance. I took off the cap, lifted the tube to my nose and sniffed. Its contents had a barely-detectable, acrid odor.

I tilted the container slightly. The contents slowly shifted, moving about like warm honey.

I did not know what it was, but I suspected it was the reason for the search. In terms of color and texture, it was a good match with what had been smeared around the holes in the window. Could the plastic vial contain that mysterious, impossible to isolate pheromone the article had mentioned? If so, I had found something worth millions in the kill-for-hire racket. I reclosed the container and dropped it and the penlight into my pocket.

After restoring the toilet-tank cover and wiping away my fingerprints from anywhere I might have touched, I went across the hall to the bedroom. It contained the usual offerings: bed, clothes-bureau and closet. I stripped the linen from the mattress and tumbled the latter from its perch upon the box spring. Finding nothing, I searched the closet and bureau.

Hidden under rolled socks in the middle-drawer, was a checkbook. Its register listed equal monthly deposits of five thousand dollars. The register also had a notation beside each deposit – 'JR'.

It was no guaranty. But I was willing to bet that 'JR' stood for Jesus Romero. For a guy who lived by his wits as a gambler, Romero had some heavy expenses.

I wiped my prints from the checkbook, did a cleanup of my presence in the bedroom and then headed back to the corpse.

When I got to the front room I heard a key scraping in the door-lock.

I quickly moved toward the sound. I was just positioning myself next to the hinges when the door opened. A second later, I watched a shadow creep into the room.

On its heels was Jesus Romero.

He did not even pause at the sight of Rodney Terrance and the piles of dead bees. Romero simply started for the bedroom, a can of gasoline in one of his hands.

Based upon his lack of surprise and the fuel-can, I assumed he had been the one who had searched the bath. I also assumed, because he had not been surprised by Terrance's method of dying, that Romero had played a part in it. Then, not having found the plastic do-da in the toilet, Romero decided to return and destroy it, and any evidence linking himself to Rodney Terrance's murder, with a not-so-little fire.

I gave Romero time to make three steps. Then I lunged, letting my right fist test the strength of his skull. As my knuckles bounced off the back of his head the gasoline can hit the carpet. Immediately afterward, Romero sprawled forward, unconscious and nearly atop Rodney.

I up-righted the gasoline can and wiped my prints from it. Then I quickly squatted beside Romero and went through his suit. The only things of interest were a wad of cash big enough to use for a baseball and his driving license with its usual address-offering. I stuffed both into my pocket. For grins, I stripped Romero down to his underwear, rose and quickly left the apartment with his clothes tucked under one arm.

On my way out of the building I set off the fire alarm, dumped Romero's clothes into a nearby trashcan and then telephoned the police. In addition to making an anonymous report of Terrance's death, I wanted to be certain that the building would be empty. If Romero regained consciousness before the locals arrived, he would likely try to complete his arsonistic intentions.

The sounds of sirens, whining their approach from some distance away, filled the night air. I smiled. Romero might be able to explain his presence in the dead man's apartment as that of a concerned friend, or even that of an employer. Elucidating the purpose of the gasoline without implicating himself in a felony, would be difficult. Particularly, when the police got to questions that focused on why he paid a call on Terrance carrying a can of gasoline while being clothed only in his undies.

When I reached the Buick, I paused to glance up at the bright moon. Although I had slept most of the day, the night had been very fruitful. It was time to head back home and relax. Tomorrow, I would treat myself to a visit with Peterson Barrows.

I climbed inside, started the engine, turned on the radio and drove off. How did that old song go? 'Knick-Knack paddy-whack?' I would hum it for Barrows. Maybe, in time, he would recall the words.

Unfortunately, best laid plans oft go astray. Not many blocks later, flashing lights of the police-cruiser variety appeared in my rearview mirror. I had not been speeding. In fact I had obeyed each and every traffic law on the books—which was unusual for me. Nevertheless, I was about to be questioned by a brain-dead local law-enforcer whether I liked the idea, or not. Based upon past experience, due to well-founded rumors concerning my unsavory reputation, such question invariably meant a lengthy stay in uncomfortable surroundings that included bars, and a bunk-bed.

I stuffed the cash I had collected from Terrance and Romero, as well as Romero's driving license, beneath the car-seat. For good measure, I added the plastic tube I had taken from the toilet to the pile.

After snuffing out my cigarette, I pulled off onto the shoulder and waited.

After cuffing me, the arresting officers read me my rights and then explained the reason for my detention. Lt. Herbie Mann had ordered my arrest. Upon investigating the shooting of Edward Little, Forensics' had found a latent print that matched my right thumb on the water tap in the kitchenette, of Room 109. Lt. Mann, forever the one who crossed T's and dotted I's, felt my presence in the room with the dead man implicated me in Little's killing. How disappointingly right he was.

When I arrived at the precinct station, I was allowed the usual phone call. I elected to telephone my bookie to find out how I had done at Hialeah that morning. Not surprisingly, my horse came in last.

After a night sharing a cell with a wheezing asthmatic, I was taken, in shackles, to interrogation room 'A'. There, the wrist and ankle hardware were removed. Then I was instructed to await the presence of Captain Weatherly, the precinct commander.

I knew Weatherly from my years in Homicide. He was hardworking and honest—unusual for an officer at that level in Austin P.D. He also harbored a gross dislike for me—not so unusual, at any level in the police department.

Interrogation room 'A' was a familiar spot, sights as well as smells. Nothing about it had changed since I'd last used it before ending a long career as a homicide investigator. Even the stench of sweat, urine and stale cigarette smoke was the same. This time, however, I was seated on the interrogatee's side of the oak table, situated at mid-floor.

The chair I occupied was also the same. It was one that many an uncooperative suspect had come to hate and fear—in the punching-bag sense of our informal chats. It was straight-backed oak with thick arms, which were suitable for padded leather lashings should the suspect become overly quiet.

There were several wooden chairs on the interrogator's side of the table. These did not have arms. After all when one was asking questions and the questionee was not answering, chair arms only hinder fast getups when coiled fists were about to be added to the question-answer scenario—not that it ever happened, officially.

I studied the unevenly scalloped table-edges looking for reminders of past successes. They were all there. Decades of cigarette burns and chip-offs. The latter were made by the teeth of suspects in one murder or another. Ah the good old days, when a cop could enjoy getting a confession from a suspect. I lit a cigarette and puffed nonchalantly. It almost felt like home, being back here.

Thirty minutes later the door opened. From down the hall I could hear the kid from *Rancho Relajar* whining, "Look, I got sick on the job and went to my parent's house. You guys picked me up when I got back to my apartment a little while ago. So I don't know anything about anything or anybody."

Then I heard the frustrated sound of the interrogator's voice, "There was a killing last night. We think we found the guy who did it. We brought you in to make an I.D. from a lineup. While we wait, I wanted to clarify a couple of things. Now lets get back to the gun…"

"Yes I saw his gun," bleated the kid. "But it wasn't like I thought he was going to kill her."

"Who's her?" the interrogator demanded.

"His wife!" the kid snapped, impatiently.

"His wife was the dead guy?"

The kid sobbed, "Aw, shit! He killed some guy, too? My ass is fired for sure."

The door shut and Captain Weatherly came into view. His coat was off and the sleeves on his white shirt were rolled past the elbows. His shoulder-holster was still on, but empty. In each hand was a Styrofoam coffee cup.

"I thought you'd need this," he said and set one of the cups in front of me.

Weatherly was as bald as an onion and as thick as one in the waist. His eyes were snake-gray within an egg-shaped face. His big nose was a network of blue capillaries. He had a jaw like the prow of a tugboat. Hard knots of muscle anchored the corners of his bluish lips. The backs of his blunt hands had a heavy coat of gray hair. Grizzled tufts of more gray stuck out of his jug-ears.

He sat down across from me, sniffed the coffee in his cup and then set it aside. Afterwards, he gave me a thorough visual scraping, like a straight-razor clearing chin-stubble.

"How long since you pensioned off, Bishop?" he eventually grunted.

"Not long enough," I replied, dryly. "You're still running things."

The Captain of Police clamped his bridgework together with a snap. The line of his jaw showed white, with irritation. "Why didn't you report the shooting?"

I spread the wrinkles out of my lips and lied through my teeth, "I called the desk-clerk and told him to do it. That way I avoided the phone-charge on the room."

His eyes flickered with justified disbelief. "Then why didn't you stay put?"

I tilted forward so he could see the fresh abrasion on the back of my head where Constance had struck me. "I received a concussion and was in need of medical care."

With a snort of disdain, he took a fat leather case from his pocket and opened it. Inside were half a dozen green Cuban's. "What hospital did you go to?" he asked, stuffing one of the cigars into his mouth.

"I stopped at St. David's. But the emergency room was packed," I explained. "So I went back out to the Buick to wait. I must've passed out. When I awoke, I immediately headed here to turn myself in. That was when the cruiser pulled my car over."

He wagged his head briefly, still not believing. "Twenty-four hours later?"

I shrugged. "It was dark when I regained consciousness. It was dark when I passed out. How was I to know that a day had gone by?"

"You admit you killed that man at *Rancho Relajar*?"

I watched him stuff the cigar-case back into his pocket and pull out a fancy golden lighter. He lit the Cuban and tucked the lighter back into his pants. Then he arched his eyebrows giving me a prompting glare as his mouth worked on the cigar and his nose belched smoke.

"The man gave me no choice, Captain."

He squinted at me sideways. "When have I heard that from you before?"

"Check the room. You'll find one of his rounds in the cabinetry and another in the ceiling. I reacted to deadly force with deadly force."

Weatherly's eyes narrowed and glistened. Then he said, "Self-defense is always debatable in a homicide—especially when the claim comes from you, Bishop." Then he smiled faintly, knowingly. "But I'd better hear your side of it just the same. The whole thing, Bishop—as if it might be the truth."

I did so in almost-complete and nearly-honest detail. I admitted to being hired by Peterson Barrows to follow Constance Dyson. I did so not in the sense of cooperation, but in hopes of making my least favored lawyer's day. I went on to tell about my fight with Rothfield, and Constance knocking me out. Then I carefully described the interaction I had with Little. The rest, however, I kept to myself for the time being.

"Prints got us nothing on the dead man," Weatherly remarked, when I finished. From the sound of his voice, he now believed some of my story. "But according to Baltimore P.D., an Edward Little is on their books as a small-time booster. Interestingly, *their* Edward Little resided at the address on the driving license. But he died unpleasantly, several months back. Curious, huh?"

"Obviously the dead man killed Little for his ID."

The Captain took a deep draw on the cigar and whistled out the smoke through his nostrils. "Maybe. But if so, why come here?" He tapped the index finger of his right hand on the tabletop for emphasis. "Why not stay in Baltimore where Little's ID might do an imposter some good?"

My front teeth nibbled at the edge of my lower lip for a moment as if I was working hard to recall each minute detail, of the night before. "I'll tell you this much for free, Captain. The dead man spent a good bit of time slurping borscht."

He looked at me, startled. "What in hell are you... Russian? Is that what you're saying?"

I nodded.

His eyes narrowed with suspicion. "Since when do you speak Russian?"

"I don't. But the old woman living in the flop next to mine is Russian. She and I haggle often—about horseracing, her daughter and several other topics. I recognized the similarity between the dead man's accent and hers. Check with immigration, Captain. I'll give you any odds you want the dead man was a frequent flyer from Chechnya."

"Chechnya?" he frowned. "I thought you said he was Russian."

"Chechnya's a little chunk of dirt, with Islamic terrorism leanings, within Russia. Nice part of the country. You should go there on your next vacation. You know, give the locals a peak at what a real American is like."

He considered my explanation a moment. "Are you claiming you're on some terrorist's kill-list? Not that I find the possibility unusual, considering the years I've known you."

"I think Constance Dyson is."

"Why?"

"Jacob Dyson threatened to kill her several months ago. Not so coincidentally, Jacob Dyson has in his employ two Chechnyans. One is named Harris. The other is named Little. I suspect the dead one is that same Little. I also believe that Jacob Dyson is Peterson Barrows's client, and the reason I was hired to follow Mrs. Dyson. Obviously, Dyson had Little in town waiting for me to locate Constance, whereupon Little would step in and fulfill Dyson's death-threat against her. See how nicely it all fits?"

"Mrs. Dyson told you that Barrows was working for Jacob Dyson?"

I said with a disinterested shrug, "She knows Barrows. She mentioned Harris. Jesus Romero mentioned Little. Rothfield admitted he was feeding Dyson information about her. It follows that Dyson is involved, with Barrows as his front-man. Can I go home, now?"

The Captain leaned forward earnestly. "Ever seen the dead man before last night?"

I wagged my head. "I told the arresting officers to contact Peterson Barrows. Did anybody bother?"

Weatherly nodded, leaning back. "I called him at home, just before I came down here. Barrows claims he never heard of you. Which pretty much shoots a hole in your theory."

"Short on memory as well as tact." I lit a cigarette. "Did you ask Barrows about the guy pretending to be Edward Little?"

A peevish look crossed the Captain's face. "Barrows claimed he'd never heard of Little." Weatherly folded his arms. "Quit stalling, Bishop. What aren't you telling me?"

"Call Dyson. Ask him about Little and Barrows."

He tugged at one ear thoughtfully. "I remember hearing about Dyson's threat to his daughter-in-law. But he was overwrought at the time because of his son's death. If he really wanted to kill her, he could've hired it done before she got back here."

"According to Constance Dyson, he tried several times."

"That still doesn't mean the dead man intended murder on Dyson's orders."

The man I shot was looking for Constance. He was carrying a gun fitted with a silencer. He was not shy about using it. He was willing to die to find out what I knew about her. I'll give you any odds you want he is the same Little employed by Jacob Dyson. I'd say that substantiates him being sent to kill her by Dyson."

He lolled the cigar-end back and forth in his mouth, using his tongue. "Then why doesn't Peterson Barrows own up about you? Barrows isn't the type to protect a client from a murder charge when doing so would put him on death row as an accessory."

"I think Barrows is up to his ass in whatever Jacob Dyson has planned for Constance Dyson. With her still alive, Little dead and me in custody, Barrows is running scared. If he admits the truth, Dyson will send Harris or someone else after Barrows."

Weatherly wagged his head. "Wanting to avoid any connection to you, I understand. It's humiliating, to say the least. But..." His voice trailed into silence. After a moment he tilted toward me belligerently. "From what I remember about Dyson he's a big-mouth who never made good on anything, let alone threats. What makes you think he did so this time?"

"This time he might not have had a choice, Captain. There's a DVD involved. From what I've learned, that DVD shows Annie Dyson being murdered. Also based upon what I've been told, Dyson is the brains behind her killing—and the DVD proves that. According to Romero, that DVD is in Austin. Constance Dyson wants it and is not about to stop trying to get it—unless someone kills her. Rothfield admitted that he intended to do so and on Dyson's orders."

"Why would he tell you a thing like that?"

"He had a gun pointing at me and was about to shoot. I don't think he figured I'd be around to spread the word."

Another bout of head-wagging. "Annie Dyson died from a bee sting," Weatherly said. "Had an allergic reaction to the venom. By the time Dyson got her to Austin in his helicopter, she was dead. The autopsy was clear on the cause of death."

"Coroners have been fooled before, Captain."

His gaze moved across me as he spoke. "Constance Dyson went where, after leaving that motel?"

"How in hell would I know? She nearly bashed in my head. I was unconscious for over an hour. Look Captain, you've got my gun. I've made a statement. I'd like to see a doctor."

He flicked about an inch of cigar ash onto the floor, ignoring my plea for medical assistance. "You must have some idea where she went, Bishop."

I gulped more coffee and tried to convince my stomach it was not lethal. The growling I got in return cast doubts upon the effort.

"Not a clue," I said, my irritation growing. "But if you check with the desk clerk at *Rancho Relajar*, he'll tell you that Jesus Romero owns that dump. He'll also tell you that Jesus Romero paid for Constance Dyson's room. So Mrs. Dyson and Albert Rothfield have probably hooked up with Romero."

"What's Romero to her?"

"From what I've gathered, Romero is the link between Mrs. Dyson and that DVD. Look, Captain, if you're shy about bringing Barrows in for questioning, take a flyer at Romero."

The Captain's face hardened. "Already have. Got the same response from him as from Barrows. Nobody knows nobody named Little." Weatherly's lip curled at me. Then that mysterious light of knowing the truth behind a lie flashed in the Captain's eyes. "I spent four hours last night, questioning Romero on an unrelated matter. He was brought in for questioning after being found unconscious at a murder-scene wearing only his underwear. Also found was a can of gasoline with his prints on it. Also found were about two thousand honeybees—dead. The coroner says the victim was stung to death."

I grinned and hit the coffee, again. "Did Romero get undressed before or after the bees arrived?"

"Romero's story changes pretty much each time he tells it," said Weatherly. "Mostly it involves somebody sapping him and leaving the gasoline after stealing everything he had."

"Did Romero claim that this mysterious thief brought the bees, as well?"

"Romero couldn't explain the bees. But a man in a beekeeper costume, using a tailgate lift to lower the hives from a flatbed truck, was seen dropping them off by one of the other tenants. She complained to the landlord about it. That was about two hours before we got the anonymous tip concerning the killing."

"Can the tenant identify the man delivering the hives?"

"Only that he was stockily built. The mesh from his hat kept her from seeing his face." Weatherly looked at me stubbornly. "The dead man was Rodney Terrance. I don't suppose you know anything about that killing?"

I wagged my head. "I've never liked bees. Why was Romero there? Was he a pal of Terrance?"

"Terrance worked for him. Romero said he went there because he was concerned that something had happened to Terrance, the night before. Romero also claimed that he was carrying over twenty grand when he entered the apartment. We found his clothing in a dumpster. But not the money."

"That's the trouble with you honest cops. You don't know a bribe-offer when you hear one. Mention you'll take plastic if he's short on cash."

Captain Weatherly bowed his head. For nearly a minute, he closed his eyes in thought. Then he looked up and asked, "What's your tie-in to Rodney Terrance?"

I made a vague gesture. "This, that and the other thing. I wouldn't say we were friends. But enemies doesn't cover it, either."

"If I search your apartment, will I find anything in the way of beekeeper clothing?" The Captain was getting impatient.

"I certainly hope not," I said, suddenly feeling a frame being fitted, ever so tightly.

"We're treating Terrance's death as suspicious because we found a hole cut through one of the windows. There was a tar-like substance around that hole. So far it has not been identified. But after examining the entire apartment, that hole is the only way to account for the bees. The hives, as we discovered during out investigation, were placed directly below Terrance's apartment."

I grinned and puffed, toying with the idea of pointing him to the pheromone theory. But I decided against that. "Are you going to charge Romero?"

"With what?" Weatherly demanded. "The gasoline was still in the can, so the chance of making an attempted-arson charge stick is damn slim." He let out a little snort of frustration. "By the time Romero talks to a lawyer, his story will change again—to him bringing in the gasoline to splash on the bees in an effort to save his pal's life."

"You could bust him for indecent exposure. At least insist upon a psychiatric examination before dumping him back on the streets."

His voice went thin with suspicion. "What have you got against Romero?"

"Actually, I've never met the man. If you don't believe me, ask Romero."

"I already did. Claims he never heard of you—which is an impossibility, considering your wide and colorful history." The Captain folded his hands on the table and looked at me squarely. "You'd better come clean, Bishop. All I need is to find a connection between you and the dead man to make the Mayor's day."

He was not bluffing. "Which dead man? Little? Or do you seriously believe I trained a bunch of bees to attack Rodney Terrance?"

"Stop playing me, Bishop," he replied. "My gut tells me you're involved in both incidents." His fingers clenched spasmodically, as though he could feel my throat. "Ever been in Terrance's apartment?"

My mind darted to the strong possibility that forensics had also found my prints, there. So I lied, again. "I did visit Rodney a few days ago."

"What about?"

"A missing person's case I was working," my lie continued. "Sixteen year old female. Rodney Terrance has quite a reputation with young women. One of my snitches told me he'd been with a girl who matched the description of the one I was looking for. After talking to Terrance, I decided he had nothing to do the case."

His eyes became puddles of hot tar. "What do you know about bees?"

"I've never been one for keeping pets, Captain. Why not cut to the chase and contact Jacob Dyson? I'm told he has all kinds of bees."

The Captain's smile went as thin as the gold on a dime-store locket. "I'm not about to bother a billionaire with political connections from here to Washington just on your claims."

"Then press Barrows for his client list and disbursement ledger. You'll find Jacob Dyson as a client and me receiving an advance."

Weatherly wagged his head impatiently. "I'm not likely to get a warrant for Barrow's records on what you've told me. But I will talk to him again." Then his brows furrowed with suspicion. "Are you certain the woman you followed really is Constance Dyson? Last I heard, she was in Indiana."

"I'm certain. Did the real Edward Little have any connections in Austin?"

"Not that we could find. According to Baltimore, he was one of those types who talked big, but invariably mimicked his own name." Weatherly drew in his breath. "Did Mrs. Dyson meet anyone at the airport?"

I nodded. "Rodney Terrance."

His eyes widened with surprise. "Why in hell didn't you mention that before?"

I gave him a vague reply in the form of half a disinterested shrug.

"As I recall she's an expert on bees," he remarked, thoughtfully. "Husband got killed by bees. Mother-in-law, too. Then a guy she hooks up with dies the same way. It makes me think…"

"The same can be said for Jacob Dyson."

A ripple of nerves went through him. "What's your connection to Jacob Dyson?"

"I've never met him, either."

The Captain leaned his arms on the tabletop. "What about Constance Dyson? Had you any involvement with her prior to being hired to follow her?"

I shook my head. "When was Terrance killed?"

His face worked stiffly. "Time of death was shortly after nine last night. Where were you about that time, Bishop?"

"In my office." I pointed at the phone. "What say we take a little trip to Dyson Island? Right now's good for me."

The Captain folded his arms in refusal. "Anything more you want to tell me about the shooting at *Rancho Relajar*?"

"Are you planning to charge me, Captain?"

Weatherly shook his head. "But I know you're playing me. The coroner says Terrance took a rough beating quite recently. Somebody who knew his business gave that man a thorough going over. Romero, I'm told, is damn good with his dukes." Then Weatherly's eyes narrowed on me as if the look could turn the object of his stare to stone. "It would've taken a damn good man to drop Romero in one blow. From what I hear you're still pretty good with your fists. Maybe you worked Terrance over, too? Maybe he died because of it. Maybe you decided to try and beat a manslaughter charge by getting a bunch of bees into his apartment to sting his corpse."

"Then I lured Romero there with a can of gasoline, convinced him to strip off, and then robbed him? Should I assume that the Mayor has been informed of my arrest?"

He laid his cigar aside, the burning end pointing over the edge of the table. It was not casually done. His placing it there had the deliberateness of a man who felt he had an unpleasant duty before him.

"Which is why we're going to go through it all over again, Bishop."

"Still kowtowing to the gods of corruption in order to protect your pension, eh Captain?" I taunted.

Blood mounted to Weatherly's face. "Take it from when you got up, yesterday morning…"

NINE

After Weatherly finally ran out of inspiration and perspiration, I was turned loose. A taxi took me took me to the Austin P.D. impound-lot. There, I reclaimed the Buick.

Surprisingly, the money and the plastic container of goop were where I had left them. I loaded these into pockets and drove over to the exit kiosk.

Not surprisingly, towing fees and storage were part of the Buick's reclamation. I paid—vowing to collect from Peterson Barrows by tapping one of his major arteries.

I was hungry after hours of nothing but bad coffee and interrogation-room queries. So on my way down Congress Avenue toward my flop, I stopped for something to eat.

Like most business districts in Texas, Congress is fronted by a collection of narrow turn-of-the-previous-century buildings. The compressed frontage for each is not the result of architectural madness, as one might easily assume. Instead, it was a workaround to limit the impact of real-estate taxes, during bygone days. In the era of Wild-West ribaldry, excises against business properties were levied according to the width of the building-face, not the construct's overall square-footage. As such, the Congress Avenue buildings run back a hundred feet, or more. But they stand barely thirty feet wide. Ah, Texas. If there is any way to get around a law, one of your politicians will proudly pursue it.

The restaurant I selected was called *Phil and Lil's*. On the front window was the message, *'Meals Fit For Any King'*. It was a big brag, even for Texas. But I went inside the place, anyway.

Immediately my nose caught the tantalizing scents of fried sausage, ham, bacon, beef, pork and Serrano peppers. That was still no guaranty of the sign's validity. Nevertheless, my nostrils flared lustily with every delightful breath. So much so, I felt a return of youthful vigor amidst an abrupt fantasy involving me, Constance Dyson, honey, and a quick fry-up of rattlesnake. Quickly, I settled into a vacant booth and grabbed a menu.

The special for the day was something called the *'All Rounder'*. It consisted of a ham-slice, a sausage patty, a strip of bacon, a pork chop, a steak and a three-egg mixture of Serrano's topped by pan-fried potatoes drenched in melted Cheddar. The only thing it lacked from being perfection on my palate was a hefty portion of deep-fried rattler. Nevertheless my nose had already convinced my stomach to expect epicurean wonderment. So with a smack on my lips and a gurgle in my belly, I waved over a waitress.

After telling her to put a rush on my order, I took out my cell-phone and rang Peterson Barrows. In my own inimitable way, I wanted to let the lowlife shyster know how pleased I was about his abandoning me during my time of emotional strife and legal peril. Further, that I planned to star in his next nightmare.

As expected, the former judge was not happy to hear my voice.

"Bishop, you damn fool!" he screamed, from the other end of the connection. "What in hell are you playing at?"

"You tell me first, shyster," I countered. "I've got Piranhas chewing my balls and you're denying all knowledge of our arrangement."

"Nobody was supposed to know about your business with me," he bellowed. "And to make matters worse, you told the police that Jacob Dyson is my client kill me, for Christ's sake! Nobody was supposed to know anything."

"Well, the cat's out of the bag now. What reason did Dyson give you for wanting her followed?"

"Damn you, Bishop! Get it through your head that Jacob Dyson is not my client. I gave you a simple job that…"

"Which got complicated, Barrows. I'm still breathing. A couple of other men aren't. Sadly, neither corpse looked anything like you."

"Killings?" he croaked, in horror. "All you were supposed to do…"

"One was a Chechnyan the police can't identify who carried the ID of a Baltimorean named Edward Little," I interjected. "The second man went by the name of Rodney Terrance. I killed Little. Terrance, however, was somebody else's kinky idea of a good time. I'm thinking you've got about twenty minutes before Weatherly hauls your ass in for interrogation. When that happens, I plan to help him strap you to the execution-gurney."

"Are you threatening me, Bishop?"

"From the tip of your bee-stung nose, right down to your lacquered toenails. I figure you for sending that Chechnyan to *Rancho Relajar* so he could kill Constance Dyson. I think you also told him to get rid of me. Once I can prove it, don't think I won't be sharing the details with Weatherly—after I've buried you."

"I didn't get your damn phone-message about that motel until a few minutes before Captain Weatherly telephoned," the lawyer protested.

"You're lying, Barrows. Only you and I knew that Mrs. Dyson was at *Rancho Relajar.* I didn't tell anyone - which makes you the leak."

There was a pause. Then he sputtered, "Mrs. Dyson? Does that mean you spoke to her, for Christ's sake? I told you that she was not to know she was being followed."

"Not only did she and I chit-chat, Barrows, but Mrs. Dyson made it very clear that she knows you. How'd that happen, Barrows? Maybe when you scammed her over that DVD? Does Wolf actually have something worth half a million, Barrows? Or is this some game you're running?"

The line went silent.

"I'll be returning your money. Goodbye, Mr. Barrows."

"Bishop, wait!"

"Look, Barrows, this whole gig stinks. Whether you're involved or not, somebody committed murder using bees. I don't want any part of it."

"Bees?" he scoffed. "Are you insane?"

"I was in Terrance's apartment, Barrows. I saw him lying on the carpet with about two thousand fuzzy-striped dead bitches keeping his corpse company."

"But…"

"To my knowledge there are only two outstanding bee-experts in Texas," I continued. "One is Constance Dyson. The other is Edmund Wolf. Both worked for or still are working for Jacob Dyson—your client."

"He's not my client!"

"Weatherly thinks Constance Dyson is the front-runner on the murder circuit. I would agree with Weatherly except for one thing. Mrs. Dyson doesn't have access to a bunch of beehives? Dyson, on the other hand, has an island full of hives. What's the deal, Barrows? Did Dyson hire you to keep her on a string until he could send her to bee-heaven? Does he believe making the authorities think some sort of bee-madness is taking place can hide her murder?"

"You must be out of your mind!"

"Two days ago I'd have said the same thing to my shaving mirror. Now I'm not so sure, Barrows. The Feds are training bees to signal when flying over roadside bombs. When the bees smell explosives they stick out their little proboscises. Pretty cute, huh? They're using them in Iraq and Afghanistan. How in hell a soldier can be expected to notice that obnoxious proboscis at any distance is beyond me. Nevertheless, it's scientific fact. Not only that, Barrows, but scientists have proven that bees can count up to four. I'm not sure what good that is when there are thousands of bees in each hive. But those little critters can do it using a brain the size of a Serrano seed. Considering all that, I think getting the little fuzz-balls to use their stingers on command would be child's play. What do you think, Barrows?"

"That's ridiculous. How in hell you…"

"I'm not finished Barrows," I interrupted. "I also had a chat with Albert Rothfield—the man Constance Dyson is currently giving a smile to. Rothfield is Jacob Dyson's chauffeur—or was. Not only that, but Rothfield admitted that your client—Dyson—was paying him to inform on her movements. Further, Dyson is paying Rothfield to kill Constance Dyson. You hooked your cart to Dyson's star and you're waiting to collect a bonus after she's dead—admit it, Barrows."

There was a choking sound followed by sudden silence on the other end of the connection.

"Have my prayers been answered and you've just died from a coronary?" I quipped. "Or are you simply playing dumb?"

"You've got it all wrong, Bishop," he squawked.

"Then correct me. Captain Weatherly is looking for Mrs. Dyson. So far he's got a case based upon probabilities. I tried to convince him that Jacob Dyson was just as good a candidate. But Weatherly doesn't like to step on politically connected toes."

More silence.

"Did Jesus Romero ever appear before you when you were a judge?" I asked the lawyer.

"He may have," the judge said, sullenly. "But what you don't understand is..."

"Romero had a key to Rodney Terrance's apartment. Romero went there after Terrance died. I saw him arrive, Barrows. He walked in carrying a can of gasoline. He didn't bat an eye at Terrance or the thousands of dead bees. Romero intended to burn the apartment, hoping to conceal what had happened. But I don't think he was there under Constance Dyson's orders. I think you told him what to do—on Dyson's orders. Goodbye, Barrows."

"Wait, Bishop! Where is Mrs. Dyson?"

"She left for parts unknown with Albert Rothfield. You should have no trouble locating them. Just look for a big guy with oak-tree connections in both fists. Watch for your refund."

"Hold it, damn you! This isn't over."

"I've spent the last six hours answering questions put to me by a police captain who knows me like a book, and has no sense of humor. I'm tired, Barrows. I've got a sore head, bruised fists and I need a shower. As far as I'm concerned, you and I are quits."

"Bishop! You can't walk out on me. If it's a matter of money consider what I advanced as a bonus."

For a man who was extremely unhappy with the quality of my work, Barrows was oddly determined to keep me on the job. I did not know whether to love, or hate him. I decided the latter would be a lot more fun than the former. But my curiosity could not be stifled.

"I'm not interested in your money, Barrows. But I might reconsider if you come clean to Weatherly about our business-arrangement."

"But if I tell him..."

"It's either that or I'll produce the tape-recording I made of our meeting in my office," I lied.

"Tape recording?" he bleated.

I smiled as I imagined the former judge squirming in his chair like a kid caught cheating on a test. "I record all client-meetings, Barrows. Would you like a copy for your files?"

"Jesus Christ! A fucking recording?"

"I promised to send a copy to Weatherly. He seemed very interested. Particularly, since you denied all knowledge of me in a statement to him. I think lying to the police in order to mislead them in a murder investigation carries a prison-term as well as disbarment as a penalty, Barrows."

"Damn you, Bishop! Okay. I'll talk to Weatherly. Just don't fold on me." There was another pause. Finally he squawked, "After Nixon's fiasco, who the fuck in their right mind makes recordings?"

"One more proviso, Barrows... I want to know the reason Jacob Dyson gave you for wanting Constance tailed."

For nearly a minute all I heard was rough breathing on the other end. Then he asked, "Any ideas at all where Mrs. Dyson might be?"

"Not as such. But I know where she plans to be in the near future. Romero claims that Wolf told him the DVD is in Austin. Did Dyson mention that to you?"

"Where is Mrs. Dyson going?"

"That's a little secret I plan to take with me to my grave —unless you come across with what I want to know."

"You can't hold out on me, Bishop. We have a contract."

"So, sue me."

Another session of heavy breathing took place on his end. Then Barrows said, "At the moment all I can divulge is that I have a client who has a legitimate reason for wanting to keep track of the woman you identified as Constance Dyson. That client is not, I repeat, is not Jacob Dyson."

"What reason for following her?"

"For her protection."

"Protection? Stop jerking my pud, Barrows. Dyson threatened to kill her. I know that for a fact. From what she said, he's tried to kill her several times. The guy I killed works for Dyson."

"I can't give you any details. But…"

"If your client isn't Jacob Dyson, is your client connected to him? Yes, or no?"

I heard more breathing. Then there was more silence. Eventually, he said, "You have to find Mrs. Dyson. It's life or death, Bishop."

"Goodbye, Barrows."

"Where are you? I'll have my secretary drop off another check."

"No thanks. Goodbye."

"Hold it!" he squealed. "Wait a second! Jesus Christ!" Then there was more silence. After which he said in a soft voice, "Let me touch base with my client. If I can bring you in on the details, I will. Give me until ten o'clock this Friday. Promise me that much?"

I wanted to tell Peterson Barrows where he could shove his request, his client and his promise of more money. But my curiosity as to the identity of his client got the better of common sense. So I agreed to his request.

"What about that woman?" he pleaded. "Bishop? Damn you, Bishop, answer me. Can you find her?"

"I can find her, Barrows, and I will. But until I get what I want from you nothing is going to happen."

I rang off and took a sip of water to wash away the bad taste my conversation with him had left in my mouth. My skull was pounding. My belly ached. And I had this unexplained desire to shave my nether regions. I chalked-up the quirky impulse for lather and a razor to low blood sugar.

When breakfast arrived, I tucked in with abandon. I would not describe the meal as fit for *any* king. But more than one would have found it worth the trip to Austin. With each mouthful my head felt better and my thoughts became more connected. With Jesus Romero in possession of Constance Dyson's jewelry, I had no doubt that the two of them would hook-up at the *Hole in One*. All I had to do was find the dump and keep it under surveillance until she showed up. There was, however, one small problem. For the life of me I could not remember my own name. It was a temporary affliction, I knew, caused by overindulgence in fried Serrano's. Once the sweat stopped pouring out of my skull, everything would return to normal. Or as normal as I ever got.

TEN

I spent the next three days checking the backgrounds of Jesus Romero and Rodney Terrance, and tailing Romero.

I learned the gambler lived in a two-story rambler on Lake Travis. I also learned he had a serious reputation for not taking losses lightly. This might explain Romero's conviction for robbing an Austin nightclub reputed to offer gambling. That gun-toting temper tantrum sent him up for five years. There had been no arrests since his release from prison, two years ago. But rumors abounded as to his connections with the Russian Mafia. It was suggested that the Russians financed Romero's gambling. The reasons for that backing, however, were vague.

Terrance had always been somebody in the wings, looking for a chance at anything close to the big-time. Although he had never been arrested, it was believed that he had done his share of smuggling as a mule for the Russian Mafia. It was through them that he and Romero had become acquainted.

Nothing in either man's history explained how Romero had made a connection to Jacob Dyson. But considering Dyson's Chechnyan connection, I suspected the Russian mob might have helped put Romero on the billionaire's payroll.

On Thursday night, I made another trip to the Hole in One. It was located on the outskirts of Leander. The nightclub was more or less a private gambling establishment built into the bank of the Colorado River. There was parking on the flatland, above. To reach the joint, a concrete staircase led down to a beach-level entrance. The public could enjoy both the restaurant and the bar. But only members were allowed into private areas for gambling and other illicit diversions.

The nightclub's interior was nothing to brag about. The walls were painted clay-brown. The floor was brown tile. The ceiling was smeared plaster. The air was putrefying from the stench of cigar smoke, and stale perfume. Still, its clientele was never in short supply. Each time I visited, the fifty or so white-clothed tables and their accompanying chairs were occupied by smiling and not so smiling people.

At one end of the place was a dance-floor replete with wooden dais atop which played a rather wooden, three-piece band. At the other end of the main room was the dining area. In between, on the left side was a spot for people in barmen uniforms who stood behind what looked to be a mile of polished mahogany. On the other side of the room one could expect to see two men guarding a set of unmarked doors. Tonight these living statues were a pair of heavy Hispanic types wearing dark suits. Behind those doors, I assumed, the membership could lighten the load in their wallets or certain bodily organs.

I settled onto one of the leather-topped stools in front of the bar and—as I had done for three nights running—carefully described Constance Dyson to a bartender.

"It's very important that I find her," I declared, in closing. "Her mother is ill. I've been delegated by her family to break the bad news."

"Is that her, Señor?" the barman asked, pointing across the room.

I turned in the direction he was indicating.

Half a dozen couples were on the dance-floor shaking all they had in time to the band's outpouring. One brunette with enormous breasts had a space all to herself. That was probably because anyone within two feet of her was risking bodily harm, from her flailing mammaries. The rest of the dancers were pretty much in synch with elbows, butts and feet. Most of the men wore skin-tight chinos, and satiny shirts. Most of the women wore short skirts and silky tops, with very little—if anything—underneath. There were, of course, a number of exceptions disposed to wearing tuxedos and gowns. But these were the upscale minority.

"Where do you see her?" I asked, still staring in the direction of his finger.

"The shadows near the back of the stage, Señor."

I squinted trying to peer into the unlit area. For a few seconds all I could see was a silhouette that could be a couple dancing cheek-to-cheek. Then, as the moving shadow edged toward the light, details came into focus. The silhouette was, indeed, a man and a woman. Both were dressed in formal evening attire. As the pair moved further into the light it became clear that if they were not Constance and Albert, they were excellent reproductions. He was big, drunk and slogging. She was redheaded and doing her best to keep his stumbling hooves off her toes.

"That looks like her," I admitted.

The dancing pair suddenly drew apart. He tried to sit down on the floor where a spotlight was making a white smear. She managed, through verbal coaxing and physical effort to keep him on his pegs. Then they slogged back into the shadows. Having located my quarry, I became curious as to the gambler's proximity.

I turned back to face the bartender and said, "That's the lady, amigo. *Muchas gracias.*" Then I asked, "Has Jesus Romero been in, tonight?"

"He's in there, Señor," the bartender pointed past me across the room to the guarded doors. "But that is for members only."

"I'm a member," I lied.

He reached across the bar and patted the bulge under my left arm. "Then you should know that you must leave your *pistola* in the car."

"I guess I forgot," I muttered, lamely.

I ordered a Manhattan on the rocks with bitters and no cherry, which got me a '*¡Muy bien!*' from the bartender. While I waited for it, I returned my attention to Constance and Albert. She still had him on his feet and moving. But he looked to be all but danced-out.

I let my eyes wander further, looking for familiar faces. That's when the double-doors opened and the gambler came into the room.

Romero quickly moved amongst the tables over to one setup for three. There, he sat down. Topping the table were glasses enough for each chair. He picked up one and drank greedily. For a man who was supposed to be a carefree gambling type, Romero did not look happy. I chalked it up to me having his money and Constance playing dance-instructress with Albert.

For many seconds he studied the sloppily moving pair enviously, his jaw-muscles working. Then, as if shamed by their romantic interaction, Romero glared down at his glass.

The music stopped. There was some desultory clapping. After which Mrs. Dyson pushed, pulled and hoisted Albert over to Romero's table. The pair sat. Then Albert rested his head on the tabletop, like a man overdue for a long nap.

Romero started to speak to Constance.

She was clearly disinterested in his gambit. Every few seconds Constance tilted her body toward Albert, as if feeling the need to be his protector.

I could not help but feel a wave of envy for the drunk. Constance Dyson was better than Albert deserved.

The lights dimmed and a single spot hit the dais. Then an aging brunette carrying a microphone staggered drunkenly into the light. The music started and she sang a torch-number in a voice that could have clawed the eyes from a lion.

At the end of her song there was clapping. But I credited that to gratitude for her willingness to vacate the stage.

The dais went dark. Then two spotlights from different angles formed a single spot. The band took that as its cue to make music. This time the sound had a country beat. A tall blonde woman in a blue sequined gown and color-coordinated microphone strode into view. A second later, the spots turned an amber color adding drama to her presentation. At that point, she started to sing.

I gave her credit for a good voice. So did the rest of the crowd. The only thing dragging down her efforts was the faraway and unhappy choice in music. I had never been one who enjoyed hearing a tune that mourned the loss of freedom for those incarcerated. As an actor so often said when in character, "If you can't do the time, don't do the crime."

At the end of her number, the stage fell dark. She made an exit to resounding applause.

A few seconds later the lights rose brightly and the band picked out a salsa tune. This tempted some of the dancers back to the floor. Most were good on their feet. Some were terrible. In between were a few who could get by without crippling each other or those nearby.

I was just getting interested in the gyrations of a buxom blonde with a bare midriff, when a movement among the tables captured my attention.

A dark-haired guy in a tuxedo was making the rounds as if he owned the joint. He paused at certain tables to tender words, probably in hopes of garnering favor. At others, he merely offered a vague nod, or a smile. Eventually, he stopped at a table off to one side and sat down. Sharing this perch was a man with whom I have enjoyed a deep and despiteful history—Salvator Portello.

Sal was dressed in his usual gray attire. Although his eyes were on the dance floor, he was not surprised by his uninvited guest.

I let my eyes wander slightly to the right, and left. At the two tables flanking Sal were his usual four bodyguards, including the two Sicilian Brothers. The other goons were rubbernecking, to keep a protective eye on their boss. The Sicilian Brothers were eyeing me with deep concern.

As far as I knew, Salvator and I had not been at serious odds—at least, recently. But the way the Brothers eyed me, I had a feeling something was amiss. That meant I would shortly be made aware of the gangsters fury. This, no doubt, would be brought to my attention in a very unpleasant manner. My toes curled slightly as I gave a small prayer that Sal's dissatisfaction would not include shoes topped by wet cement.

The tuxedo leaned across the table toward the Mafia Don and said something. Sal rubbed the side of his thin nose, intently listening. Then both men looked towards Romero, Albert and Constance.

The tuxedo seemed concerned. He made more remarks and then lifted his shoulders, as if in despair.

Sal gave no indication, either way. But after the gangster said something, the tuxedo got up and moved off.

Sal pulled out a pipe and stuffed its stem between his jaws. But he did not light it.

It was then one of the Sicilian Brothers leaned toward him and pointed out my presence. When Sal's fulminating eyes found mine I gave him my usual greeting—a Gaelic gesture of contempt. The gangster frowned with annoyance.

My drink came and I paid for it. After tasting the cocktail, I called out to the bartender, "*¡Esto es excelente, mi amigo!*"

He tendered a slight bow.

The music stopped, again. This time it remained quiet, as the band set down their instruments before filing off the dais. The dancers weaved over to their respective tables, some more happy than others about the break.

I let my eyes drift back to Romero's table. Albert was now shoulders-down on the cloth, his arms dangling limp below his knees. Romero was still trying to catch the interest of Mrs. Dyson. From her body-language, Constance would have preferred both men to be somewhere else.

I sucked an ice cube into my mouth and rolled it around with my tongue, pretending to be interested in all that was the *Hole in One*. Every few seconds I returned my stare to Jesus Romero. He was still talking but his demeanor was becoming more and more grim.

Some men are willing to kill for a woman. From the way Romero pursued Constance Dyson, I strongly suspected he was that type. Somehow, I found that tantalizing. Probably because Salvator was only yards away. Her threats to Romero at *Rancho Relajar* had suggested there was something between she and the Mafia Don. If so, Romero might be forced to shoot Sal in order to claim

Mrs. Dyson. I smiled at that prospect.

Naturally, should that unpleasantness occur, I would make myself available to her. After such an experience Constance would need seduction by a P.I. type who was short on class and wardrobe, but long on creative bedroom games. I would offer to dump Albert in a cab and give her a lift to my flop. Whereupon, my irresistible personality would come into play. Then, after a few drinks and my usual obscene coaxing, her libidinous desires would swing in the direction of my bed. Well, perhaps tilt slightly—if an earthquake rattled her in the right direction and she was blind-drunk.

My dirty thoughts were interrupted when Constance gave Romero's face a resounding slap. The sound echoed across the room, and back. It was then I decided that gamblers should leave romance to experts in the art of seduction, like me.

As Romero rubbed the red blotch on his cheek, the rest of the place broke into giggles and claps.

I took out my cell-phone and rang Peterson Barrows. Although no one answered my call, I was able to leave a message. I told him that I was in contact with Constance Dyson. However, I did not disclose her location this time. I also advised him that if he wanted more details he had better fill me on his client when I arrived at his office tomorrow.

As I rang off, Romero shuffled his chair closer to the redhead's. One of his arms casually draped across Constance's shoulders.

He was talking once more.

She was staring at him like a woman wishing she was armed with something that could neuter the entire male population.

Romero paused in his spiel long enough to clasp one hand at the back of her neck, and jerk her head close to his. From his clumsy efforts it looked like he was trying to get her lips in line with his, but he wasn't sure where the noses should go.

As expected, Constance put up a game struggle. However, the gambler had strength and weight on his side. It was not long before he prevailed.

For nearly a minute he chewed her face. During these boyish efforts, one of her hands groped across the table as if searching for something. When her fingers touched a glass, she grabbed-up the tumbler of liquor. Then Constance dumped the drink into his lap.

With a cry of surprise heard round the room, Romero let go of her and jerked back, one hand instinctively reaching down to claw at his soaking crotch. Romero's eyes snapped with rage, his face turning purple. The room, as expected, broke into hoots and catcalls.

A moment later, Romero's mouth twisted into an ugly snarl. Constance scornfully tilted her chin away from him.

He leaned toward her, speaking fiercely.

The redhead dragged one forearm across her mouth to wipe away his spit while making a disgusted face.

To all who watched, it looked as if the gambler tasted like something a dog might deposit on freshly cut grass.

Romero stopped talking, his body going tense with rage.

Unruffled, she offered a quick retort that was punctuated by her spitting into his eyes.

The gambler let go a roar that drew more derides from the onlookers.

Constance, then, said something that Romero liked even less. But I couldn't hear her words.

With an outraged cry Jesus Romero jumped up, grabbing her shoulders hard enough to leave bruises.

Although Constance struggled to get free, Romero managed to drag her erect. Then he used brute force to crush her body to his.

People pointed and laughed, mostly because of the wet blotch covering his groin. He reacted to the ongoing humiliation by trying another shot at kissing.

Surprisingly, Constance gave the impression that she enjoyed it. But a second later, after his defenses were down, she gave a quick movement from her lower body which brought up a well-practiced and pain-inflicting knee. It hit his wet-spot with a force that caused me to whimper in empathy.

Romero's knees buckled and he let out a whimper that was loud enough to be heard from Heaven to Hell. The room exploded with laughter. Applause followed. When the gambler toppled back into his chair, both hands gripping his groin and his face contorted by agony, cheers and whistles broke out.

I joined in the ruckus with a clap of approval.

Mrs. Dyson stood quite still, glaring down at the gambler. She was obviously undaunted by Romero's crudity.

When the ruckus died down, Constance warned him in a voice loud and clear for all to hear. "Touch me again, Jesus, and I'll kill you." With that, she turned and stalked off.

The gambler, twisted painfully in his chair to glower after her. I stood, intent upon following Constance. But she remained within the club, moving obliquely between the tables.

I resumed my seat, still exuberant over her defensive actions. That was when I noticed the Tuxedo hurrying over to the Romero's table.

Although Tuxedo had a better grip on self-control than Mrs. Dyson, he verbally lashed out at the gambler.

Romero countered by getting to his feet with the aid of the table and went into a verbal counter-tirade. Both men's arms, at that point, began flailing with fury. The way Romero was coming on, I expected Tuxedo to back off. But the man did not retreat one step. Instead, Tuxedo simply ended the interaction by pointing toward Salvator Portello, at whose table Mrs. Dyson now sat.

Romero shoved Tuxedo aside and strode toward Salvator, like a raging bull intent upon reclaiming a fickle cow.

Before Romero arrived, Sal's two goons rose and gathered close to their employer. That was when the gangster said something that caused the Sicilian Brothers to leap between Sal and Romero.

Romero stopped. Then he spoke to Thomaso—the older of the Sicilian

Brothers—while pointing at Mrs. Dyson.

Without even glancing at Romero, Sal snapped his fingers.

Instantly, the Brothers went into a well-rehearsed routine. While one gave Romero's neck a not-so-loving hug, the other proffered sharp thumps to the gambler's kidneys.

I could not help but whimper again in empathy with Romero's newfound misery. By morning, each urination would cause Jesus to scream as he pissed blood.

Mrs. Dyson glanced vindictively at Romero, a pleased smile tugging at the corners of her mouth.

I glanced over at Tuxedo and noticed that he was watching the gambler's remedial manners-training without taking any action to stop it. Tuxedo stood stone-still, his face broadened by a smile. After a few seconds, he turned and walked away. Whatever the outcome, he communicated through his departure, it was not his concern.

Fifteen seconds later Jesus Romero was on the floor in squirming anguish.

Sal nodded his head in approval. Immediately the Sicilian Brothers took up a defensive position near his table. The brothers were no longer watching Romero. Instead, both were staring across the room at me.

I gave them a thumbs-up in appreciation of their efforts.

Pietro grinned in reply. But Thomaso remained stoically concerned, by my presence.

At that point Sal twisted slightly in his chair as if suddenly aware of the gambler's predicament. Sal's lips moved slowly and with purpose, his face devoid of emotion.

I could not hear what the gangster was saying. However, I had a good idea what was being conveyed. More than once I had been on the receiving end of Salvator Portello's verbal remonstrations. Invariably these included chidings with respect to impulsive actions. And always, he included a reminder that the worst way to die was by way of Sal's favorite toy—the dip-tank.

When the gangster finished speaking, Romero got up on shaking legs.

Sal tilted back, offering Mrs. Dyson a reassuring smile.

Romero backed away, both his hands pressed against his lower back as if trying to stop a blood outflow. Sweat glistened across his pale face.

Jesus Romero was not yet in clinical shock. But from his deathly coloring and wet complexion, that was probably going to close out his evening's entertainment.

For the casual observer it must have seemed like God had intervened. Salvator uttered a few quiet words. And all became right for the Hole in One. At least right, for everyone except Jesus Romero.

The gambler turned and staggered out of the club. I got off the stool and quickly followed. I still had not recovered Mrs. Dyson's jewelry—something I intended to do. I felt now would be a good time to broach the subject with Romero. Considering the night's events, he probably would like to be shed of any obligation to Constance.

I caught up with Romero in the parking lot, above the nightclub.

Before I could explain myself, he jerked out a sap and came at me.

I assumed the gambler thought I worked for Sal and intended to finish the beating started in the club. But despite my assurances that all I wanted was a friendly chat, he pressed his attack.

The gambler swung the sap at my head.

I did a quick sidestep to avoid it.

Clearly, his plans included giving me in spades what Salvator's men had given him. He swung again. This time I replied with a hard right. But my fist barely clipped his chin. With his free hand reaching, Romero made a lunge and caught hold of my right wrist.

The gambler was tougher than I had expected. His grip on me was like the tentacles of a feeding octopus. I could not jerk free. Then, using his weight, he bulled me off-balance.

That was when the sap came back into view. He intended for the leather-covered lead to catch the side of my face.

I swung with all my strength trying to put my fist through his puss. That redirected the sap, but it still caught me, landing on my shoulders.

Again, I tried to wrench free of his grip. But he managed to retain it and raised the sap overhead for another strike.

At that point I made a left-foot lunge against the gambler, putting all my weight into the move.

When our bodies contacted, my weight pushed him off balance. That's when I caught the back of his left knee with the heel of my right foot. He twisted away, avoiding a fall. So, I swung my free fist. This time I connected. But even with my legs behind the blow, it was not enough to drop him.

A split second later the sap hit me on the forehead, dancing me onto one leg. Jesus lunged forward intending to make another pass with the leather wrapped club. In response, I twisted toward him and at the same time jerked my right knee up.

The blow caught him in the groin with everything I had behind it.

Romero let go a squeal like a pig being castrated. Then he turned sideways, releasing his hold. Not wanting to leave a job unfinished, I quickly cocked my right arm and threw a heavy punch to the base of his skull. A moment later he was sprawled upon asphalt, slack-jawed.

I glanced around to see if anyone was in sight.

The parking lot looked empty so I quickly squatted beside Romero and gave his clothing a search. That netted me his wallet, another bundle of cash and a set of keys.

After pocketing the cash, I stood. Then I pressed the remote-entry device on the key-ring and watched for car-lights.

A few rows over, a new Mercedes beeped its horn and flashed its headlamps. I squatted back down and stripped the gambler to his underwear. With his clothes tucked under one arm, I jerked out my cell-phone and hurried over to his car.

Deadly Sting

I telephoned the police to report a man indecently exposing himself to women at the nightclub. Then, I climbed into his Mercedes and opened the glove box. It had the usual things a man likes to keep in a car: roadmaps, tire-inflation gauge and a box of condoms. I released the trunk latch, climbed out and hurried around to the rear of the Mercedes. Inside the boot, I found a bonus to my knuckle-busting efforts—a woman's jewelry box.

I opened the foot-square, wooden container to find piles of what looked to be castoffs from the crown jewels. I closed it, tucked the box under my free arm like it was a suckling pig, and trotted over to the railing on the far side of the lot. There I gave the keys, his clothes and wallet a toss into river. Then I ran over to the Buick and secreted the cash and jewelry-box into its trunk.

About a quarter mile away, I spotted police cruisers approaching with lights flashing and sirens blaring.

I raced across the parking lot and double-timed it down the steps back into the nightclub. No doubt Jesus Romero would have a great deal to say about his lack of clothing and the guy who must have taken everything when the locals arrived. But giving consideration to my call, his lack of attire, and the fact that he had been previously arrested in the same state of disrobement, I doubted anybody would take his words seriously.

The bartender greeted my return to the stool, casually. "Getting a little fresh air, *amigo*?"

I nodded. "I like to dazzle my good lung once in a while."

I ordered another Manhattan. Then I looked around.

Sal and Constance were in the midst of what looked to be a very intimate conversation. He was stroking her forearm with the fingers of his left hand. She was giving a pink-cheeked look in return. Both seemed to be offering more than casual consideration to the other.

Her end of the verbal intercourse, I understood. Sal was a man nobody refused. But the gangster's interest in Constance—despite her beauty—was completely out of character. For his entire adult live, Salvator Portello had conducted himself as the consummate Sicilian businessman, leaving work only to attend church. Money and power had been his sole pursuits. And, yet, the Mafia Don was sitting there with Constance, looking like he was having the time of his life. Maybe he was, at that.

When the bartender delivered my drink, I pointed to where Sal sat and made a vague question about the man in the gray suit.

"That is the new boss," he proudly proclaimed. "Mr. Salvator Portello, himself. He bought this place last week."

"Had it been up for sale long?" I asked, in bewilderment. Again, I was hearing something completely out of character for the Mafia Don.

The bartender wagged his head. "Not ever. But Mr. Salvator came in, met with the old owner, and then came out and announced that he was the new owner." The bartender gave a shrug. "That was it—all in less than ten minutes."

"Did the old owner comment on the sale?"

Another head-wag. "He went out the back door and ain't been back."

"Sal does have a way with people," I remarked, dryly.

Forcing the sale of a business was in line with Salvator Portello's Tiger-tactics. But doing so to get a toehold in the liquor-retail market was not. That end of Austin's business-sector had always been left to the illicit control of Blind Ray. Old Frank Portello, Salvator's father, had made peace with Ray by agreeing to forgo competing in Ray's business-line. That decade-old commitment ended what had become a gang-war of attrition between Sicilians and blacks. How Blind Ray Wilson would react to Sal's new acquisition was yet to be seen. But I suspected that Ray would not take long in venting his displeasure. That, in turn, would likely start the war again. So why had Salvator done something so foolish?

I suspected it had something to do with the beautiful redhead whose eyes he was staring into, dreamily. There was nothing like first-love to make a man behave foolishly.

I sipped my drink. It was obvious by they way Sal and Constance huddled together with wide grins and lots of giggles, that both were on an emotional rollercoaster. For Salvator, it must be feeling like a rocket-ride. So, why had he not intervened when Romero was mauling Mrs. Dyson? Sal had never been shy about meting out immediate retribution to anyone who might cause problems for those he cared for. He certainly did not hold back when Romero came after Mrs. Dyson. So why had he not stopped Romero earlier?

At first it made no sense. Then it came to me. Constance Dyson had not been in any real danger. If Romero had gotten too rough, Salvator's men would have gone to her aid. By purposely holding back his protection, Sal conveyed an important message to her. She would get his protection against anyone or anything. But it would come at a price and be made available, only on his terms.

"Does Salvator come here often?" I asked, the bartender, the next time he came near.

"Every night since he bought the place," the bartender said. "Personally, I think he's been waiting for somebody." Then he thrust a finger toward Sal's table. "And from the way Mr. Portello is looking at that redhead, I think she's the one. I hope you are not the jealous type, *amigo*. I know you came in here looking for her. But you have only one *pistola*. He has many, many more."

"It's strictly business with me," I told him. But I was jealous. Constance Dyson was giving Sal looks that a man gets only when a woman loves him more than life itself. Whether she was acting to keep his interest, or truly adored the gangster, was yet to be determined. Regardless, at that moment I would gladly give my life to be on the receiving end of her attentions.

The band resumed its position on the dais. Then the drummer ran off a roll, and the lights went out.

A white spotlight centered on the stage. Out of the darkness came a slinky brunette, strutting directly into the glaring beam. She had on a gold, floor-length dress that clung to her body like thin paint on skin. The fabric was held together across her ample breasts and hips by a long zipper, which looked to be short on staying-power.

Deadly Sting

The brunette began barking out a naughty song and gyrating her body like a snake trying to shed its skin. Her voice was hard, and low, the kind that warns any man taking a lusty interest that he had better be up to the job.

After a few seconds the band fell in synch with her movements, providing bump-and-grind accompaniment.

A few seconds later, she began to slowly pull down the dress's zipper.

When a gap splayed from neck to ankles, she suddenly stopped singing, letting go a shrug that dropped the garment from her shoulders. Then she shimmied like something from my favorite dream to force the dress from her arms.

As the cloth hit the floor, there was a cymbal crash. There was another as she stepped clear. This left her wearing only a white bra and panties. The effect of which brought a sigh from the male members of the audience. The brunette reached down and grabbed up the dress with one hand. Making a long windup in time to the continuing beat, she spun the dress overhead like a flag in a windstorm before giving the gown a toss.

The garment flew in the direction from which she had come, causing another sigh from the audience.

With hips gyrating, she took another flyer at the song. Then she performed a slinky strut back and forth across the stage that not only promised good things to come but brought out beads of sweat on my forehead.

In appreciation, the men in the crowd let go encouraging claps and cheers.

That was when her voice cracked with delight and she stopped splay-legged in the spotlight. I grabbed my drink and gulped.

Her body undulated like a horny cobra trying to climb inside a man's pant-leg. She shimmied, as if the snake had moved up the pant-leg to where a snake would be least appreciated.

There was another bang of cymbals. Immediately she discarded her bra with a jerk, exposing silver pasties covering nipples on milky breasts.

The newly exposed flesh seemed to glow.

My heart began to race.

There was another cymbal-bang. In response, her panties snapped off and I nearly choked on an ice-cube.

She now stood before God and my throbbing gearlever with her nether-region protected only by a silver G-string.

There was another clamor from the drummer. In response, she turned her back to the audience, bent down into what I can only describe as my favorite viewpoint before contact.

A drum-roll started. She slowly waggled that view while sliding hands down legs, to grab ankles.

I was almost ready to leap from the stool and race for the stage when a bong thundered.

Instantly, the spotlight went off and she was gone. My disappointed gearlever dropped back into neutral.

After the lights came on the crowd clapped and whistled wildly. But the brunette did not appear for an encore. I moved my eyes back to Salvator's table. He and Mrs. Dyson were still speaking in earnest; their heads close, their bodies tilted toward each other. Now she was the one touching, her fingers lightly stroking his folded hands as if the Texas Mafia Don was God's gift to womankind.

I set down my glass and was about to wave the bartender over for a refill, when Constance Dyson stood and looked across the room at sleeping Albert.

Sal got to his feet like a man about to be led to the death-chamber. His brow puckered in pleading, as her eyes returned to his.

He said something. She reached out and momentarily her fingers touched his cheek.

The gangster, in his old-fashioned way as a suitor, caught the hand and kissed her palm. It was as if she represented all that was wonderful in his life. Maybe that was true, considering his frightening history.

From the blush I saw jump into Mrs. Dyson's cheeks, Constance was more than pleased with his folksy attentiveness. The gangster's idea of being the romantic might be out of date. But it still worked.

Constance said something to Salvator Portello.

Instantly, the gangster snapped his fingers. His two goons rose like robots ready for battle.

Sal spoke.

The two goons hurried over to where Albert dozed, and heaved the drunk upright.

Mrs. Dyson tilted toward Sal and said something—presumably offering appreciation.

Sal responded with a bow that might have been hokey except for the stoic man making it. On him, that bow looked like the offering of a lifelong commitment—or for as long as she would accept him. My amazement continued to grow.

Constance turned and quickly made her way toward the exit.

Sal eyed her departure like a thirsty man watching the world's last case of beer being delivered to someone else.

Sal's goons followed her, dragging Albert Rothfield between them. The Sicilian Brothers, however, remained near their employer, continuing to be occupied with my presence.

I left the bartender a tip, then hurried after Constance Dyson. From the corner of one eye I saw Thomaso informing Salvator of my less than coincidental departure.

The gangster glared after me as if I was about to hijack that mystical case and use the beer for my own perverse pleasure. Frankly, after the impact that stripper had on me, I was seriously considering it.

By the time I reached the parking lot, a handcuffed Jesus Romero was being dumped into a police cruiser. He was screaming bloody-murder that he it was he who was the victim. But the locals were not interested in anything the gambler had to say. The evidence condemning the gambler was clear—his lack of clothing. No doubt Romero would get more than a mention in the *Austin Gazette* in the morning.

I waited until the police cruiser left. Then I trotted over to the Buick. Half a dozen parking spots over from where I stood, Salvator's goons were having trouble getting Albert into the back seat of a compact rental-car. I climbed inside the Buick and started its engine. By the time I had the seatbelt in place and cigarette lit, Albert was in the rental and Constance was behind its steering wheel. I gave her several blocks of space after she drove out before following.

An hour later, Constance Dyson drove into the parking lot of the *Hampstead Extended Stay Motel.*

I parked where I could see her car, and watched. Somehow she got Albert awake, out of the vehicle and moving. Despite a couple of wobbling missteps that dropped the big man to his knees, she managed to get him up the nearest staircase to the motel's second floor.

They stopped at the room on the end, number 223. Rothfield was, more or less leaning his weight against the building, face-on. Constance stuffed a key-card into the lock and then swung the door open. She reached for him, but at that point, Albert's mobility ended. His knees buckled and he hit the passageway-deck with a jarring thump, his face having slid down the building much like a watermelon might skid across a bed of pebbles.

Mrs. Dyson, with practiced precision, grabbed hold of his suit-collar and dragged the big man inside the room.

I waited until she removed the keycard and closed the door. Then I put the Buick into gear. As I drove off, I could not help but notice a heavy tarp covering a stack of something about six feet high near the end of the building.

I took my foot off the brake and nosed the Buick toward my office. I wanted to put the money and jewelry into my safe. I intended to return Mrs. Dyson's property. But I also intended to wait until I had spoken further with Barrows before doing so. The jewels, Romero, Salvator Portello—it was too odd a combination to fit into the simple scenario the lawyer had laid out. Whatever his client had in mind, there was something sinister behind it. And I wanted to know the details before trouble took roost on my doorstep.

* * * *

Two hours later I unlocked the door to my flop. I was planning on a long restful night. Little did I realize the complexities of going to bed until I pushed the door closed.

That's when a not-so-nice group of people stepped into view from my front room.

There were five of them, all men. Each man was completely fluent in the vagaries of the Sicilian dialect. Each man carried a gun. All the guns were out and pointed at me—except for one. That item remained quietly out of sight safely holstered under a nattily tailored gray suit, its use intended for emergencies only.

"Slumming, Sal?" I quipped.

The Mafia Don went to the kitchen table and sat. Then the Salvator

Portello pointed to the chair directly across from him.

I went over and settled into it, feeling like a guest in my own home.

"What's your interest in Constance Dyson?" Salvator Portello quietly asked.

"What's yours, Sal?" I countered. "Don't tell me you've found romance in your twilight years? Love for the first time at your age could be fatal."

The gangster nodded curtly at his men. Two seconds later Pietro stood beside me, his silencer-equipped Glock pressed firmly against my temple.

"Last time, Bishop," droned Salvator. "Constance Dyson? What gives?"

From the disinterested look on Salvator Portello face, he was not bluffing. Neither was Pietro. One wrong word on my part and I was dead. One word on Sal's part, whether I spoke wrong or not, and I was dead. A finger-cramp on Pietro's part, and I was dead. Considering the odds, I decided that honesty—of a sort—was my best chance at surviving the gangsters' visit.

"An attorney named Peterson Barrows hired me to tail her," I explained. "I was not told why. I was paid in advance. Another man was looking for her. He was a Chechnyan using the ID of a man from Baltimore, named Edward Little. I don't know who hired him. I don't know what his intentions were. He never said. But I assumed he planned to kill Mrs. Dyson. I killed him. You can verify that through Captain Weatherly of Austin P.D. That's all I know, Sal."

Salvator face became suddenly grave. He mulled my answer for nearly a minute, his hands folding atop the table as if in anticipation of a prayer, before nodding. The gun at my temple promptly disappeared, along with its owner.

"I heard you took-out some punk," remarked Salvator, with a snort. "They all think they're tough as body-armor when holding heat. But they all buckle once the action is equalized. There ought to be a bounty on those gutless bastards. They give my people a bad name." He paused a moment to study me. "Did that creep say why he was after Constance?"

I shook my head. "But he was willing to die trying to find out where she was."

"Why?" Sal's brows rose in bewilderment. The gangster let go a desolate sigh. Then a far-away look came into his eyes as though he were replaying the most wondrous of memories. "Why," he resumed softly, "would anybody want to kill a beautiful thing like her?"

"Some men don't have your finely tuned eye for a good woman, Sal. Tell me something… Does Jacob Dyson have connections with the Russian mob? I know Romero does. Are the Russians the link between those two?"

The Mafia Don got to his feet. He came around the table to where I sat and gave me a light tap on the cheek. "You keep clear of her, understand? Whatever business you had with that shyster, it's done. I'll be giving him the same message. Constance Dyson is nobody's interest except mine. Understand?"

"Who is she to you, Sal?" I asked. "Seriously, and with all due respect."

He went over to the door and then glared back at me. "Stay clear, Bishop."

After they left I fried up an egg-and-onion sandwich to give my stomach something to work on during the forthcoming Sicilian-related nightmares. The whole time I cooked and ate I could not come to terms with Sal's devotion to

Constance Dyson. *Amore a prima vista?* The lightening-bolt of love? Had it made its mark on the least temperamental Sicilian, in Texas history? Or was there more than adoration for a beautiful woman at stake?

I munched and thought. Then an idea came to mind. What if Jacob Dyson were to die? Could Constance Dyson, as his daughter-in-law, claim his estate? There would be billions in that pot. Perhaps Mrs. Dyson had offered Salvator a piece of that prize? If so, Jacob Dyson was about to get some help along life's final stretch.

ELEVEN

Several hours later, a tapping sound on my apartment door awakened me. It was erratic and insistent.

I glanced at my watch. The dial showed the time coming up on four a.m.—not my favorite hour for visitors. Nevertheless, I crawled out of bed and pulled on a robe before staggering into the kitchen.

At the apartment door I looked through the peephole. A figure in black stood in the hallway; scarf wrapped atop head, black jacket over black shirt and black slacks down to wherever. My first assumption was that Azreael, the angel of death, had arrived for his annual P.R. visit. That theory quickly dissipated when my eyes focused upon a couple of nice points beneath the jacket that promised vibrant femininity.

Dropping caution in favor of fantasy, I opened the door a crack to leer. My visiting angel was none other than Constance Dyson.

"I hope you brought your own jammies," I told her. "I don't have extras."

"I must talk with you, Mr. Bishop," she pleaded.

I stepped back, pulling the door wide.

Mrs. Dyson slipped across the threshold like a ghost floating on a layer of fog. I shut the door and tightened the belt on my robe. Considering Salvator Portello's interest in her, I felt it was important to keep anything that might get excited by my caller's presence from popping into view.

"You'll forgive me if I don't offer a libation," I told her. "After that crack you gave my head at *Rancho Relajar* I'm reluctant to turn my back."

She stumbled over to the kitchen table and leaned against one of the chairs. Her breath came and went in ragged, heaving gasps. "I'm in trouble."

"Not the first time, I'm sure," I remarked, unsympathetically. "Are we talking about Salvator Portello's pent-up passions about to spill over into several months of sexual torment? Or something insignificant, like you being a plague-carrier and I'm your first stop before the entire world is annihilated?"

Her agitation became more pronounced. "Albert was murdered."

"Sounds like you were worth getting up for. Take a load off. You're less dangerous that way." I watched as she settled into a chair, my eyes running over her delightful form with lustful intent. Then I said, "Salvator Portello's at your beck-and-call. Why not let him do your killing?"

Constance twisted toward me frowning with impatient bewilderment. "*I didn't kill Albert.*"

A sudden chill went down my spine as I envisioned Salvator being the perpetrator of Albert's death with jealousy as his motive and me staying out of it, as his intent. "Did Salvator arrange the hit on Albert to clear a pathway to you?" I asked, quickly locking the door. "Or, did he do it on your nickel? And, more importantly, did his men follow you here?"

"Mr. Portello didn't kill Albert." A faint tremor went through her body. "I've never seen anything like it."

"I'm relieved to hear that Sal was not involved. But how can we both be absolutely sure? He is so very, very good at murder."

"It was Jacob Dyson." Her brow knitted into a puzzled frown. "I'm certain it was—almost certain. That's the only way it makes sense."

"Sense, how? Dyson had no reason for killing Albert. The corpse who used to be in your dreams was feeding Dyson information about your travels. Albert admitted it during our punch-out." I folded my arms, still studying the drama in her beautiful face. "Jacob Dyson had no motive for killing Albert."

Constance smoothed back her red hair. "Albert was helping me by giving Jacob misinformation."

"I find that hard to believe, Mrs. Dyson."

"It's true."

"Even so and supposing Albert got tripped up doing his double-agent act, Dyson isn't going to risk a murder conviction by using lethal retaliation."

She twisted to look at me. "Albert was also blackmailing Jacob."

"Blackmailing Dyson, over what?"

"Annie's death." She tilted toward me, her eyes searching mine for reassurance. "Annie was Jacob's wife."

I nodded, thinking back to the news-service's dramatic description of the incident. "But you told Romero that Wolf's DVD proves it was someone else who killed her."

"I said that, yes." Her hands covered her face and she began to quiver. As her hands dropped away she sniffed, "But I was lying. I knew Romero was helping Jacob keep tabs on me. So I told him that to make sure my words got to Jacob."

"To what end?"

"I thought if Jacob believed there was nothing on the DVD to link him to Annie's murder, he would stop looking for it."

I did not buy that explanation but I let it pass. "Does Albert have something more condemning than the DVD?"

Constance shrugged. "Whatever Albert had on Jacob, he got it after the two of us left Indiana," she explained. "Albert went to Dyson Island to see Wolf."

"He actually met with Wolf out there?"

"Exactly. Wolf showed Albert what was on the DVD. Albert told me the only person involved in Annie's murder was Jacob. The DVD clearly showed Jacob injecting Annie with something after restraining her. When she passed out, Jacob untied Annie and carried her away—presumably to his helicopter."

"Whereupon Jacob Dyson, playing the frantic spouse, flew her to Austin for medical help," I said, thinking out loud.

"Annie, of course, was dead when he landed."

"If Albert had no trouble getting onto Dyson Island and back, why was Romero so reluctant?"

"Because he's in cahoots with Dyson."

I nodded noncommittally. "I thought bee-venom was fast-working."

"It is. That's why Jacob couldn't risk injecting her with it on the island. If he had done so, Annie would've died in minutes. Then there would've been no need to make those frantic radio-calls demanding a medical team be available when he landed. But by drugging her and then giving the fatal injection just before he landed, Jacob was able to play his part as Annie's grieving husband to the press. The net result? A slipshod investigation into her death."

I studied Constance Dyson's face, trying to tell if she was lying. When that failed I headed over to the counter and dragged a bottle of pinch from one of the lower cabinets. Then I retrieved two glasses from one of the upper cabinets, and set the bundle on the table. There was nothing like unfurling a sail or two in the wee hours of the morning to improve my good eye and make her truthful.

"How did Albert get to Dyson Island? As far as I know, it's not a tourist stop."

"He chartered a boat."

"Must've cost a bundle. Didn't Dyson try to stop Albert from landing?"

"Jacob didn't know Albert was there," she said. "Albert arranged it so the boat arrived after dark. Then he sneaked into the main house and down to Wolf's laboratory, as prearranged."

"Why would Wolf cooperate with Albert? You told Romero that Wolf had refused to say who killed Annie Dyson."

Constance looked over at me, with obvious impatience. "Albert told Wolf that there would be no sale if he did not see what was on the DVD, first."

"I guess that makes some sense," I said. "But if Albert was on Dyson Island, why didn't he bring Dr. Wolf back here? See what I mean? If Wolf truly wants off Dyson Island; if Wolf is being held there against his will, as you've indicated, then Albert having a boat would've made escaping easy."

Mrs. Dyson fingers clawed at her hair in response, not saying anything.

"I think you've been led down the garden path concerning that DVD," I remarked. "I doubt there's anything on it."

"But Albert told me…"

"Even if what he said is true, I find it very careless of Dyson to get caught on video killing his wife." I poured two drinks and set one of the glasses in front of her. "Too careless."

"You wouldn't think so if you'd known Annie." She pulled the glass close but did not taste the booze. "Annie was paranoid about being murdered."

"Murdered by her husband or in general?"

"By Jacob. That's why she had a video camera hidden in the ceiling of her room. It recorded everything that went on to a series of DVD recorders."

"Must've been colorful, at times."

Mrs. Dyson gave me a confused look. Then color came to her cheeks. "Oh, that. It didn't happen. She and Jacob lived separately."

"That, so I'm told, is what makes for a good marriage. Nevertheless, why didn't Dyson destroy the DVD after killing his wife? He must've known about the equipment. Some guy showing up to install a camera in a ceiling in a house on a private island gets noticed."

Constance shook her head. "I can't explain it. All I know is that only she and Wolf knew about the recording setup."

I felt my eyebrows arch in surprise. "Mrs. Dyson was having an affair with Dr. Wolf?"

"Probably. I can't say with any certainty. What I do know for sure is that they both hated Jacob. So at the very least they were friends against a common enemy. As such, I suppose she told Wolf about her fears and the DVD equipment so that should she be killed, Jacob would be brought to task."

"So after she died, Wolf went in there and took the recorded DVD's—presumably while Dyson was flying Annie to Austin?"

"I know this may sound foreign to your experiences. But everyone on the island suspected Jacob of killing Annie."

I considered her words and then wagged my head. "It doesn't work. Why didn't blackmail rear its ugly head when Dyson returned to the island? With billions on the come to Dyson through inheritance, Wolf should've given Dyson a good financial shaking. Instead, Wolf offered that recording to you."

She made a frustrated gesture with one hand. "How could he approach Jacob? Wolf is trapped on the island. Harris would've killed him if he'd made a blackmail threat."

"Why didn't Annie divorce Dyson? Failing that, why didn't she leave the island?"

"I guess because of Phil. I really don't know. Maybe despite her fears she still loved Jacob."

I fumbled with my lower lip for a time, thinking. Constance's claims had a sort of sense about them. But parts of her story were completely off the beam as far as human nature was concerned. Still, anything was possible.

"How well do you know Salvator Portello?" I asked.

She drew her breath in with a little hiss of surprise. "I know that Mr. Portello doesn't paw. I don't like men who paw."

"Neither do I. It's the pixie in me. From what I saw at the Hole in One things are moving pretty quick on the romantic front. At least from Sal's prospective. Are you in love with him?"

"Mr. Portello is always a gentleman," she said, a little obscurely. "He makes me feel like I'm the only woman in the world. It may not be love. But it's very special."

"Sal *is* very special, I grant you." I settled into the chair directly across the table from her. "He is the Godfather of crime in Texas—not to mention his ever-expanding stranglehold on parts of surrounding States. Sal tortures, butchers and generally makes life unpleasant for people who cross him, or people he's taken a liking to. He bribes politicians and the police to keep Texas in its current state of peerless corruption. He is extremely possessive. Anyone trying to take what Sal thinks is his will die in a most agonizing way. I bring that last tidbit to your attention because your new boyfriend was here a few hours ago. Sal has long-term plans for you, pretty lady. As part of that, he warned me to stay clear of you."

She frowned. "I said nothing to Mr. Portello about you."

"Salvator Portello does not make idle threats. Did you know that Salvator owns the *Hole in One?*"

Her head wagged in surprise.

"He acquired it quite recently. I say acquired, because I doubt that money actually changed hands. Like all things he wants, Sal merely shows up and explains the importance of cooperation. Naturally, the owner of what Sal desires never objects."

"Surely you're exaggerating," she scoffed.

I shook my head. "What's more, in the decades that I've been involved with the Portello clan, there has never been an interest in that type of business. Not until now. Not until you came into Salvator's life. It's not because there isn't enough profit potential. A cash-business like a bar is perfect for the Portello's money-laundering racket. But Old Frank—Sal's father—made a deal with another local gangster by the name of Blind Ray. The agreement was founded on the promise that the Portellos would never invest in anything that competed with Ray's business-interests. Ray, in turn, would not tread on the Portellos' turf. Ray's bread and butter comes from liquor-serving, and various forms of entertainment. That means the Hole in One will probably cause a gang-war."

"It has nothing to do with me."

"Yes it does. You see, you're the reason Sal owns the Hole in One. He wanted to impress you. He wanted you to see a little bit of flash in his otherwise dreary and murderous life."

Her chin dipped. "I can't help it if Mr. Portello likes me."

"Like? Hell! That man is in love with you."

I pulled the cigarette pack from my robe's pocket, sloughed one out and stuffed it between my lips. Then I lit it from the book of matches pinned behind the pack's cellophane wrapper. After which, I blew smoke toward the ceiling.

Constance picked up her drink and gulped. I tasted mine, stared at her and wondered what was going through her beautiful head.

When her eyes returned to mine, her right hand reached into her windbreaker's slash pocket and pulled out the gun she had pointed at me in her room at *Rancho Relajar.*

I said, "Can killing the bearer of bad news concerning your love-life wait until I've finished my drink and smoke? I hate dying with my system low on addictive drugs."

She looked down at the gun. Her lips parted as if to speak. Then they closed, sealing in her thoughts. Constance set the weapon onto the table and shoved it across, as if it were an evil thing. Then her hands settled into her lap and her chin dipped again. She looked like a little girl caught playing a shameful game with someone's little nephew.

"Mine is a lot longer," I quipped, wondering how the gun might relate to the demise of Albert Rothfield.

She pointed at the pistol. "Can you tell if it's been fired?"

Wonderment over and assumptions rapidly taking control, I gave the weapon a reluctant, sidelong stare. I had never touched it, as far as I knew. On the other hand I had been unconscious when she and Albert had left *Rancho Relajar*. My fingerprints could have been placed upon the gun by someone with a vindictive bent. It would also have been easy for someone to have fired the weapon while holding it in my hand in order to leave telltale nitrates embedded in my skin. This, of course, would set the stage for an airtight frame. There was the question of motive, of course. Albert might have done something along those lines to make up for my decking him. But he hadn't the brains for such a sham. Constance, on the other hand, had brains to spare. She, also, had a strong motive. I was the dirty old man who had slightly mussed her in the motel-room.

"Did you tell Salvator about Albert's death?" I asked. "Did he send you here with this bright and shiny toy?"

Her face took on an almost fluorescent pallor. "Of course not." Constance raked her fingers through her hair and glanced about the room as if suddenly becoming aware of her surroundings. "It was my idea."

I leaned forward and sniffed the end of the pistol's barrel. My nose immediately detected the pungent odor of freshly-burned gunpowder. Then I detected other scents not normally associated with pistols—fired, or otherwise. It was the odor of talcum and latex. Although an unusual combination as weaponry scents, it was not completely beyond my experience. Usually it meant that someone had worn latex gloves—with their usual internal dusting of talcum powder—in the act of firing the gun. This, to keep fingerprints at bay and burned nitrates from hitting the hand holding the gun as it went off. I leaned back, studied her staring eyes and wondering.

"It has been fired, hasn't it?" she said.

I nodded. "Quite recently. Did you fire it?"

"Of course not."

"Cops are funny when it comes to guns. They're also sticklers for holding P.I.s to licensing requirements. If I touch it, I'll have to turn it over to the authorities. When that happens they'll check its registration. No matter what information they get back, they'll demand to know how I got hold of it. They'll make all kinds of threats if I choose to remain silent—including jail-time. In the end, I won't have any choice but to point to you as the supplier. Is that what you want?"

"Albert wasn't shot, Mr. Bishop." A grimly humorous smile stole across her visage. "He was stung to death."

Deadly Sting

A chill ran down the back of my neck, causing me to lean across the table. "First your mother-in-law was killed by a bee, if we ignore rumors to the contrary. Then your husband was killed by bees. After him, was Rodney Terrance. Now, your latest romantic interest is dead by the same means? Lady, have you mentioned this curse to Salvator Portello? Because I think he'd like a little forewarning."

Constance gave me a gaping look. "Rodney? Dead? When?"

"At least you didn't offer an alibi as your first words after hearing about it," I remarked. "Don't you read the newspapers? Or watch TV? Or listen to the radio? Rodney Terrance made headlines on all counts because of the way he died—probably the only thing the man ever did that deserved recognition."

"I never listen to the news," she murmured, the light in her eyes dying. "It's too depressing."

I tilted back, nodding in understanding. "Considering what keeps happening to your friends, I'm not surprised."

"You're making fun of me."

"Not by a bee's stinger, if you'll excuse the pun. Mrs. Dyson, do you know what the odds are against those bee-stinging incidents? The ones that keep occurring in your life? I don't. And I've spent a lifetime calculating odds and gambling my hard-earned money away. But I'm fairly certain it's close to being incalculable."

"Surely you can't think I had anything to do with those deaths." She fanned her hands.

"One guy stung to death in Austin during any given decade might be nature's way of tormenting humanity over the atrocities we inflict upon lower forms of life. But three men dying in that manner during a single year? It cannot happen, Mrs. Dyson. Not unless the process is getting help."

She sank back in the chair as if I had struck her. "You're saying I'm involved, aren't you?"

"I'm saying the finger of suspicion can't help but point to somebody. How is it you weren't there when Albert died?"

"He started vomiting after we got back from the Hole in One," Constance explained. "I went out to get Albert something to soothe his stomach." She sneaked a look at me as if to see if I believed her. "When I got back, he was dead, the room filled with bees."

"Can anyone verify your little mercy-mission?"

"The clerk where I bought the antacids will probably remember me. He leered down my blouse when I was writing a check. I told him what I thought of his embarrassing behavior. If you need more than that to accept the truth, I do have the receipt."

"I'd rather have a peep at what the clerk saw. How well did you get along with your mother-in-law?"

Constance looked down at the tabletop, guiltily. "Not very well. Annie felt I wasn't good enough for Phil. I thought she was an overprotective bitch."

"Considering your looks and brains, Annie Dyson must've been insane."

"She hated me," Constance declared.

I took another drag on my cigarette. "I know all about mother-in-laws and hate. Each of mine hated me. I think it had something to do with my harem-complex. For some reason, they felt that a wandering eye negated marital bliss."

She glanced up stifling a grin.

"Who is or was George Lipton?" I asked.

There were several seconds of surprised silence as Mrs. Dyson stared at me. "George was a scientist who worked for Jacob. Why?"

"Did he also die because Jacob Dyson ordered it?"

"I think so." She hesitated. "George didn't fit in with the others. Jacob became suspicious of him. In part, I must admit, because of me."

"What do you mean?"

"I used to see George sneaking around, at night."

"Kitchen? Outside windows with a camera? What?"

"The laboratories are in the main house's basement," she replied. "Each scientist has his or her own lab. But they're all in the same area. I'm the type of person who cannot rest until problems are solved. So when testing didn't go well, I didn't sleep. More often than not, I would go down to my lab and reread the day's notes, trying to find out what went wrong. On several of those occasions, I found George down there. Not in his lab, but in one of the other scientist's. He always had an excuse—needed a pencil, notebook or something. But it happened far too often for those types of things to be his real reason. George, to my mind, was illicitly collecting information to sell. At first I kept that idea to myself because I had no proof. Then one night I saw him taking photos with a miniature camera—in my lab."

"Of what?"

She shrugged. "My research-notes."

"Did you confront him about that?"

"No. But at that point I decided to report George's wanderings to Jacob. I told my father-in-law of my suspicions the next morning. The following evening, George did not appear for supper. When questioned about where George might be, none of the others could recall seeing him that day. As a matter of fact, I had not either. After supper when he still had not appeared, we all became concerned. I suggested we go looking for George. One of the others found his body among the hives, behind the main house."

"Stung to death?" I asked.

She nodded, grimly. "Murdered."

"Mrs. Dyson," I said. "Between you, me and these walls, I think someone who knows a whole lot about bees is behind these fatal stingings. But for the life of me I cannot figure out how it's being done. Could someone commit murder using bees?"

One of her hands became momentarily animated. "It's quite easy, if you know how."

I picked up my glass and drained it. "Like bees finding explosives in the Middle East?"

She gave me a surprised look. "Not many people know about that."

"I read the articles in *Playboy*, now and again. Did you have any involvement in that military effort?"

She blushed. "I was contacted by the Pentagon about its feasibility."

"You said it could or could not be done?"

"I told them it could, of course."

"Let's focus on Sal's favorite hobby—killing people. Is making bees attack harder or easier than what the military is doing?"

"Much easier. The bees being used in Iraq and Afghanistan go through a specialized training. Since their lives are very short—one to four months—that means ongoing training of other bees. It's expensive and time consuming." She bit her lower lip in thought before continuing, "Stinging, however, is instinctive —no training required. The difficult part is getting the chemistry, right. After that, anyone can put the bees to the task."

"Chemistry? You get the bees hopped up on something that makes them go berserk?"

Her reply was prompt and decisive. "In a way," she said. "The 'something', as you put it, is a particular type of pheromone."

"Ah," I said, agreeably. "I read about pheromones and bees, recently. But my understanding, based entirely on the article, is that the correct pheromone is impossible to find."

"I'm an expert. And I'm telling you that's incorrect." Then Constance gave me another surprised look. "I'm astonished that you know about pheromones."

I shook my head. "It's just a word to me. But whatever they are, if they let me point a hive of bees like a gun at the man in my nightmares, they're going to be the most fun I've ever had."

One of Mrs. Dyson's eyebrows arched the merest trifle as if her assessment of my abilities had fallen a tic. "Pheromones are chemicals that elicit base-responses through interaction with the senses."

I refilled my glass. "You'll have to simplify that, Mrs. Dyson. I operate at gut-level, and directly below."

"Okay," she said, "you smell something. That scent causes you to react."

"Like fried onions on burgers and salivation?"

She scooted her chair nearer the table. "More like Bartholin glands communicating a woman's sexual arousal to your penis through your nasal receptors."

I gave her a disbelieving frown. "Are you trying to tell me that all those people died because of bee-sex?"

Her arms rose and fell in frustration. "Mr. Bishop, I'm trying to give you an example that you'll understand." Constance paused a moment before snapping her fingers. "Let's try this approach. Think back to the last time a woman put a smile on your face."

"That might take some doing, but I'll try."

"Your nose collected the scent exuded by her sex. You got excited. Your own pheromones hit the breeze in response, which caused her to get even more aroused." She crossed her legs and her chin sagged into the palm of one hand as its elbow hit the tabletop. The fingers of that hand pulled gently at her cheek. After a moment of contemplation she said almost wistfully, "The pheromones thus passed back and forth caused your penis to erect and put her vaginal lubrication into high-gear. Are you still with me, Mr. Bishop?"

"I'm certainly getting excited. But I still don't see how it all comes frantically banging together—if you'll forgive my naughty jargon."

Constance smiled cynically at my feeble attempt at wit, and shifted upright. "Each creature—including humans—sends off many different types of pheromones. One of these elicits a sexual reaction. Others communicate fear or anger or hunger or something else. In the case of bee-attacks, the bees are reacting with their stingers thinking they must defend their queen. That panic-stinging—the aftermath you witnessed with respect to Rodney Terrance—was instigated by a pheromone. Whether human intervention was part of the event, I cannot say. But a pheromone *was* involved. Otherwise it would not have occurred."

I tilted towards her in confusion. "Panic-stinging?"

Her eyes narrowed rather prettily, like a cat's when spotting a mouse. "The members of a hive attacking an intruder—*en masse.*"

I leaned back rubbing my glass against my cheek, still bewildered. "You're talking a bit above my head. Let's take it one step at a time. What's the first thing I have to do to begin what I think will be my next hobby?"

"You would hire someone with extensive expertise in isolating pheromones."

"Of course. Silly me for not thinking of it. Who, for example, would you recommend?"

She laughed sardonically. "I think you're trying to trap me into saying something akin to a confession."

"Meaning you might be the only one who can do it?"

Without hesitation she nodded.

"What about Dr. Wolf?" I asked. "He's a bee expert, isn't he?"

"It takes more than expertise with bees. The methodology to isolate specific pheromones is extremely complicated and time-consuming. It also requires very expensive equipment and a great deal of persistence."

"Okay, I've hired you and you've done the isolation bit. I have the pheromone. Then what?"

"For practical reasons, you would want to synthesize the pheromone." Constance put the back of her hand to her mouth to stifle a yawn, and looked at me over it. "You would not want to repeat the isolation process each time you needed to replenish your pheromone supply. It's too difficult."

"Which means I would need to hire a chemist, right?"

She nodded. "That part Wolf can do and has done. But everything he can lay claim to is based upon my having previously isolated the correct pheromone."

"This pheromone thingy... I'm trying to get its usage clear in my head. If I spray this stuff around, it will cause an entire hive to go on the attack?"

"Nearly the entire hive. The bees that tend the Queen, and the Queen herself, would remain within the hive. There would also be some bees left near the entrance to guard against intruders." A shadow of anxiety crossed her beautiful face. "And you couldn't just spray it around. You would have to use it in a limited space between your intended victim and a hive. Close enough so the bees would detect the pheromone. Otherwise they would not react."

"But if I did this in the proper way…" I snapped my fingers. "Just like that, the action starts because the bees get a whiff?"

"Think back to my example," she said. "Did you or did you not react without thinking when you were near your female consort?"

Bee-murders or not, I had to agree with her on that. No thought was needed—hopefully it never would be.

"Okay," I said. "I'll buy the pheromone sex angle. But humans wanting to make whoopee is a big stretch from putting bees into assassination-mode."

"Not at all," she declared. "Most low-level communication—meaning that which takes place without sounds or miming—occurs through pheromones. In the case of insects—because they live so intimately with one another—it's done almost entirely in that manner." She took time out to think, as if formulating her next words. "Pheromone communication is instantaneous. More importantly it is absolutely precise. There are no mistakes because of language translation-errors or cipher decoding screw-ups or misspelling problems, such as occurs in typical human-to-human interaction. Each bee receiving the chemical message interprets what is at risk and what she must do—with unqualified accuracy."

I took another drag on my cigarette. "Let's get to the fun part. You know, where those little critters kill on command because I'm pointing a finger at someone of Sicilian ancestry."

Constance Dyson considered my quip with a vague shrug. "You simply make the bees think their Queen is about to be killed."

"And this unique pheromone does that?"

She nodded. "In the natural world, that pheromone would be released ONLY when the hive is invaded—by a marauding bear, for example. In such a case, there would be no checking to see if Queenie is still alive, safe and happily producing eggs. Instead, the bees would attack the nearest moving target NOT part of the hive's population."

I crossed my legs and rested my forearms on the tabletop. For the first time in years I was seeing science from an entirely novel and potentially profitable prospective. "So all I have to do is dump a hive near Salvator's bedroom window, bust the glass and then let go this pheromone stuff?"

"Essentially, yes." She leaned back in surprise over my direct question. "But you would want to be far away at the time to avoid sharing his fate. You would also want to make sure he's moving. If Salvator is asleep, the bees would not view him as a threat and therefore not attack. They would buzz around in confusion for a period of time, and then leave."

"Don't think I wouldn't be heading for a deep hole long before that occurred, just in case the bees didn't get the job done," I muttered, wryly. Then another thought came to mind. "Let's say I didn't have you to provide the expertise needed for isolating pheromones. Couldn't I buy that particular pheromone somewhere?"

Her head moved in a small gesture of denial. "Not at this time."

"But you and Wolf have synthesized the stuff so it could be mass produced?"

She nodded. "Absolutely. But as far as I know, that has not been done."

"Considering that Dyson has a supply of this pheromone and an expert to replenish that supply anytime it's needed, Dyson is holding the smoking gun," I muttered. "I know he has hives on his island. The only wrinkle keeping him from becoming my prime suspect is getting hives from there, to here?"

"Hives are completely portable," Mrs. Dyson explained. "Each spring and fall you'll see trucks hauling them around the country. Farmers and orchards lease the hives—the bees, actually—to pollinate crops and blossoms." She squared her slender shoulders as if dedicating her next words to posterity. "So if Jacob wanted hives brought to Austin, he would simply fly them here. Once landed, the hives would be trucked wherever he desired."

"I saw some brown, sticky stuff around the hole in a window at Rodney Terrance's apartment," I remarked. "Could that be the pheromone?"

She took a long time to answer. "If you were to examine the torn screen outside the window at the motel where Albert and I stayed, you would see just what you've described. But I could not attest to it being the pheromone without actually seeing a sample."

"I noticed several hives outside Terrance's apartment."

"On the ground, directly below the motel window, is a large hive."

"But at Terrance's apartment, the hives are thirty feet below the window."

She was studying me openly. "A large amount of pheromone could be detected by bees at that distance. But that would be nearing the maximum span to orchestrate an attack."

"You did not notice the hive when you left the motel to get Albert's meds?" I asked.

"No. But I saw it when I got back. At first sight, I assumed someone was playing a dreadful joke on the people staying in the motel. It wasn't until I got up to our room that I realized what had actually happened."

"How many stings would it take to be fatal?" I asked.

"For the average person, about fifteen hundred," Constance replied. "For someone allergic to bee-venom, only one is required—as in Annie's case."

"Fifteen hundred?" I asked in disbelief. "How many bees are in a hive?"

"That depends on the hive. Many thousands, in some cases."

"But is that number of stings exact?"

She shook her head. "It's a guestimate based upon a rule-of-thumb calculation. For every pound of bodyweight, there must be ten stings by a honeybee. A wasp, hornet or bumblebee uses a different calculation. But it's along the same lines." She shuddered, as if chilled by the memory of Albert's death. "In any event, someone lighter than average would die after receiving fewer stings and someone heavier would require more."

"Death being caused by a heart attack, I assume?"

"No." Constance hunched her thin shoulders up. "Your victim dies from paralysis of the nervous system. There would be other damage, such as hemorrhaging and destruction of red blood cells. But those are secondary."

I snuffed out my cigarette in the ashtray on the table. "I've seen beekeepers taking honey from hives. The bees are buzzing around a lot—they're obviously pissed about what's going on. But for the most part they are not stinging the beekeeper."

Constance was very still for an instant, frozen in the act of thought. "First of all, beekeepers use smoke to confuse the bees. Secondly, they are taking the honey from the supers—those shorter boxes above the hive - not from the hive, where the Queen resides. Because she is larger than her bees the queen cannot get through the narrow slit purposely installed between the hive, and the first Super – but the bees can, in order to store the honey."

"So when honey is collected from the super by the bee-keeper, the Queen is not at risk so no pheromone is released?"

"Not the one warning of the Queen impending peril." She stroked her brow with a gesture of infinite weariness. "What you saw was primarily a pre-stinging defense-tactic."

"You mean the bees blow their little bugles at the guy to warn him off?" I teased.

She smiled slightly. "No. They butt their heads against the trespasser. Honey Bees realize instinctively that they have one shot at stinging because their stinger is barbed. It gets lodged in the skin of their victim. When the bee pulls back the stuck stinger tears the poison sack from the bee's belly, killing the bee. Consequently, honeybees bump an intruder and then back up in flight only to bump again—at least for starters. It's a curious sensation on the face, quite pleasant. Almost like a fuzzy butterfly-kiss. If the trespasser retreats that ends it. But if the intruder advances, the bees' reaction escalates. Hornets and other members of the bee family sting at the first sign of intrusion. But they have no barbs on their stingers. That means they can repeat their attack as often as desired."

"Wouldn't my intended victim smell this pheromone stuff? The bees do."

"A large amount would be noticed," she agreed. "It smells rather bitter." She turned her hands palms outward. "But it's not a suspicious odor."

I lit another cigarette. "When I was a kid, honey came with a good dousing of bee-legs as part of its charm," I remarked, and stood up. "So I thought all the risk from getting a jug of the stuff was on the bee's end."

"Bee-legs must be filtered out, these days." Constance Dyson passed her hand over her eyes and leaned back. "My grandmother always complained that doing so takes away a lot of the flavor. Still, much of Honey's mystery relates to what is added during the honey-making process."

"What do you mean? I thought honey came from flower-nectar."

"Some does." She breathed and then sighed, wearily. "Some comes for the anal droppings of certain types of Aphids. It's called Honeydew – quite thick and darkly colored." Constance grinned and licked her lips. "Mmmm. Tasty."

"I think I'll save my taste-buds for bee-collected flower-nectar, thank you."

"I'm afraid there is more in honey than just nectar," she said. "There is a step that most people don't know about. The bee, after returning to the hive with her load of goodies, masticates the nectar for about thirty minutes."

I made a grimace. "You mean I've spent the last fifty-some years swallowing bee-spit?"

She laughed. "Don't worry. Honey is a natural anti-bacterial—probably because of the bee-spit. In fact, next time you cut your finger, daub a bit on the wound before covering it with a bandage. It will heal remarkably fast. The Pharaohs were firm believers in its medicinal properties."

"I think I'll stick to commercially created chemicals for my damaged parts. Something healthy on my skin might cause a bad reaction. Sit tight. I want to show you something."

I went into the front room and rummaged through my suit until I found the plastic container I had taken from Terrance's toilette. Then I returned to the kitchen and resumed my seat.

"Take a look at this." I set the plastic tube on the table.

Constance picked it up and took off its cap. After sniffing the contents she reclosed the container and set it down. "Where did you get it?"

"Rodney Terrance had it hidden in his apartment. Is that the pheromone we've been discussing?"

She nodded.

"As I recall, your husband was found in Ainslie Park."

"Phil went there to meet someone—he did not tell me who." Constance Dyson looked at me. Her lovely face was eloquent despite the weariness she was obviously feeling. "I'm certain it was his father who lured Phil there—so Jacob could kill my husband."

I wagged my head. "I don't buy that, Mrs. Dyson." Then I jabbed a finger at the tube she was holding. "That little item makes me think Rodney Terrance killed your husband, hoping that you would come his way afterward. Didn't Terrance ever approach you with romantic ideas?"

Constance gave me a slightly revolting look. "Rodney telephoned several times. But even with his limited mental processes, he could not assume that I would be interested in sex with him right after my husband died." She paused a moment to chew her bottom lip. "Why would Rodney keep this—something that would obviously implicate him in Phil's death?"

"I think Terrance kept it as his backup-plan to force you into whatever arrangement he wanted. You would either comply, or he would prove to the authorities how you killed your husband—by pointing the finger of suspicion at you, and telling them what to look for. The police would search your home and find that tube. Whereupon you would be arrested. Because Terrance's claims could easily be proven or disproven by testing that stuff in front of a beehive, your conviction would be all but assured. Did your husband have any extramarital affairs?"

Her cheeks reddened.

"Who was the lady?" I asked.

Constance leaned back in the chair as if a load of manure had been dumped onto the table. "My sister."

"Whereupon you had a fling with Jesus Romero?"

"How did you know that?"

"I have big ears, remember?"

"What do you want me to say?" Her lips curled with scorn. "That I'm a whore?"

"Nope. But if you should take up the profession, put me at the top of your client-list." I picked up the tube of pheromone and waggled it. "Why didn't you prove your theory to the police? This would've done it."

"Before I could do so, Jacob had me arrested for embezzlement. Since then I've either been in prison, or on the run from him." She held out her hand. "May I have that? It will give me a chance to demonstrate my theory to the police."

"Of course."

I dropped the tube into her hand. Then I picked up the weapon and carefully slipped the magazine out of its butt. In addition to the expected light coating of oil, it had very fine, white particles clinging to it. After counting the cartridges, I spread the estranged parts on the table.

"Leave the gun with me," I said. "I'll see that the police find it during their investigation into Albert's death. But I'll make certain there is no link between it, and you. In the meantime, I need you to go back to the motel."

Her eyes widened. "I can't go back there," she pleaded.

"You have to. The police are already looking for you."

"Police? Why would they be looking for me?" She rested her wrists upon the tabletop.

I drained my glass. "Because whoever turned those bees loose on Albert would've called them," I explained. "When you arrive, act surprised. Then give your best teary-eyed account of your visit with me because of your concerns over Salvator Portello. Be sure to emphasize how I brutally attempted to molest you. Whatever you do, don't mention the gun or that you knew beforehand about Albert being dead. If they ask any questions about a gun, say Albert had one. Keep your answers very short and to the point. Don't expand on your story or change it in any way no matter how many times you are asked to repeat it. If anyone gets unpleasant, demand a lawyer and then keep your mouth shut." I pointed to the table. "Leave your wallet."

She leaned forward across the table, her palms flat on its top, her fingers splayed. "Why?"

"Because you abandoned it when my sexual advances forced you to flee against the onslaught of my well-known, unfettered lust."

"How does that help?"

"Returning your wallet will be the reason I'll use for showing up at your motel-room a few minutes after you get back there. That way my story will corroborate yours. When I return this to you, be sure to slap my face."

After setting her wallet on the table, Mrs. Dyson walked over to the door. There she opened it, stepped out into the hall, stopped and turned back.

"I could get used to you, Bishop," she declared.

"Sal wouldn't approve."

"I can't believe you're afraid of him," she declared.

I nodded. "From my shivering tippy-toes right up to my terrified hair-roots."

With a small laugh, Constance came back to me and pressed her lips to mine. It was a soft, far too brief caress. But one that clearly held my attention. After which she stayed near me, staring into my eyes.

I stared back thinking how nice it would be to do some pawing, probing and all the other things that make foreplay such great fun. But I decided against it. It wouldn't be much wise for either of us to test Salvator's omniscience. With a disappointed shrug, Mrs. Dyson turned and walked away.

I picked up the gun and clip. After giving each a very thorough wiping, I went into the front room and got dressed.

TWELVE

The Hampstead Motel's parking lot was lit up with blinking red and blue lights when I arrived. Milling about were gawkers in jammies and tired-looking blue uniforms.

I parked on the street, stuffed Mrs. Dyson's wallet into my suit-coat pocket next to her pistol, got out of the Buick and headed toward the gathering. I intended to drop the pistol down a sewer-drain a few blocks farther on. But before I did that, I wanted to make sure Mrs. Dyson's alibi was situated.

A young patrolman stopped me at the steps leading up to the motel's second floor, and demanded to know my business. I identified myself as the coroner. Then I told him I was there to perform an impromptu autopsy for channel seven.

Despite my not having any type of bag to hold whatever instruments coroners might carry for impromptu autopsies, the young cop gave me a nod of respect before waving me on.

I took the steps up, two at a time.

Number 223 was not much to look at. Pea-soup colored walls, matching twin beds and a big pine dresser with a white blaze on its top. Near the blaze sat a Bible that looked untouched and a dog-eared phone book. One of the beds had a tear in its green coverlet. A lamp with two green globes shaped like tulips had been plopped on a small table between the beds. There was a telephone in front of the lamp. It was color-coordinated to match the walls. Beyond the beds, fronting a pair of windows, a couple of brown chairs crowded the round table between them. Green drapes bracketed the windows, in moth-eaten fashion. The room's heating-cooling unit jutted into the room just below the windows, like the lips of a hungry Cod. At the room's entrance where it had worn thin, the carpeting looked like mold growing from the concrete. There was a tiny kitchenette to my right. There was an open door leading to the bath, on my left. Directly in front of me, sprawled upon the floor, was Albert Rothfield.

The dead man was face down with one arm tucked under his chest, and the other flung out. The hand of the latter was coiled into a fist as if his last act was trying to slug someone, or something. Rothfield still wore the pants and shirt I had seen on him at the Hole in One. Dead bees by the thousands were all over the room, many piles of which lay atop his body. On the back of the dead man's shirt I spotted a peppering of dark dots, presumably stingers. I started to count the markings but quickly gave up. There were hundreds and hundreds of them, far too many to calculate at this early hour.

A forensic tech, with a good collection of bee-corpses clinging to the paper-coverlets on his shoes, squatted beside the body. As I watched, he began putting plastic bags over the dead man's hands. This is done to protect what might lie beneath the victim's fingernails. The idea being, the deceased might have clawed his killer or killers, before dying. In this case, I doubted there would be anything but bee-fuzz.

My eyes scanned the room looking for Mrs. Dyson. Captain Weatherly chatted with another suit near the kitchenette. Several technicians hovered around the counter and microwave, dusting for fingerprints. In a corner near the windows, three uniforms huddled together. They were laughing—probably about bees as the future of assassination. The open bathroom door gave me an unobstructed view of its interior. No one was within. I let my eyes scan the room again. But nowhere did I see my erstwhile visitor.

Mrs. Dyson's absence could mean that she had been taken into custody immediately upon returning to the motel. If so, she may have been brought to the nearest precinct-house and dumped into one of the holding-cells. Or a sympathetic cop might have taken her to a café for a cup of coffee. My years of experience with Captain Weatherly negated both possibilities. Weatherly was a staunch believer in using the psychology of a murder-scene as the core to his interrogation technique. If Mrs. Dyson had driven back here, she would be sitting right in front of Rothfield, awaiting Weatherly's less than comforting efforts.

I tried to convince myself that Constance Dyson had panicked at the sight of the police cars, and driven to another motel. The prospect of being interrogated as a suspect in a murder is terrifying, even for the innocent. Flight to avoid that experience is a common first-impulse. But my gut-feeling was that Constance Dyson had never intended to return to the motel. She purposely left me with the pistol that was growing heavier and heavier in my pocket, in order to fit me to a frame.

Mentally, I tried to dump suspicion on Salvator Portello, as the impetus for the pistol-delivery. But Sal was not a frame-type of guy. That form of revenge would be too oblique for his tastes. Salvator preferred the direct approach to everything. When it came to retribution, Sal enjoyed hearing his enemies' screams during their last week of life, as Sal spent hour after hour dipping the object of his hate in a vat of Nitric Acid. If he wanted me permanently out of the way, Sal would have sent the Sicilian brothers to get me out of bed, not Mrs. Dyson.

That, of course, brought my suspicions back to her. But if I gave credence to Mrs. Dyson's claims that bees will not sting inanimate objects, I had to believe that Albert Rothfield had not been shot as she had claimed. Otherwise, the thousands of dead bees spread around the room would be alive. So had she been forthright in her tale about the gun? Had a third-party taken it from the motel room while Albert was passed out, used it, and then returned the weapon? If so, who had been shot? Certainly it must have been someone known to Mrs. Dyson. Otherwise why go to the trouble of returning the weapon in a feeble effort at framing her for the shooting? In any event, had that third-party also been responsible for the bees and a very dead Albert Rothfield?

I started to turn, intending to leave before Weatherly spotted me. But I was a tic short on my timing.

"How in hell did you get up here, Bishop?" the Captain demanded, as he strode over.

"I've got pull with the mayor," I quipped, wishing I had not answered Mrs. Dyson's knock. "What's going on?"

"A bee invasion! What in hell does it look like?"

I pointed past Weatherly to Rothfield. "What'd he try to do? Sleep with his pets? From the looks of things, Rothfield crowded the queen."

Captain Weatherly jabbed a finger at me. "What are you doin' here?"

I took Mrs. Dyson's wallet from my pocket and held it up. "Constance forgot this when she left my place a few minutes ago. I was returning it. Is she here?"

He grabbed the wallet. "No. But I've got an all-points bulletin out for her. Did Mrs. Dyson tell you where she was going when she left your apartment?"

I shrugged. "She mentioned nausea. I think that might be in South-Texas."

His eyes held a curious mixture of belief and doubt. "Suppose you tell me why Mrs. Dyson visited you at this hour?"

"Constance dropped by to shoot the breeze about Sal. Our least favorite mobster's become a little over-attentive to her. So she wanted advice on how to let him down easy."

"Since when has Salvator Portello ever taken more than a passing interest in any woman?"

"Trust me. Even the most dedicated misogynist could take a turn after seeing Mrs. Dyson in tight denims."

The captain's thick, square jaw shot out like a thrown brick, and his teeth clicked. "What sent her to you, of all people? Stop playing me, Bishop."

"I have a certain romantic flair."

He held up her billfold. "Which caused Mrs. Dyson to leave this as a keepsake?" he scoffed. "Not likely."

"No. She dropped it as I was trying to maneuver her into bed. I came here hoping she'd be willing to trade passion for the return of her belongings."

Weatherly grimaced with disgust. "Extorting sex. That is so like you."

"At my age I get any way I can, Captain. Give her my regards, will you?"

He snorted impatiently, "Not so fast. Did Mrs. Dyson tell you that Rothfield was dead?"

I rubbed my left cheek pretending it was sore. "No. But I can tell you this much for free, she definitely has an aversion to honey being daubed on her nipples."

He said, giving my chest a tap with one accusing forefinger. "First Terrance and now this." Weatherly twisted to glance down at the corpse. "We're treating this and Terrance's death as suspicious." Then he turned back to me and said, "In my opinion, someone's worked out a way to get bees to attack on command. Only trouble with that is, the experts claim it can't be done." He pointed down at Rothfield. "What's your theory on this?"

"I don't have one. But if what you suggest is true, then it follows that both Terrance and Rothfield were it by the same perpetrator."

"Considering the M.O., I agree with you."

"Who better to do the job on Terrance than a guy with a key to his apartment?"

Weatherly smiled slyly. "Such as who?"

"Jesus Romero. You did say you found him in Terrance's apartment. Since Terrance was dead, it follows that he didn't let Romero in. Therefore, Romero must've had a key."

I saw a telling crimson tide rise up his neck and settle in his face. "Why would Romero kill Terrance? Terrance worked for him."

I shrugged. "Some employers take a dim view of pay-raise requests."

"A stake-truck with a lift on the back of its bed was seen dropping off what we now know are beehives at this dump. They were stacked just below the windows to this room. One man handled the unloading. We think it was the same guy and truck spotted at the Shar-Pei Apartments, based upon descriptions by witnesses." He tilted menacingly closer. "You had a run-in with the dead man at *Rancho Relajar.*"

I nodded. "But I didn't send him a bee-gram."

He tugged at his big nose for a few seconds. "If anybody was up to this kind of thing, it would be an expert on bees. Somebody like Mrs. Constance Dyson. Wouldn't you agree?"

I shook my head. "Mrs. Dyson certainly has the qualifications. But she just arrived in town. Therefore she would not have ready-access to a bunch of hives. Were I you, I'd talk to Jacob Dyson. Dyson also has an island full of beehives. He's also got his own resident bee-expert by the name of Dr. Edmund Wolf. Not only that, but Rothfield was blackmailing Dyson over Annie Dyson's death."

Weatherly weighed me on the balance of his eyes. "Wolf is dead. Shot with a .25 caliber automatic."

A knot formed in my belly. I now knew who the pistol had been used on. Romero told Constance that he would bring Wolf to Austin. He must have done so. But after the humiliation Mrs. Dyson had given Romero at the Hole in One, the gambler had decided to repay her in spades by killing Wolf.

I reached down and tried to flatten the weapon's silhouette. Although I had a permit to carry a concealed pistol, the one in my pocket had been fired but carried no fingerprints—very suspicious. Not only that, but it was wrapped in a towel—also suspicious.

"When was Wolf shot?" I asked.

"About the same time this happened. An anonymous tip brought an investigation team to Ainslie Park. Wolf died near the spot where Phil Dyson was stung to death some months back. I think that coincidence may be important, don't you?"

"Meaning, Mrs. Dyson suspected Wolf of complicity in her husband's death? So she lured him there for revenge?"

"That's how it looks to me. She screamed until she was blue in the face that her husband had been murdered. But nobody listened after several other bee-experts claimed that such a thing was impossible. The coroner also says that Wolf had been tortured—beaten—before being shot."

"You can't think her capable of that."

"No. But I think a guy who's willing to extort sex from her might be willing to help in other ways, with the same type of compensation in mind. When did you last talk to Wolf?"

"I've never met the man."

His brows furrowed in disbelief. "Then how do you know so much about him?"

"I read newspapers."

"Did Mrs. Dyson at any time discuss Wolf with you?"

"She was too busy being uncooperative. Can I go, now? The sight of all this death is going to raise hell with my digestion. I don't think I'll be able to face honey, again."

"You're not going anywhere any time soon." Then he grabbed my arm and dragged me into the room before giving me a shove toward the nearest chair. "Get comfortable. We'll be going over this until I believe you've told me everything." Suddenly his eyes dropped to the bulge that Mrs. Dyson's automatic was making in my suit. "What else did Mrs. Dyson leave behind?"

I tried to think of an explanation for the pistol's presence and wrapping, on the chance Weatherly was going to frisk me. Admittedly, pistols are often used for non-criminal activities, such as target-practice or plinking at vermin. Unfortunately, those pursuits rarely occur during the wee hours before dawn. And in only the most impossible to explain situations does a fired-gun not carry at least on person's fingerprints.

"Only my disappointment," I replied. Then I redirected his focus away from the bulge by asking, "How did the bees get in here?"

He gestured toward a window. "It was raised up a few inches. The screen was cut." Then Weatherly made a thoughtful face. "What do you know about bees?"

"I know they make honey, can count to four and have barbed stingers that play hell with my baby-soft skin."

"Mrs. Dyson knew both Terrance and Rothfield, didn't she?"

I nodded. "So did Jacob Dyson—no matter how loud he denies it."

Weatherly looked at me imperviously. "So did you. When did you last see Albert Rothfield alive?"

"A few hours ago at the Hole in One. He was a lousy dancer. Kept wanting to sit down."

He thumbed his lower lip, his eyes returning to the bulge in my coat. "Did Romero know Wolf?"

"I'm told he had a business arrangement with Wolf. I was also told that the business arrangement was not going as planned. It involved a DVD."

His lips formed a circle, as if he were about to ask another question.

"Rumor has it that Dr. Wolf wanted out of his job with Jacob Dyson," I quickly interjected. "Rumor has it that Dyson was keeping Wolf on Dyson Island by force."

Captain Weatherly shoved his hands into his pockets and jangled keys and coins. "So your theory is, that Dyson killed both Terrance and Rothfield, correct?"

"Not personally," I said. "Dyson would've hired it done by someone working for him. Someone like Jesus Romero."

"Then why would Romero kill Terrance and Rothfield using bees, but shoot Wolf?"

"He probably ran out of hives."

More silence as Weatherly dropped back into thought. I sat down, crossed my legs, closed my eyes and wondered how long it would be before Weatherly had her gun in his sweaty hand?

He made an exasperated splay of one arm. "Why not just shoot all three? Why go to all this trouble?"

"Crazier killings have occurred, Captain."

"Name me one, Bishop."

I took a cigarette out and lit it. "Have your people lifted prints from any of the hives?"

He nodded. "Several. They're being scanned into our database for comparison." Weatherly looked from the corpse back to me. "Can you prove that Romero works for Dyson?"

I shook my head. "But if you dig deep enough you'll find corroboration that Rothfield worked for Dyson. Since Dyson lied to you about that, what makes you think he would tell you the truth in denying involvement with Romero?"

Captain Weatherly turned and yelled at the uniforms, "Pickup Jesus Romero!" Then he returned his attention to me. "I spoke with immigration, this afternoon. They identified the man you shot at *Rancho Relajar* by his fingerprints as a Chechnyan terrorist named Sergei Ignatchenko Popovitch. The Russians have been after him since that school takeover, several years back. So how is it you knew he was Chechnyan?"

I blew smoke into his face. "I'm a trained detective, Captain."

THIRTEEN

It was not until well after sunrise that Captain Weatherly finished questioning me. I returned home, showered, shaved and slipped into my best suit. Then I headed out to the Buick intending to find breakfast before driving to the offices of Peterson Barrows, Esq. Unfortunately, somebody had other plans for me. Standing next to the Buick were the Sicilian Brothers, Thomaso and Pietro, Salvator Portello's personal bodyguards. They unbuttoned their coats, as I drew near, each sliding one hand toward a shoulder holster.

"No trouble, Mr. Bishop," warned Thomaso, as I approached them.

"Yeah," chimed Pietro. "No trouble, Mr. Bishop. Mr. Portello wants a word."

"Mr. Salvator, Pietro," Thomaso scolded. "We must be precise."

"Yeah, Mr. Salvator wants a word, Mr. Bishop."

There was no avoiding it. I meekly nodded my head and followed them to their car.

Forty minutes later, I was sitting in Salvator Portello's office at his home, in West Austin.

"You think I'm enjoying this?" Salvator yelled after I finished complaining about my missed breakfast. "I'm up to my ass in misery because of you. Lt. Mann dragged me out of bed at the crack of fucking dawn claiming you told Weatherly that I owned the Hole in One!"

"You know how Herbie Mann is, Sal," I protested, lamely. "Always a guy for dumping the source of world problems onto your shoulders."

The gangster came around his desk over to where I sat, glowering. He started to say something. But before he could get out the words Momma Portello stormed into the room. She stalked over to me and slapped my face as hard as she could.

"That's for what you did," Momma Portello shouted. Then Momma slapped me again, just as hard. "That's for not making it right!" Momma started off, turned, hurried back and kissed both my cheeks. "And that's to make my boy all better," she whispered in my ear. With that, the Portello Matriarch giggled like a schoolgirl and hurried out of the room.

Sal looked from this mother's receding back to me. "What in hell was that all about?"

"I must've forgotten to call on her birthday," I muttered, completely

102

confused by the incident.

"Momma's very sensitive about her birthday, Mr. Salvator," said Thomaso, with a confirming nod of his head.

"Yeah, Mr. Salvator," chimed Pietro. "She's very sensitive. That's why Thomaso has her birthday written down, so's we don't never forget."

Thomaso gave is brother a brow-furrowed look. "No, Pietro, you have it written down so's we don't never forget."

"You mean you forgot to write it down so's we don't never forget?" demanded Pietro. Then he pointed over at me. "You want us to get hit, like him?"

Salvator turned to the Sicilian Brothers and ordered them out. Thomaso and Pietro left amidst protestations that I was still a danger to Sal due to my habit of getting 'miffed' each time they dragged me in front of their boss. However, the Mafia Don insisted. After following them to the door and shutting it, Salvator Portello returned to his desk and sat down.

"Rita's in Sicily—knocked up. Did you know that?" he demanded.

I gave my head a worried shake. "Nobody tells me anything."

His face became thoughtful for a moment. "Momma's been nutso like you saw ever since Rita announced she was pregnant. Did Rita say anything to you about the guy who's responsible?"

I knew exactly what Salvator had in mind. And it included a swim in the dip-tank for whoever had sowed his seed in the Portello clan's only hope for perpetuating the family line. So amidst worried stomach-rolling, I quickly calculated the last time Rita and I had been physically intimate. No matter which way I figure the date, it had been long enough for the usual pregnancy tests. Could I possibly be the father? No. Not a chance. It was not like Rita to keep such a thing a secret. Threatening to cut off my balls if I did not marry her because I had gotten her pregnant—that was Rita's style.

"You're accusing me?" I demanded, hoping against hope that her forthcoming progeny was not of my making.

"Of course not!" he snapped, making a disgusted face. "Rita has more sense than to hook up with a loser like you. But this whole thing…" His hands went to his face and he groaned between his fingers, "I'm humiliated as hell. Never in my family's history has there been a bastard!"

"Perhaps not in the legal sense, Sal. But on the colloquial front I think you're exaggerating just a trifle. Otherwise, how do you explain Dom?"

His paws fell away, his jaw-muscles working. "Don't start with me, Bishop." The gangster stood and leaned his hands on the desk, tilting across it toward me. "Rita must've told you something about the guy."

"Usually my conversations with Rita end when she threatens to kill me— which is pretty much each time she starts talking," I replied, still evaluating pregnant possibilities. It had been four or five months, since my last interlude with Rita. Surely in that length of time she would've suspected and telephoned me? "As such, I'm not likely to hear many confidences." My mouth went dry as I asked, "Did Rita mention a name?"

Salvator wagged his head, grinning sourly. Then he straightened up, and adjusted his suit. "My sister really hates your guts, don't she?"

I nodded, trying to chuckle—again counting days. But all I managed to do was start my lower lip trembling not unlike a tattered rag on a stick in a high wind. "When is the happy event?"

Salvator Portello shrugged. "Four, Five, Six, seven, eight months—how in hell do I know?" His arms flailed the air in frustration. "Rita announces she's gonna' have a kid. Momma insists that Rita goes back to Sicily to have it. So my sister takes off leaving me so fucking embarrassed I can't face the people I do business with. Making it worse, my mother starts bragging to the world about it." He adjusted his pale, gray tie. "The both of them should be ashamed. But are they? Not on your fucking life! They think it's great. Those two cuckoos have been buying shit I can't even spell, let alone know what it's for. Bassinette this. Bassinette that. Receiving this. Receiving that. It's costing me a fortune!" He shook a finger at me. "There are a hundred and forty-two baby blankets in Rita's bedroom closet, and another twenty seven on backorder. Not only that, but Momma shows up daily with more bills—all because of some bastard I'm going to dip until I see his eyeballs floating." He made a fist. "I want the bastard responsible, Bishop."

I smiled wryly, slightly more confident. "So talk to Rita."

The gangster looked quickly to the right and then to the left, as if concerned he might be overheard. "I did. All she does is giggle and wink at Momma. They both know, Bishop. I know they both know. But will they tell me?" He stopped for a moment before growling, "That's why you're going to find the bastard!"

"How? It's not like the guy is going to brag about it."

"How in hell do I know, how? You're the so-called detective." His eyes grew dark with distant lights, in them. His mouth opened, and shut in a grim line. Then he said, "Just find the bastard."

By my latest figuring Rita had not been in bed with me for five months and one week—which, if Salvator's expectations were correct, left me clear of any prenatal complicity on the far end of his time-estimate. Unfortunately, I was well within target considering his inside estimate. No. Rita would never keep a thing like that from me. Or would she? If she thought telling anyone but Momma might get me killed, she might. No. It could not be. Me? A father? After all these years? Not a chance. It had to be some poor soul who had unwittingly contributed his genes to improve hers during some drunken outing. Regardless, my finding him would guaranty the brain-dead bozo a swim in the dip-tank.

That left me with mixed emotions. On one hand, I could make a chunk of change finding the guy. On the other, I would be bringing about the death of a man Rita cared for. Fortunately, I never allowed my personal feelings interfere with the practicalities of business.

"Fine," I said. "It'll cost you five thousand, up front. No guarantees. No refunds."

Salvator Portello's head jerked as if I had tightened a noose around his neck. "Five grand?" he shouted, in objection. "Are you out of your fucking mind?"

"If you don't like the price, stop complaining about Rita's baby," I countered. "What do you care who the father is? Momma's getting a grandchild —something you and Dominic would not provide. That's going to keep Momma out of your hair for the rest of her life—something you've wanted for as long as I've known you. Rita will settle down to being a mother and stop running around, nights—which you've complained about since she got out of school. So where's the harm?"

He thumped his chest, came around to the front of his desk, and took a perch on its edge. "My goddamn name!" The gangster's eyes seemed to focus inward, on an image in memory. "My father must be rolling in his grave." Then he blinked, as though that distant image lay under glaring light. "What my people must think. My family's supposed to set an example, for Christ's sake." He dug into his pocket and pulled out an overstuffed money-clip. "You're gonna' do it for a grand and like it."

"Like hell I will, Sal! That won't even cover gasoline."

He peeled of twenty one-hundred dollar bills, and dropped the pile onto the desk. "Two grand—and you'd damn well better not fail me." Then the gangster spoke quickly. "When I get my hands on that bastard… I'm gonna' start by filleting his goddamn feet. Then I'll work my way up. And when I got each and every one of his fucking nerve-endings all naked to the world, I'm gonna spend a week dipping the bastard!"

"Did you consider the possibility that this guy proposed marriage and Rita turned him down? It's not his fault if she refused to become an honest woman."

Salvator looked over at me, his eyes cynical. "He shouldn't have touched her in the first place."

"Rita gets what Rita wants, Sal—no matter what it is. Tell me different without lying."

"Go to hell!" Salvator Portello dragged his hands through his gray hair, as if trying to smudge out a fire. "Okay. I did figure maybe the guy might've offered marriage. So, I asked, okay? All I got from Rita and Momma was more fucking giggles—like this is some big joke on me!" Then he patted his stomach. "I got an ulcer. Did you know? An ulcer." Then both his hands went to his head. "I think I'm getting' migraines. Christ the pain, some days. Between guts, brain and heart, I'm as good as dead." His mitts momentarily joined as if in prayer. "And do you know who's to blame? I'll tell you who's to blame. My goddamn family, that's who's to blame!" His hands flew overhead, in frustration. "I talked to Momma about the guy. I told her we had to do something to save the family name. But will she tell me anything? All I hear from her is 'Don't touch him or I'll put a curse on you.' My own mother, for Christ's sake, and she's threatening curses." More finger waggling. "You know what that means don't you? It's a guy from the old neighborhood. And when I get my hands on that bastard…"

"The old neighborhood was bulldozed to make a strip-mall."

Salvator jabbed a finger at me. "Don't you think I know that? I'm sayin' all you gotta' do is find which of those yokels was dating Rita, and you got the bastard."

"Why don't you ask around?"

"What? You think those losers from the old neighborhood are gonna' tell me the truth? Whoever did it knows he's dead." One of his hands suddenly gripped his chest. Then his voice whimpered in pain as he added, "You're gonna do this, Bishop, I don't care if it kills me."

Considering the mood Salvator Portello was in, I decided to take the cash-offer rather than try to negotiate a better rate. Worst case I could dun Sal for expenses later on. Or, I could conveniently discover that Rita's paramour committed suicide in some far off foreign land because she had rejected him—without me turning a cog. I stood up and grabbed the money.

"I do this under protest," I said, feigning disgust. "But I'll find the guy for Rita's sake—and her kid. A kid should carry his father's name—and enjoy his father's love and guidance. Tell me I'm wrong, without lying."

"Don't you think I know about fathers?" he demanded, his arms flinging wide. "Don't you think I want the same thing for her kid? What do you think I am, some animal?"

"Which means no dip-tank, Sal."

He batted the air. "Ah, fuck you!"

It was my turn to shake a finger at him. "Remember Momma's curse."

"If the bastard agrees to marry Rita I'll forgive and forget—maybe!" Then the gangster gave the desktop a thump with one palm. "If Rita's condition isn't bad enough, my idiot brother is running me right up a wall. His fucking furniture-business went down the toilet. Did you hear?"

I shrugged. "These things happen so often with Dom that nobody makes mention, anymore."

The gangster dragged his bony hands across his pale face. "'Only top of the line shit, Sal' he told me. 'Gonna' make a fortune, Sal' he told me. Fortune, my ass! I got half of my biggest warehouse stuffed with the shit he was flogging, and no takers on the horizon!"

"Why not have a fire-sale?"

"Don't think I haven't considered it." Salvator stalked behind his desk shaking a fist. "D'you know what that investment cost me? A goddamn fortune, that's what that investment cost me. And since then—you will not fucking believe it. Right now—that crazy bastard's raising bees, for Christ's sake."

I swallowed hard to keep my stomach down. What were the odds that Dom had not played a roll in Terrance's and Rothfield's deaths? About the same as three men being stung to death in Austin, in any given year.

"Honeybees?" I asked, still not believing my ears.

Salvator nodded, letting go a madman's cackle. "The idiot can't figure out how to get the goddamn honey from 'em. But he's got bees up the ying-yang!"

"Why bees?"

"How do I know, why bees?" the Mafia Don bleated, his arms spreading. "I told him, remember from school when we heard how bees stick pollen into their little pouches? Maybe all you gotta' do is empty them damn pouches to get the honey? He said he didn't want to try that alone. So would I go with him? I did. We opened one of this fucking hives and tried to grab a couple of bees – you know, just to see if they had any honey in them pouches. Well, take it from me that is *not* going to happen again!"

"Where did Dom get the idea for bees?"

The mobster's arms flung wide, again. "Where he always gets his goddamn ideas. He jerks them out of his ass, that's where he gets them. I had to lay out another fortune to get a bunch of fucking bees shipped here from fucking Greece! Did you know there were bees in Greece? Not me. Not 'til last year when I handed out blood to a bunch of goat-screwing Greeks to get them bees here. And then last night that idiot…" He paused to take a whimpering breath, a hand clutching at his chest, again. "Dom shows up for supper, okay? His goddamn face full of stingers. He said he read where bees put honey in wax combs. He said he read that all he had to do was use smoke to get the bees out of the hives, so he could grab the combs. Simple, right? So what did the idiot do? He sticks a fucking rolled-up chunk of newspaper into one of them hives, lights it. The whole goddamn thing goes up in flames. The bees went crazy! They came out of every hive and attacked him like there was no tomorrow. He had to run for his life. And if that ain't bad enough, he starts in on how…"

"I take it that Dom gave you a song and dance about somebody stealing his hives?" I interjected.

Salvator threw his hand to his hips, gaping at me. "How in the fuck did you know that?"

"Little things—like people being killed by bees. The police are asking questions—part of which involves where the hives came from. They also found prints on the hives."

He sagged back into his chair massaging his middle. "Christ almighty! Are you telling me my idiot brother's undercutting my business by selling discount-hits… using bees?"

"Considering Dom's shortage of brains, I doubt it," I replied, wondering how intimately Dominic and Mrs. Dyson had become. Not once in Dominic's entire life had he ever figured out anything for himself. "The immediate problem is the fingerprints. If those hives belong to Dom, he will become the prime suspect."

"Dom hell! They might've found *my* prints on 'em," he shouted, jerking upright. "I'll kill the bastard! A man can be expected to take only so much. So help me God I'll kill him, I don't care what Momma says! I don't care if Pop crawls out of his grave and comes for me. My brother is a dead man!"

"Did Dom ever mention a guy by the name of Rodney Terrance?"

Salvator started pacing, again rubbing his middle. "Some punk he used to hang out with. What of it?"

"He was one of the victims. What about Albert Rothfield?"

The gangster stopped and gawked at me. "Poker pal of Dom's. Is he…"

"Another victim. I also found evidence that probably links Terrance to Phil Dyson's death."

He strode back to his chair, sat down, reached into one of the desk drawers and dragged out a bottle of liquid antacid. After gurgling down several ounces he croaked, "Constance's husband? That was a bee-hit by my brother, too? What in the hell am I going to tell her?"

"I doubt Dom played an active role in any of them, Sal. But if he knew all the victims, I'm betting Dom is unwittingly involved."

"Of course he's unwittingly involved," shouted Salvator. "He's got shit for brains!"

"Did Dom know Phil?"

Salvator nodded. "That's how I first got introduced to Constance. She was still married to Phil." He gave his head a mournful shake. "Christ, when she finds out that my brother…"

"How long has Dom been in the bee-business?"

He shrugged. "Ten or eleven months. I swear to God, I'm going to need a rubber room before much longer."

"Do you or Dom ever do business with Jacob Dyson?"

The gangster rolled his eyes. "Him, too?"

"No, but Dyson may be the one orchestrating things to make Dom the patsy."

"Sure, we know the guy." Sal was looking at me fixedly. "He was making death-threats against Constance. So we went out to that rock where he lives to let him know that she's untouchable. The son-of-a bitch! I should'a capped the bastard, right then and there. But I'd heard he had some big government contract. So knocking him off could've brought the Feds down on me like stink on a snake."

"Does Dom know Jesus Romero?"

He jumped to his feet. "Christ, how many bee-hits where there?"

"Two."

Salvator sighed with relief and gave his head a grim nod. "Romero is Dom's gambling buddy—the fucking jerk." Then he batted the air with both hands. "What my brother doesn't lose pretending to be a businessman he throws away shooting craps, with Romero." The gangster's brows abruptly furrowed in thought. "Couldn't those hives belong to Dyson? Dyson's got all kinds of bees —more than two thousand hives—that's what Constance told me. Not one of which, I might add, is from Greece."

"The hives could be Dyson's. That was my first surmise. But after what you told me about some of Dom's going missing, I no longer think so. I know Romero's on Dyson's payroll. But I can't figure out what Romero does for Dyson."

The gangster's lips tightened. Then he said, "Romero's his legman for rounding up the freaks Dyson hauls to his island."

"What do you mean by freaks?"

Salvator did not reply at once. "You know." Then he shrugged his narrow shoulders, almost philosophically. "Air-heads who think they can leave their bodies and fly around the world. Dyson brings 'em out there to test this new drug he's working on." He tugged one ear a second. "I had an uncle who said he could leave his body. He used to run around the neighborhood stark naked, telling everyone he met that they couldn't see him. The family finally had to lock him in the loony-bin. But he swore it was his destiny to live outside his body. One day he got up on the hospital-roof and leaped off—flapping his fuckin' arms clear to the ground. He'd still be flapping, now, if we hadn't buried him."

"Constance told you about those freaks of Dyson's?"

Salvator took a silver cigar case from his suit. He selected one of the pencil-thin smokes and put it in his mouth. But he did not light it. For a long time he sat there with the unlit cigar drooping from between his lips, as if his mind was working out how best to reply.

Eventually he said, "She says it can actually be done. Do you believe that?"

I shook my head. "Where are Dom's hives?"

"Remember that church he built? The one where everybody was fucking everybody and my idiot brother was peddling cocaine to those sex-crazed loonies? There are over two hundred hives out there."

"Is anybody keeping an eye on the hives?"

"Of course not." Salvator Portello's arms flailed the air impatiently. "The one thing I don't need right now is more expense." He clawed at the back of his neck. "Momma wants me to buy a villa in Milazzo? She says it's the best place to take a kid for the summers. Can you believe it? A villa? Like I print my own money, for Christ's sake."

"You do print your own money," I grinned.

"Don't even joke about that."

"Other than your talk with Jacob Dyson about Constance, have you had any trouble with him?"

A silence fell between us. He averted his eyes from mine, scanning the carpet. Then he stood. Eventually his words came with determined confidence, "Not me. Not with Jacob Dyson." But a moment later he was looking at me, as if no longer sure of himself. "But Dom had a go-round with Phil Dyson."

"When?"

"Early last year, I think. Just before Phil died."

"Over what?"

"How the fuck do I know, over what? I got better things to do than worry about than who wants a piece of my idiot brother."

"Could it have been about Constance?"

He made a fist. "Don't go in that direction, Bishop."

"Why bees from Greece, Sal? Was that Dom's idea, too?"

He smiled thinly. "Can you believe it? 'Why?' I asked. 'Because they make better honey that's why,' he says. 'Honey is honey, for Christ's sake,' I told him! But he said he wanted the best. And the best bees for my stupid brother only come from Greece. I should kill him in Greece."

"Or maybe because there would be enough distinct differences between local bees and those from Greece, to point the finger of suspicion at Dom?" I suggested.

His brows furrowed. "A setup?"

"It's possible."

The gangster's jaw muscles knotted as he tugged at his belt, the fury in his being barely controlled. "Who? The Russians? Blind Ray? Who's tryin' to set us up?"

"You broke your agreement with Ray, by latching onto the Hole in One. It wouldn't be like him to ignore that."

Salvator thumped his chest with both hands, in gorilla fashion. "That deal with Ray was my father's idea, not mine!"

"I don't think these bee-killings were Ray's idea. They require too much specialized knowledge. What about a guy named Dr. Edmund Wolf? Has Dom ever mentioned him?"

His eyes widened. "Wolf? That creep who works for Dyson?" His face abruptly became doubtful. "What would a brain like him want with my idiot brother?"

"I'm just shooting in the dark, Sal and purposely avoiding the main target."

"Meaning what?"

"Meaning Constance."

"You are out of your fucking mind!" he screamed.

"Am I? How well does she know Dom?"

Then he gave me a hurt look. "Dom? She'd never do anything like that to me."

From the quiet way he said the words, I knew they were intended to convince himself, rather than me. "Did Constance ever date Dom?"

Salvator's face colored. But after a few seconds he gave a sheepish, nod. "It was when he was in some shit-hole called Minnesota. Back when he was trying to keep his trucking business, afloat." The Mafia Don's voice rose in fury as he added, "If it wasn't blown engines, it was lost cargo. I swear to God, that man is cursed!"

"Constance was teaching at the university, there?" I asked.

He shrugged. "I guess. Why anybody would live in Minnesota, I can't figure. They build hotels out of ice? Did you know that? It gets so fucking cold there your dick tries to fuck your asshole for heat." The gangster came over and settled into the chair next to mine. "Have you heard something about Constance and Dom?"

"No. But Captain Weatherly's looking for her."

Salvator Portello went white. "What for?"

"He's got two suspicious deaths involving bees and she's the only living expert on bees in the area."

"But Wolf…"

"Wolf is dead—shot."

The gangster's head wagged as if trying to rattle the sound of my voice out of his ears. "Constance wouldn't hurt a fly." He started to say something more.

Then his eyes narrowed suspiciously upon my face. "How 'bout an explanation about you being with Constance? How 'bout that, huh? And after I told you to stay clear of her. Didn't I tell you to stay clear of her?"

I started to open my mouth in a lie.

"My men followed her to your flop, Bishop. So, don't start blowin' smoke up my ass."

"Constance did come to see me," I admitted, suddenly realizing how smart I had been to ignore her romantic eyes. "She said she was in trouble because Albert Rothfield had been stung to death. I offered to help—because I thought it was what you'd want me to do."

I went on to give him a blow-by-blow account of my meeting with her, including the pistol, and my later meeting with Captain Weatherly. When I finished, Salvator Portello looked as grim as I had ever seen him.

"That gun makes it look like she capped Wolf, don't it?" he said, in a worried voice.

"She had a motive, Sal."

The gangster looked at me as though I had suddenly lost my mind. "What for would she kill him?" he bellowed. "What the fuck would she get out of doin' a hit on some bee-freak?"

"Because Wolf has a DVD that Constance claims links Jacob Dyson to the murder of Jacob's wife. She blames Jacob Dyson for Phil's death. She wants that DVD to take revenge on Dyson."

His arms flopped. "Why didn't she come to me, for Christ's sake? I'd have gotten what she wanted from Wolf—no questions asked. I'd have demonstrated the dip-tank, on Dyson. She could've had it all."

"This probably started before you and she got involved," I suggested. "Once in it, she probably didn't want to get you implicated."

He nodded his head slowly. "That's like her. But she should've come to me, anyway." Then he leaned forward, almost embarrassed. "Constance was supposed to meet me for breakfast, this morning. But she never showed. My men said they saw her leave your flop. But they lost her, after that. Did she tell you where she was going?"

I lit a cigarette. "I sent her back to the motel."

Salvator's face twisted in rage. "How could you do that with the cops waiting for her?"

"I was giving her an alibi, Sal. She was to go there and when questioned tell the cops she'd been to see me. I was to arrive with her wallet in hand to confirm her alibi. That's how Weatherly cornered me."

He slumped into his chair, looking like sick kid after a carnival ride. "The wallet was good thinking. That kept her out of it. I owe you for that, Bishop. But it doesn't tell me where she is."

"Constance probably panicked when she saw the cops and went someplace to think it over. I'm sure she'll be in touch. If she does call, it'd be best for all concerned for you to fix her up with a lawyer who will turn her in."

He hands twisted into worried knots. "I'll take care of that." Then he looked over at me, offering a crooked grin. "I thought maybe you'd given her some shit about me being some asshole she shouldn't get involved with."

"Would I tell tales out of school, Sal?"

He started to wag his head, caught himself and flared, "I wouldn't put nothin' past you, Bishop." Then his voice went soft. "You still got her gun?"

I nodded. "Back at my flop."

He got up twisting his fingers. "Is she in cahoots with Dom on those bee-hits? If you know, tell me."

"Maybe. Maybe not. Ask Dom."

"The asshole would just lie to me. He's always lying to me." The gangster whirled away from me and started to pace. "Constance can't do this to me. Not after the commitments I made. She can't. It ain't right. So help me God, if she and Dom are... I'll kill 'em both!" Salvator suddenly stopped and offered me a hurt look. "You think she conned me, don't you?"

"I didn't say that, Sal."

"But it figures, don't it? Phil Dyson, Rodney Terrance and Albert Rothfield. They all knew her, didn't they? All done in the same way? My brother had the hives. She knew how to rig the action. What's the plan? Am I next? So she and Dom can run things?" He blinked as if trying to hide tears. "I actually told her I loved her, Bishop. I'd never told any woman that, before."

"Then you'll do what's best for her, Sal—no matter what."

Salvator stalked across the room to the door. He was completely white and weaved on his feet, like a man about to faint. When he jerked it open he shouted at the Sicilian Brothers, "Get in here, you two."

The two thugs scurried in looking from me to their boss trying to figure out what was going on and whether they should shoot me there or somewhere else.

"Get Dominic," Salvator told them. "You drag his ass here—I don't care what the fuck you gotta' do. If Mrs. Dyson is with him... well, you bring her, too."

The Brothers gave me a questioning look. All I could do was shrug in response.

"On your way to Dom's apartment you take Bishop to his flop," Salvator continued. Beads of perspiration rose up on his forehead. His hands were quivering. "Bishop has a pistol I want. You bring it here after you get my brother. Clear?"

"Sure, Mr. Salvator, sure," said Thomaso, his voice low with concern. "You feelin' okay, Mr. Salvator? You don't look so good."

"Yeah, Mr. Salvator," chimed Pietro. "You don't look so good. Maybe we should get you a doctor?"

"Never mind that." The gangster wiped the sweat from his brow with one hand. "Just do what I told you."

"You know you can count on us, Mr. Salvator," said Thomaso.

Salvator gave his nose a wipe on the back of one hand. "This time, it may come down to testing that."

"No matter what," I urged, the Mafia Don. "Give Dom and Constance a chance to explain."

Salvator Portello's eyes narrowed with malevolence, as he turned toward me. "You just get your ass out there and find that bastard I paid you to find!" he growled. There was a mean line around the corners of his mouth as he added, "Don't be giving me shit on how to run my family."

After being returned home and handing Mrs. Dyson's pistol to the Sicilian Brothers, I nosed the Buick toward the Lester Hampton Building on the West end of Congress Avenue, in Austin. It was time to bring things to a head with Peterson Barrows.

FOURTEEN

The Lester Hampton Building was built about ten years ago. It was one of those high-rise, luxury-constructs of glass and steel that everyone notices and admires. It was the architectural dream of its namesake, Lester Hampton—political-infighter, pseudo-entrepreneur and swindler.

For nearly three years, Mr. Hampton spent every waking moment arranging the necessary construction-funding through bond-sales to Texas investors. His tireless perseverance to make the Lester Hampton Building a reality was lauded by every politician from the Mayor of Austin up to the Governor's office. There were fundraisers on his behalf, stock promotion spots on local television paid for by political contributions, along with public gatherings where the famous-of-Texas gave speeches to entice the public into making the Hampton one of Austin's most memorable landmarks. During this time, a carnival atmosphere followed Lester Hampton everyplace he went. As a result everyone who was anyone among the political elite, wanted to be part of this hurricane of publicity and promotion. Why not? At that time there was nothing better than to have one's political future linked to the charismatic Lester Hampton.

Then one rainy Sunday Morning several months into the building's construction, the *Austin Gazette* reported a rumor that abruptly burst the investment-bubble. According to the news-article, an unnamed source had provided information that claimed the Hampton Building's investors were being defrauded. Hundreds of millions in construction-dollars were missing with no trace as to where that money had gone. The article also claimed that Lester Hampton was the perpetrator of the theft.

Lester Hampton, when confronted by these allegations in a televised broadcast the next day, fervently denied any wrongdoing. Further, he demanded an accounting-audit to clear his sullied name. Hampton's emotionally-charged denial had the Mayor of Austin, the Texas Attorney-General and the Governor, all vowing to stand by Lester Hampton.

Another televised news conference, later that evening, gave thousands of nervous investors reassurance that all was well with the Lester Hampton Building. And to fend-off future rumors, each politician at the broadcast vowed to take action against anyone who besmirched Lester Hampton's wondrous name. Hampton, sobbing in front of the cameras over this unwavering support by State and local politico's in the face of what he called slanderously insurmountable accusations, closed out the telecast by vowing to fight for an uncompromised vindication.

However, all was as it seemed—at least in terms of the rumor. While the public, police and politicians patiently awaited the audit's outcome Mr. Hampton became busy—secretly liquidating his personal holdings.

Then a week after Lester Hampton's televised denials, more bad news came from the Fourth Estate. Not only did the audit prove that hundreds of millions were missing, but so was Lester Hampton—also gone, without a trace.

William Hawthorne Bank, the financial institution that provided the initial outlay of monies for the Hampton Building's construction, immediately stepped into the financial fray and funded the entire building's development. This, of course, was touted as the only rational thing to do by Austin's venerable Mayor. Unfortunately, the effort did nothing to assuage the financial burn received by Texas-investors. Nevertheless, there is no doubt that completing the project did save Austin's taxpayers millions, in terms of tearing down what would otherwise have been an unfinished high-rise.

Curiously, upon completion of the Lester Hampton Building, William Hawthorne Bank immediately sold the high-rise. This not only resulted in the recovery of the bank's investment, but returned a substantial profit. The identity of the purchaser was kept a secret, per the terms of sale. But some banking insiders claimed an offshore investment-cartel made the acquisition. Although, it is still not clear what transpired immediately thereafter it is believed the cartel did a quick and complicated paper-shuffle. This passed the Hampton Building to a Cayman Island investor-group called, the Nilhists.

Naturally, there were complaints among the Hampton's investors over the bank's refusal to share its profit on the sale. But as the Mayor quickly pointed out, William Hawthorne Bank had ignored tremendous financial risks in order to serve the people of Austin. Therefore the bank justly deserved its high-risk reward. The Mayor made no mention, however, of being on the bank's board-of-directors and its major stockholder. He also failed to disclose the massive bonuses paid to the board members as a result of the Hampton's sale.

That might have ended the matter, sending Lester Hampton's name into Texas history, except for two things. First, there were the incessant rumors about the Nilhists Group being led by the missing—and much sought-after—Lester Hampton. Secondly, Rita Portello was one of those who had lost her investment in the high-rise swindle. That, in turn, brought Salvator Portello into the financial aftermath.

For the next eight years Salvator Portello, never one to give up a search or forgo retribution, tirelessly followed paper trails and rumors concerning Lester Hampton. Then, two years ago, Salvator mysteriously acquired ownership of the Lester Hampton Building.

It came as a complete shock to everyone—particularly Austin's Mayor. Some local speculators claimed that the Hampton was purchased in a highly-leveraged transaction that would ultimately bankrupt the Portello clan—much to society's betterment. Other rumors countered that claim with words to the effect that Salvator Portello had obtained title to the building without paying dime-one.

Salvator denied all the rumors, of course. However one cannot help but wonder if it was pure coincidence that the Sicilian Brothers spent nearly six months searching every nook and cranny in the Cayman Islands. What or who occupied their time on that venture is still open to speculation. But one might make certain assumptions based upon the timing of the Sicilian Brother's return to their usual duties as Salvator Portello's bodyguards.

On that day, Salvator announced his acquisition of the Lester Hampton Building—lock, stock and proverbial barrel. Also on that day, a news-report announced the discovery of a man's body floating in the ocean a few miles offshore from Cayman Brac. The nude corpse, although badly damaged due to feeding fish, had been irrefutably identified as Lester Hampton.

Although the cause of death could not be determined, it was put forward that Mr. Hampton's demise had been orchestrated by the Portellos as an example of what lay ahead for Hampton's Cayman Island business-partners. This, many observers claimed, resulted in those frightened partners offering up the Lester Hampton Building as a pacifier.

Regardless, for Salvator Portello, ownership of the Lester Hampton Building was a massive social coupe. The gangster was suddenly in the spotlight as Austin's largest legitimate business-operator. For the first time in Portello history, the family patriarch was being talked about in business circles not for his criminal activities, but for his savvy business practices.

Realizing the reputation-purging value of positive publicity, Salvator further preened his mafia-discolored feathers by nesting in a suite on the Hampton's main floor. There, the Mafia-Don began the task of keeping the building's rental spaces filled, while quietly continuing the Portello clan's nefarious and not so nefarious business operations.

When I entered Peterson Barrows's private office on the fourth floor of the Hampton Building, a few minutes late for my appointment, the former judge was pacing as if there was a cattle-prod shoved up his ample backside.

"Dammit, Bishop, you were supposed to be here twenty minutes ago!" the lawyer nagged, as he waddled back and forth amidst his office's white-on-white surroundings.

"I was busy with a guy of an extremely insistent nature." I went over and settled into one of the Harvard chairs fronting the lawyer's massive, marble desk.

"What in hell are you up to?" he railed, still pacing. "After I cleared things up with Captain Weatherly about you, he accused me of everything from bee-theft to terrorism."

While Barrows moved, each squeaking step caused the lawyer's black shoes to glint under the room's ceiling-lights, like freshly chipped basalt. I settled back, lit a cigarette and let the wrinkles in my suit bond with the chair's glove-soft leather.

"Sounds like this gig has moved you up in Weatherly's estimation." I blew smoke in the lawyer's direction. "Heretofore he's claimed you were a brain-dead ambulance chaser."

"Don't smart-mouth me, Mister!" snapped the former judge, irascibly. "If I'd have kept my mouth shut I wouldn't be in trouble, now."

Although my clothes had that much sought-after slept-in look, I did feel some envy for Peterson Barrows's ensemble. He was the epitome of business-style in a blue nattily-tailored number, replete with vest, silk shirt and crimson tie. One glance and I knew Barrows's ensemble was probably a close second to the price of a new Buick during the Austin dealerships' annual scratch-dent-and-repossession sale. In fact, he looked almost good enough to pose for an advertisement in a fashion magazine. The only limitations to achieving that society-endearing tribute were his swollen nose, red cheek-bumps and the raft of painful-looking blotches clustered upon his neck, forehead and hands.

"Quipping's the only thing that makes this visit bearable," I said, with disinterest. "What about your client?"

"My client's dead," the lawyer grumbled.

"Sure, Barrows," I scoffed. Then, I had a sudden suspicion.

The lawyer turned on me like an angry rat, his eyes distended. "How do you think I got all these bee-strings? I went to meet him, last night, and was attacked by a whole damn hive!"

The deaths of Philip Dyson, Annie Dyson, Albert Rothfield and Rodney Terrance brought about a sudden interest in Barrows's obviously painful condition. However, I continued to make light of his ailment by offering the lawyer my biggest grin, and an unsympathetic observation.

"Those fuzzy-striped girls with built-in stingers have a natural disdain for you, Barrows," I snickered.

Displeasure gathered on the lawyer's face like a rumbling storm-cloud. "Go to hell!"

"First, tell me what name will be chiseled into your client's headstone—as if I cannot guess?"

He glowered, giving his chest a dramatic thump. "Dr. Edmund Wolf." The lawyer paused a moment before adding in a whimpering voice that held sincere torment, "I was lucky to get back to my car alive."

"Sounds like you were setup to get a little stinging, when you arrived to meet Wolf. Someone wants you dead, Barrows." I paused a moment to enjoy the worry crossing his face. "Wolf being dead means there's no need to delay showing me the DVD," I observed.

Barrows thrust his hands into his pockets and squaring his shoulders as if having disclosed bravery not heretofore demonstrated by the legal profession. "I can't. The DVD represents his estate. It can only be released to Wolf's heirs."

"What you really mean is, you plan to pick up where Wolf left off with Mrs. Dyson."

"That would be completely unethical."

"Which fits you like your suit. I don't want to own it, Barrows, just look at it."

"Nevertheless, I must refuse."

"Did you see anyone at the park?" I asked.

"It was as black as sin," Barrows replied vaguely, the red bumps on his face twisting into tiny purple hills over my impudent question. "I couldn't see more than ten feet in front of me."

"Did you hear anything?"

He bit out his reply, "Buzzing."

"Did you see a stack of hives?"

"Why in hell would there be hives in that a park?"

"The bees came from somewhere," I said.

He scratched the stings on his neck. "I got to where Wolf told me to wait. I didn't see him, so I called his name. Then the bees started in… I wasn't about to hang around. I didn't hear about Wolf being shot until this morning."

"How did Wolf get off of Dyson Island?" I asked. "I'd heard he was pretty much under lock and key."

The lawyer shrugged.

"How was the meeting arranged?" I pressed.

"She telephoned and said that he was in Austin and that we had to meet."

"She, who?"

"Dyson's secretary. Denise."

"If Dyson didn't want Wolf to leave the island, why would Denise telephone you?"

His arms flailed the air as he bleated, "How in hell do I know?"

"Did Wolf ever mention a man named Harris?"

The attorney nodded his head. "Dyson's butler." Then he turned toward me with breathless apprehension. "You think Harris killed Wolf?"

I blew more smoke at him. "I'm thinking it was someone closer to home. Who suggested the meeting-place?"

He dragged one hand pink paw across his sweating forehead. "She, of course. Denise. Do you think I'm stupid enough to suggest a nighttime visit to a park? I could've been mugged."

"Which makes me wonder why you were stupid enough to agree to the meeting?"

"I had to. Dr. Wolf insisted on it."

"No, it was Denise who insisted." I eyed the lawyer cannily. "Obviously, Dyson set you up."

He shook his head sharply. "I've done nothing to Dyson. Why would he have anything against me?"

"You possess the DVD—something he probably wants. I'm surprised your office wasn't burgled while you were out."

A dull red crept up under his cheeks. "Actually it was. But whoever broke in couldn't get into my safe. That's where the DVD is."

I controlled my impatience with effort. "How nice for you."

He chewed the air before choking, "You've got to be mistaken about the bees. Bees can't be programmed to attack."

"On that, you are wrong. In fact, it's the current fad among Austin homicides." Then I switched my attack and said, "The truth this time, Barrows. Did you tell Wolf about Constance Dyson being at *Rancho Relajar*?"

He gulped. "I don't recall, exactly. What difference does it make now? Wolf is dead."

"I like the idea of the guy I killed being sent there by you."

Barrows turned white enough to blend into a snow bank. "I didn't send anybody."

"Stop lying. The clown I shot knew my name."

He quivered in reply, "I may have told Wolf that you had located Mrs. Dyson."

"Did Wolf pick me, or did you?"

The lawyer scurried behind his desk, opened a drawer, took out a marble ashtray and slid it across to me. "Wolf gave me your name." Barrows offered-up a sheepish look. "Frankly, I tried to talk him out of hiring you because of—shall we say—your colorful history. But he insisted."

"All this was done via telephone, I assume?"

"Radio telephone, yes. But that does not make any difference in terms of contractual obligation."

I flicked a long stretch of tobacco ash accumulating on the end of my cigarette, onto the floor. "Scrambled connection?"

Barrows flushed purple. "Not at my end."

"Then you can't be certain of who was on the other end."

Peterson Barrows paused in silence for a moment. Then he looked up at me, his eyes going wide. "Dyson listened in, didn't he?"

I shrugged. "I suspect it was him you were speaking to. How did you get the DVD?"

"It was mailed to me with a note to hold onto it. Enclosed with it was five hundred in cash. Wolf—or so he claimed to be—called a few weeks later. It was then we discussed the arrangement involving you."

"So during the interim between the DVD arriving and you getting a call, Wolf must've told Dyson where he had sent the DVD."

The lawyer suddenly shifted in his chair away from me. But just as suddenly he shifted back. "How can you possibly assume that?"

"I have that kind of mind. Then, again... During your conversations with Wolf, was the voice always the same?"

He shrugged. "As best I can recall."

"How many times have you spoken with Denise?"

"Just the once."

"So there's no way to be certain if that was she, either."

"Have you located Mrs. Dyson?" he croaked, rising out of his char and tilting forward, as wide as the desk.

"I had as of last night. But since then she's disappeared. Now the police and Salvator Portello are looking for her. Which could get complicated should we all find Mrs. Hyssop at the same time."

"The police?"

"Weatherly suspects her in the bee-sting killings."

Barrows eyes bugged. "Why is Salvator Portello looking for Mrs. Dyson?"

"If she's gotten careless with Dominic's bee-hives and personal attributes, as Sal suspects, he plans to kill her. If she's been on the level with him, he'll probably marry the woman. Either way, Mrs. Dyson does not have a whole lot to look forward to."

"The Portellos have gone into the honey-business?" He gaped, in disbelief.

"One of them. But so far Dom's not much competition to anybody else in the profession. What reason were you given that necessitated Constance being followed?"

He looked at me steadily for twenty or so seconds, his tongue flitting across dry lips. Then with a defeated shrug Barrows muttered, "None, actually."

I reached over and snuffed out my cigarette butt. "Weren't you even curious?"

He hesitated, drumming on the desktop with his flat fingertips, waiting, seeming to be selecting his words carefully. "Frankly, my current financial situation is such, that I was afraid of asking too many questions for fear of losing the business."

It was my turn to get nervous. "You mean your check might bounce?"

"Of course not!" Barrows scowled.

I took a deep, thoughtful drag on my cigarette. "What would Jacob Dyson have to offer Chechnyan terrorists?"

"From what I've been told, Wolf perfected a way of spying without physically going to the place of interest." Barrows rubbed one hand through his thinning hair, uncertainly. "If true, that would be of great value to any nation."

"But why not this nation? Why Chechnya?"

He fell silent, considering. "I don't know. Possibly because Wolf exaggerated his accomplishments and our government was unable to confirm those claims."

"Meaning, he was running a con and found some suckers with money in the form of Dyson and the Chechnyans?"

Barrows laughed suddenly. "I didn't say that."

My memory raced back to Salvator Portello's words about Romero's arrangement with Dyson. "That type of spying would be linked to what is typically called, 'out of body experiences?'"

He settled back into his chair. "Exactly."

"I'm having a hard time understanding why a billionaire like Jacob Dyson would cut a deal with terrorists to pocket the few million they might have."

The lawyer made a vague gesture. "Perhaps because those billions are nothing but air."

It was my turn to gape. "You know that as fact?"

He shook his head. "Not as such. But I'm reliably informed that after Phil came of age, he expressed an interest in finance. Annie Dyson thought Phil was a genius."

"Mothers of idiot sons often make that erroneous assumption."

"In any event, Annie handed him the job of managing the family fortune. According to a stockbroker-friend, Phil lost all of it by investing in Enron, MCI and a couple of other failed corporations."

"Did his mother ever find out?"

"Who's to say?" said Barrows, making an indistinct movement with one hand. "Phil went bust and she promptly died. Then Phil died. It must've been a terrifying awakening for Jacob Dyson when he realized the truth."

"So nobody inherited anything?"

Barrows shrugged.

"Does Constance know there's no money?"

"Annie Dyson died intestate—meaning, there was no Will. That means Jacob would've inherited everything of his wife's," said Barrows. He licked his lips thoughtfully. "As such, there was no reason for Constance Dyson to be informed. But that's not to say Jacob Dyson did not discuss the situation with her. Especially, if he suspected that Constance was the reason behind Phil's bad investments."

"What's on the DVD?"

The lawyer leaned back, sighing. "I don't know."

"You must've looked at it."

He hesitated before shaking his head.

"The man is dead, Barrows. Mrs. Dyson is under suspicion of murder. If that DVD shows Jacob Dyson killing his wife with Bee-venom, it could redirect the current police-investigation."

The lawyer nodded in understanding, still ill at ease. "That changes nothing. I have Wolf's estate to consider."

"How did Wolf approach Constance initially? Through you?"

He nodded. "Wolf asked me to arrange a meeting. That was impossible what with her in jail at the time and him being trapped on Dyson Island." Barrows eyed me over. "So I arranged for a telephone connection. They spoke privately. At the end of their discussion, I met with Constance at the jail." He shuddered slightly. "She, to say the least, was interested. But Wolf wanted a million in cash. Constance didn't have that. So with me as the intermediary, negotiations began. Wolf finally agreed to trade the DVD for half that amount —which Constant claimed she could pay."

"Payment being Annie Dyson's jewelry?"

The lawyer nodded his sore head. "Initially I assumed those jewels belonged to Constance." He shrugged as if shuffling off a load of guilt. "Otherwise I would not have continued in my capacity as negotiator."

"Of course not," I said, dryly. "But this whole thing could've been set up to get Annie's jewelry returned. The DVD is probably blank."

The lawyer gave me a startled look. "But that would mean…"

I nodded, grinning. "That you won't get dime-one for it. How did Romero get involved?"

Barrows's shoulders drooped, in disappointment. "He was Wolf's idea. I discussed Romero with Constance. Surprisingly, she agreed."

"What was Romero's end?"

"Fifty thousand." Barrows made vague motions as he spoke. "Payment was to come from Constance. But she stipulated that Romero would have to take a particular piece of jewelry as his end—not cash. Romero was not happy with that idea at first. However, he finally relented."

"Jacob Dyson led you and Constance down the garden path to get back what was rightfully his."

"Then how do you explain Wolf's murder?"

"I think a beautiful redhead got Wolf here and killed him when he could not produce the DVD. What made Constance Dyson think she could trust Romero?"

The lawyer made a moue. "During my conversations with her, I got the impression that she did not. But the DVD was of such importance that she felt there was no choice."

"But if the DVD is valid, why couldn't Romero cut Wolf out of any deal with Constance?"

"Because Wolf created the DVD with an access code," explained the lawyer, giving the desktop a fingernail-tap, for emphasis. "Without that code, it was useless to the possessor."

"A code you know?"

"I am privy to it, yes."

"Did Romero know about the access code?"

"Not that I'm aware of." Barrows smiled crookedly. "That knowledge was to remain between me and my client..."

"So if your client received payment..."

Barrows glanced over with impatient eyes. "If the Jewels were passed as agreed, Wolf was to contact me and I would deliver the DVD to Constance along with the code."

"Romero made the comment that Jacob Dyson had gotten involved with a woman," I said. "Did you hear anything about that?"

The lawyer lifted his right hand like a witness before swearing to tell the truth. "Not in as many words." He licked his lips and drew a deep breath. "But from the sound of Denise's voice—his secretary—she's a very young woman. I would not be surprised if she and Dyson were involved."

I gave a noncommittal nod. "Romero suggested that the woman Dyson was involved with murdered Annie and Phil Dyson."

Barrows grimaced. "I doubt that a mere secretary would have the mental capacity to create such a murder-scheme."

I did not believe it, either. "What do you know about Denise Myer, other than that she is young?"

His brows arched in surprise. "Nothing. But I'll make some calls. I might be able to get a lead on her family." He paused a moment scratching at the scab on the end of his nose. "I was contacted by Jacob Dyson, shortly before you arrived."

"With regard to what?"

Peterson Barrows leaned his elbows on the desktop. "Dyson wanted to know if Wolf had given me anything to hold," he said in a confidential manner.

"Meaning the DVD?"

"Exactly. Naturally, I could not admit to anything." His eyes became like slits with the importance he felt by his next words. "Dyson wasn't satisfied. He offered me a million-dollar finder's fee. He knew Wolf was dead. He even went so far as to accuse Mrs. Dyson of killing Wolf." He paused a moment before saying, "She did kill Wolf, didn't she?"

"Romero had as good a reason as she," I said, purposely being vague. "So did Dyson—assuming the DVD is as claimed. But my money is on her." Then a sick realization suddenly flooded my gut, and it had nothing to do with my fast-food breakfast of sausage and Serrano burritos. "I'm wrong. It was Dyson," I said, more to myself than Barrows. "Jacob Dyson grabbed Constance after she left my flop. That's why she wasn't being interrogated by Weatherly. That's also why Wolf was killed—probably by Harris. With Constance at Dyson's beck and call to finish the work for the Chechnyans, Wolf was no longer needed."

He cocked his head sideways. "But…"

"I've had it wrong from the beginning," I said. "Little was at *Rancho Relajar* to bring Constance to Dyson Island, not to kill her. Wolf had already made his escape and was hiding in Austin. Dyson sent Harris to find Wolf. But Harris came back empty-handed." I stood up feeling grimly outmaneuvered. "How can I get to Dyson Island?"

Barrows scrawled several lines on the notepad, tore off the top sheet and then handed it to me. The note read, *'Lake Travis Ferry. Janine Kirkland.'*

"What are you going to do when you get there?" he asked.

"I want you to call Dyson. Tell him I've got the DVD. Tell him I've seen it. Tell him I'm willing to cut a deal. Tell him Constance is the price."

The lawyer's face fell. "To what end? If Dyson needs Constance so badly that he abducted her, he's not about to give her up." His words came from a voice that was unmanned, more along the lines of a hysterical boy's.

"I don't expect his cooperation."

Peterson Barrows looked at me in horror. "You're going there to kill Dyson, aren't you?" His face contorted into deep, ghastly lines. "That's cold-blooded murder."

"I'm going out there to bring her back, here. As long as nobody does anything stupid, there won't be any killings."

"But if you do kill Dyson, that DVD won't be worth anything."

"I thought you had not looked at it."

He cleared his throat carefully. "I haven't. I'm just going by what Wolf told me."

"When I get back, you and I are going to look at that DVD—I don't care if

I have to strip you naked and tie you to the top of a beehive."

"If you think I'm going to cut you in…"

"Mrs. Dyson doesn't have a dime, Barrows. That makes your only sales opportunity Jacob Dyson."

He snorted confidently, "I'm sure I can convince Mr. Romero to adhere to the agreement."

"I doubt it. You see, *he* doesn't have the jewelry either."

The lawyer's eyebrows arched in despair. "Then who does?"

"Not a clue, Mr. Barrows." I pointed at the telephone. "There's no sense in delaying this."

His demeanor underwent a sudden and almost painful change, then. Fear ran crooked crevices over his face, like a razor in a shaking hand across a sheet of wax. I lit a cigarette as he picked up the telephone receiver. I waited until Barrows had Dyson on the line. Then I turned and left.

FIFTEEN

"I thought you P.I.s were fearless, Bishop," Janine Kirkland chided. Then, she gave me a peek at her even, white teeth. "You're as pale as a ball of rice."

I did not return her smile. Not that I perceived female pilots as unappealing —quite the contrary. There is something very sexual about a woman who is in complete control of a plane old enough to predate mankind. Especially, if that plane is flying several thousand feet above a moonlit ocean, hell and gone from everywhere.

"Normally, I'm the gung ho type who's first into the fray," I declared. "However, sitting in this vibrating tin coffin dampens my courage."

Janine was a fit, fortyish, full-lipped brunette with a well-formed face, and small delicate ears. There were a few freckles on the bridge of her exquisitely chiseled nose and squint-lines at the corners of each dark eye. Those, to my eye, enhanced her beauty. She had long, smooth fingers with nails covered in a clear lacquer. Death-trap-transport-with-wings aside, Janine Kirkland was everything a dirty old man like me desired in a woman. Well, almost everything I desired. She had an irritating habit of taunting my innate fear of flying.

"I supposed you'd rather be driving on I-35, risking life and limb at every tick of the odometer," she scoffed.

Janine wore a brown leather jacket, a beige sweater that covered two nice bulges, tan slacks and western boots. A white ribbon tied her long hair into a loose, gray-flecked ponytail. The latter coiled across one of her jacket-applets like a cat's tail.

"When was the last time you had the engines overhauled?" I complained. "I think they're sharing pistons."

"About a hundred hours, ago." Janine tossed me a wry grin. "The vibration comes from the exhaust manifold. The gasket's wearing thin. I'll have to replace it. Nothing to worry about, though. In fact if I sit in the right position, the vibration can be absolutely exquisite."

"Sex, sex, sex. Is that all you women-pilots think about?"

"As if that wouldn't be the answer to your prayers," Janine snorted. A muscle twitched in the right side of her mouth, forming a crooked smile. "How about your engine, Bishop? If that suit is any indication you're long overdue for an overhaul."

"For your information, I'm better now than I was at sixteen. I just don't feel like proving it as often."

She gave her head a dismal wag. "How disillusioning to hear you had the sex-drive of a worn-out old man back then."

Despite the bruising my ego continued to receive from her venomous digs, I quickly came back with, "Have you ever crashed this airborne execution-chamber?"

We were nearly three hours into the flight. Three hours of buffeting winds reminding me my tenuous hold was on life. Three hours of remembering how old I was. Three hours of realizing how much younger she was. Three hours of trying to analyze how best to approach the trouble awaiting me on Dyson Island. Three hours of droning engines vibrating every part of my body until I had concerns for the well-being of certain areas equipped with delicate attachments. Three hours of me enjoying her nearness, hearing her breathing, smelling her hair, her skin and sweat without being able to do anything about it. Three hours of her rattling my cage at every opportunity, as if I was God's punishment to women. Three hours of me wishing I could climb out on a wing for a quick smoke. Three hours, into a flight that never seemed to end.

"Nothing serious in the crash-category," declared Janine. The words came out flatly. Then she cocked her head to one side, and studied the gauges. "But if you're nervous I won't take offense to prayers being said. Or aren't you the religious type?"

"My priest, Father Drapula, claims I have the potential for strong religious leanings. Of course he's been locked in the loony-bin for the past year. Nevertheless, I'm certain it would please him to know that I've been chatting with my maker ever since you and I left the ground."

The plane let go a series of sharp rattlings. These sent unnerving jolts through my feet and up my legs. "Dear God, what fell off this flying coke-can?"

"One of the props is slightly out-of-tune after chewing up an albatross during takeoff my last trip to Dyson Island." Her nose wrinkled slightly as if she were still evaluating the incident. "Nothing serious. But wind-sheers make it hiccup. I'll have to get it replaced."

"Hiccup, hell! It feels like the angel of death just roosted on the tail of this flying funerary-urn."

"You're a pessimist, Bishop. Worst case, an engine mount breaks and drops half a ton of rumbling steel into the cockpit."

I offered her a pleading look. "That's something you can deal with, right?"

"Absolutely," she said without hesitation. Then she tossed me a teasing wink. "All I have to do is join you in prayer while we await a life-saving miracle."

I looked away from Janine with a new sense of appreciation for planet earth and the lack of fragility in the female species. "Is a falling engine likely to happen?" I demanded. "Or are you punching my buttons, again?"

"You've actually gone from white to green, Bishop," she laughed, her voice sounding like silver bells tinkling in a soft breeze. "There's a sick bag under your seat if you need it."

"What I need is my usual rush-hour spot behind the Buick's steering wheel, with all four tires grabbing pavement while I'm cussing a blue-streak at the slow-driving bastard in front of me, between puffs on my favorite weed."

Still smiling she hit me with, "Get out of panic-mode, Bishop. Give air-travel a chance. You might like it."

I tried to settle more comfortably in the co-pilot's seat, but without success. There were pedals on the floor where my feet wanted to be. There was a stick topped by a cut-down steering wheel moving back and forth directly in front of my middle. And the off-key drone of the two engines mounted to the wing above the cockpit was deafening.

"Being up here is all I've ever wanted," Janine remarked.

I looked over at her, again. The plane's instrument lights glowed softly upon her tanned face. To some men, Janine might not be the ideal beauty. I considered her breathtaking.

"Touching the face of God and all that?" I quipped.

"I see that priest was right about your religious potential." Her eyes gave me a swift, flickering glance. "With a little luck you'll be a true-believer by the time we reach Dyson Island."

"What make of plane am I in?" I asked. "Or, don't records go back that far?"

"Grumman Goose. Sometimes called a Flying Boat. They don't make them anymore."

"I'm not surprised. A trip in this is akin to suicide."

As if in response to my latest zing, the plane offered-up a bone shaking shudder. Then it took a sharp dip, followed by an equally abrupt rise. I grabbed for the co-pilot's controls. But this time I caught myself before she batted my hands off the wheel.

I heard Janine mutter a curse. Then she jerked on the stick, while her feet kicked the pedals. Slowly the Grumman stabilized.

"Should I assume one of the props gnawed the head off another albatross?" I complained. "Or did something serious happen? Like the boat part of this thing fell off?"

"It's the extra fuel tanks," she casually explained. "I've got six hundred gallons in the wet-wing tanks. But I had a pair of three hundred gallon cans added in case of headwinds. They hang near the struts. They get battered during cross-gusts and raise hell with aerolon-control."

I gave Janine a worried look. "Is that your way of telling me, we're going to crash?"

"Not the way those tanks are attached." Her eyes twinkled with amusement, in the lights from the control panel. "It's more likely something would fall off of you, at a very inopportune moment."

"I may be old but I've still got what it takes," I proudly protested.

"I'd say you were sixty, maybe a year or two on either side of death." Janine looked at me suddenly, before looking away again. "As for what it takes…"

"How much longer before I kiss rock and fondle tree?" I interjected impatiently.

"Not long." She tossed me a curious look. "If Jacob Dyson isn't a friend of yours, why this trip?"

I was still annoyed. "He's a friend of a friend, so to speak."

A vague smile moved the corners of her mouth, and then went away. "Meaning, Dyson's not going to want you there?"

"Under other circumstances, he'd probably object even if I put a gun to his head. But I think Jacob Dyson will welcome me with open arms this time."

"What makes the different?"

"I've got something he wants."

She laughed without humor. "How badly?"

"Enough to kill for, if I'm any judge of character. How close are you to Dyson?"

Janine shrugged faintly, as though she didn't believe my reply. "Strictly business. Dyson's all right. But he's got hired help I don't care for."

"How so?"

"One is supposed to be the butler—if you believe the monkey-suit." Janine suddenly tilted forward over the stick as if trying to look at something barely visible along the dark horizon. Her eyes were grave and her hands knotted on the wheel. After a moment she eased back, once more relaxed. "His name's Harris. He's got an automatic holstered under one arm. I saw it on one trip to Dyson Island when his coat blew open in the breeze. So, I'm thinking he's actually Dyson's bodyguard. The other guy is a creep called Little. He's supposed to be a foreign-exchange student studying bees. But from what I've seen, Little wouldn't know one end of a bee from the other if it stung him."

"What makes those two clowns special to Jacob Dyson?" I asked.

"I don't know where Dyson dug them up." She turned her head briefly and looked at me. "Nobody likes either of them—yours truly, included."

"I heard rumors that Harris is from Chechnya."

Janine said nothing for several seconds, staring out at the blackness surrounding us, her hands riding on the dipping and rising wheel. "Neither Little nor Harris are from this country, I know that. Both men have distinct accents. Chechnya's part of Russia, isn't it?"

"As far as the Russians are concerned. But the Chechnyans think it should have its own flag. To get their point across the terrorist membership pressured Moscow by shooting little kids in a school. Apparently, that group doesn't have spine enough to face armed opponents."

"Why would animals like that work for Dyson?"

"A good question. Especially when another rumor has it that Dyson sold those guys a bill of goods. When the Chechnyan funding runs out things are liable to get very interesting for Jacob Dyson if he can't provide what was promised."

Janine considered my remark for a few seconds before nodding. "And that is?"

"Out of body stuff."

She tossed me a naughty grin. "Are we talking foreplay or afterglow?"

"More along the lines of leaving their bodies to commit whatever atrocity the average terrorist finds tempting."

"Nobody's stupid enough to believe that." She smiled teasingly. "Or have I misjudged you?"

My burning cheeks over her sarcasm sent my mouth into brag-mode before I could stop it. "I admit I'm not a Ph.D. But I know what's-what and what goes where, when it comes to bodies."

"I don't know whether to take that as encouraging or something to despair over. Are you the type who likes to do it the same way each time?"

"Not a chance. If I get that out-of-body business mastered, I plan to do it on the ceiling."

She licked a finger and struck the air and giggled. "That's one for you, Bishop."

"When was the last time you saw Little?" I asked.

"I flew the creep to Austin two or three days ago," she replied.

"You won't be flying him back."

She gave me a questioning look, her eyes snapping with confusion. "Dyson fired Little?"

"Little's dead."

Her mouth gaped for a moment. Then Janine sputtered, "Dead? Little just dropped dead?"

"Officially it was self-defense."

Janine gave me a double-take. "You mean you…"

"We were playing gun-tag," I went on. "Little cheated. I played by the rules. He lost, with penalties. Did you fly Wolf to Austin from Dyson Island?"

She nodded, still glancing over at me in shock. "I brought out a load of medical-supplies. Wolf jumped in the plane when Harris stated loading the boxes onto the golf cart they use for running around the island. Wolf told me there was an emergency. He said he had to get to Austin, pronto."

"How did he look?"

"What do you mean?"

"Was he banged up? Like somebody'd knocked him around, a bit?"

She considered my question for a moment and then shook her head.

"Did you notify Dyson about Wolf's departure?" I asked.

"Wolf said Dyson had flown the helicopter to Austin and had been injured in a crash. It wasn't until we were several hours away from Dyson Island that I realized I'd been suckered. Dyson radioed me. That's when Wolf produced a pistol and told me to ignore the call, and keep flying. I did. When I landed, Wolf ran across the tarmac to a waiting car. I radioed Dyson and told him what had happened. He said to forget the gunplay and that he'd make it up to me with a bonus."

"What kind of car?"

She shrugged. "Newish. It was parked in the shadows so I can't give you a description."

"Who knew you were making that trip to Dyson Island?"

More thinking. "Dyson, of course," she said. "He ordered the supplies. Juan. He's the gardener-cum bee-keeper. He would've told Harris." She paused a moment. Then her eyes got big. "And Romero. He stopped by my office just before I left. He wanted to arrange a trip out there the next day. I told him it would have to wait a day because I'd have too many hours without a break. He said it wasn't important and that he'd check back. He did this morning." She paused again. "You think Romero told Wolf I was on my way? And then Wolf waited for me to land so he could fly here to meet Romero?"

I nodded. "I also think Romero gave Wolf a beating after getting him to Austin in order to get his hands on the DVD Wolf was peddling. Then he killed Wolf."

Janine Kirkland looked over at me as if I had lost my mind. After realizing that I was not making a bad joke, her eyes snapped wide open and she caught her breath. "Wolf is dead, too?"

"Shot dead. Not by yours-truly."

She said thoughtfully, "I flew Harris to Austin yesterday morning. Isn't it more likely that Dyson ordered Harris to…"

"I don't think Harris would've killed Wolf. With Wolf heading-up Dyson's research, there would've been too much to lose on the Chechnyan front. But Romero would've been out nothing by killing Wolf."

"Are the police looking for Romero?"

I nodded. "But I don't think they've linked him to Wolf's killing, yet. Why?"

"I flew him to Dyson Island this morning."

"That doesn't sound good for me. You didn't hear about Wolf's death on the news?"

"I don't tune-in. There's never anything good to hear. Where did it happen?"

"Ainslie Park. What makes you think Harris might kill if Dyson ordered it?"

"Harris has the disposition for it," Janine said resolutely.

"As does Dyson?"

"I'm not sure. He's the chubby, nervous type." Janine's eyes sparkled with new appreciation for me as she returned them to the plane's gauges. "Were you hired by Wolf's family to investigate what happened?"

"Nope. My reason is redheaded and built to please. What can you tell me about Harris?"

"He's big and brawny. He drinks too much—or so I've been told. He's real short on tact—that I tell you from personal experience."

"Harris threatened you?"

She screwed up her mouth, trying to think of the right words. "Let's just agree that he's not much for light conversation."

"What time was it when you landed Wolf in Austin?"

"Sevenish. It was getting dark."

"Did you see Harris after that time?"

She nodded. "This morning. He was with Romero on the flight. I barely had time to powder my nose and refuel the Grumman before you showed up this evening. Is the lawyer you told me to bill for this trip good for the money?"

"Peterson Barrows? How can you ask such a question? He used to be a judge."

She grinned. "That's no recommendation and you know it."

"Did Harris or Romero mention anything, during the last flight, about Wolf?"

"They sat in the back of the passenger compartment, and argued. I couldn't hear what was said. But from the tone of Romero's voice he was angry as hell." There was nearly a minute of silence before she said, "You're telling me straight about Wolf and Little? They really are dead?"

I nodded. "Little carried a Lugar with a silencer and thought he was tough as belt-leather. Sound familiar?"

More sparkle from her eyes followed by a smile. "That's Little. Funny thing for a student to have—an old gun like that."

"How did Harris get from Dyson Island to Austin?"

She shrugged. "Dyson must've flown him there in the helicopter."

"Why didn't Dyson fly Harris back?"

Another shrug. "Maybe Dyson was hauling something or somebody, back. His helicopter's a two-seater."

"Dyson was expecting Romero's visit?"

Her head nodded. "I think something's up."

"How long have you worked for Dyson?" I asked.

"I work for myself." She glanced over and gave me a wink. "Dyson contracted with me to supply air-shuttle service about two years ago. I'm allowed to have other clients. But the agreement states he gets priority. I've got no complaints. He pays on time. In return, I fly whoever or whatever shows up at my door to his island and fly back anybody or anything he puts on my plane." Janine paused a moment to chuckle. "Deacon Bishop. I knew your name was familiar. Damn! You're that ex-cop the mayor of Austin hates, aren't you?"

"I'm hated by lots of people. It comes with my pleasing personality. Tell me about the 'whoever' you fly to Dyson Island?"

"Psychics, palm-readers and spook-hunters. They're cocky when they climb on board. They're scared shitless by the time they make the return-trip." She was silent for a moment. Then Janine turned her eyes to mine. "I don't know what happens to them on Dyson's island. But whatever it is, it turns their spines to jelly."

"Anybody else on Dyson's payroll beside Harris?"

"Wolf and Little—or they were. There's Juan and his wife, Margarita. Nice people. There's a cook and a secretary. Then there are the six scared disciples— or, rather five."

"Disciples?"

"That's what I call them." She tried to smile, but somehow it didn't come off. "Three sweaty men and two chain-smoking women. They're tweedy, university-types. Very nervous crowd."

"Are any of them friends with Harris?"

"I doubt it. They're not even friends with each other. Particularly since Cry-baby disappeared. After that, nobody trusts nobody."

"Cry-baby?"

"The sixth disciples. I gave him that moniker because he spent each trip sobbing. It was like somebody was out to get him and he had nowhere to hide." Janine tapped a gauge. Then she adjusted the plane's course. "Something's happened to him. He's not been seen for months."

"Do you know Cry-baby's name?"

Janine made a face. "George Lipton. He was the last of the disciples to move to Dyson Island. Poor guy. He didn't last three months. He was German, I think. Had an accent, anyway."

My memories flashed with recollections of Constance Dyson's words to Romero about George Lipton. "I think Cry-Baby's dead."

"You're just full of good news." Her head shook and the dark cattail flicked. "You didn't tell Dyson you were coming, did you?"

"He knows I'm coming. He just doesn't know when... or how."

She paused for a moment. "Well, now it's my turn to deliver bad news. Harris knows the when and how of your visit, which means Dyson does. I hope you're not married."

"Not recently, anyway." My stomach formed into new knots. "You told Harris you were bringing me?"

"Per procedure, I radioed Juan before takeoff." A tight, hard smile, ever so faintly sardonic, formed at the corners of her mouth. "His instructions are to relay my ETA and any details of my flight to Harris. Harris is supposed to tell Dyson. What really happened between you and Little?"

"He was looking for a friend of mine. Little thought sending a slug a little wide in my direction might make me talkative. I was brought up the hard way— watching westerns on TV. Consequently, I don't believe in idle chit-chat or wasting ammunition."

She gave me another look, worried, this time. "Harris'll be on the dock when we land. He won't hesitate to use his gun. That doesn't worry you?"

"Nothing and nobody scares me—at least, not any more. Not after flying in this tin-tombstone."

Her mouth worked silently for many seconds as if she were having trouble forming a question. Eventually, Janine asked, "Why did Little come after a friend of yours?"

"To bring her to Dyson Island," I said. "That's the theory I'm operating under, anyway."

"Kidnapping, you mean?" I got a look of surprise this time. "Why would Dyson order Little to do that?"

"Because Wolf ran off and Dyson did not expect to get him back. The redhead is Constance Dyson. She used to be married to Phil Dyson. Do you know her?"

Janine made a small sound and took a sudden interest in the plane's instruments. "How is it you do?"

"I was hired to follow her by the lawyer I told you to bill. I get the feeling you know Constance?"

She nodded. "Constance is my sister."

I tried not to gape. "When was the last time you saw your sister?"

"Not for over a year." Janine gave me a sheepish look. "We're not on the best of terms since..." She broke off with a swift intake of breath. When she finally continued, Janine said, "Dyson wouldn't dare force Constance to go back there."

"He might—if dying is his other option."

"You mean Harris?"

I nodded. "My information claims that Phil lost the family's billions. Any truth to that?"

"Indirectly," she murmured. "Phil thought he was a financial wizard. The truth was, he could choose a sound investment if it kicked him in the ass. Just before he died, Phil was a frantic case of nerves. I'd never seen him like that, before. I suppose losing all that money was the reason." She frowned. "What makes you think Dyson had Constance kidnapped?"

"Wolf is dead. Your sister disappeared at the same time. Your suggestion that Harris flew back with you because there was no room in Dyson's helicopter further supports that belief."

"Why?"

"Because Constance was the second person in the helicopter."

Janine's hands flexed on the wheel, as her worries grew. "So what do we do?"

"You don't do anything but come back tomorrow."

She swore under her breath. "If my sister's been kidnapped, I'm going in with you."

"Not a chance. I'll have all I can do to keep myself in one piece without worrying about you."

She snorted, "How do you plan to stop me?"

"I'm just playing with probabilities, Janine. If I'm wrong you'll lose your business with Dyson."

"And if you're right?"

"I'm not noted for my lucky-streaks. You wouldn't want to be along if things go wrong."

"Constance is my sister. I have to chance it."

"Don't you have some way of contacting her? To verify that she's okay?"

Her head slowly shook.

"Let's work it this way," I suggested. "If I'm all wet about Constance being there against her will, I'll have Dyson radio you. If you don't hear anything, then assume she's in danger and notify the Texas Rangers."

"Dyson Island is owned by the Venezuelans. The Rangers won't do squat."

"Austin P.D. is looking for Constance. The Rangers will come."

She gave me a frightened look. "Police? What for?"

"You really don't catch the news, do you?"

She looked startled. "Stop stalling, Bishop. What the hell for?"

"The suspicious deaths of Rodney Terrance and Albert Rothfield."

"Rodney and Albert? Dead? What are you, the angel of death? What happened to them?"

"The same as Phil Dyson—you do remember, Phil?"

Her cheeks darkened. A convulsive tremor rippled through her body. Then her fingers tightened on the wheel.

"Constance told you, didn't she?" Janine murmured.

I shrugged. "I don't think your sister cares, any more—if that helps."

"What makes the cops think she killed Rodney and Albert?"

"Your sister had good motives. Rothfield was informing on her to Dyson—she knew it. Terrance got rough with her and she didn't like it. As for motive to kill her husband... You fit the bill. What was the draw for Constance to hook up with Albert Rothfield?"

Janine shrugged. "Protection, maybe. Albert was tough enough for ten bodyguards."

I smirked, "Not tough enough, in my case."

She gave me a disbelieving look.

"I knocked him flat on his ass, and then out for the count," I told her, proudly.

"Sure, Bishop," she smirked. "You and your other army, I suppose?"

"How is it you knew Rodney Terrance?"

"Constance was going to marry him." Janine hesitated. Then she appeared to go listless. "Then my sister met Phil."

"You were dating Phil, I take it?"

"Yeah. But that's love for you. It never goes as planned."

"How was Terrance on the scale of men?"

"Okay, I guess. Not my type. But Constance thought he was dreamy. I always had the feeling Rodney was hiding something. He was always snooping, digging."

"Blackmail, maybe?"

"Ah," she sighed. "That would fit."

"What do you mean?"

"I flew him out to Dyson Island right after Phil died. He met with Jacob Dyson. I guess because Romero had arranged the meeting. But afterward, Rodney stuck around for an extra day. Later, I had a quick chat with Juan and found out that Rodney had been asking questions about Phil's death—talking to the Disciples. Implying that there might be something more to it than what the cops said." She glanced over, still concerned. "What do we do when we land?"

"You're going to listen for a radio-call, remember?"

"No offense, Bishop, but you're past it." There was a flicker of pity in her eyes, as she stared at me. "You can't do this alone. I've got an automatic under my seat. I know how to use it."

"If Dyson and Harris are waiting for me with ugly intentions, you'll get killed. Then what happens to your sister?"

"Okay. I'll leave and come back." Her voice was soft, and sure. "They won't expect a thing. You just hang tough if they grab you. I'll show up and threaten to blow Dyson's head off if they don't turn you and my sister loose."

I frowned in disbelief. "Can you actually get to Dyson Island unnoticed this noisy chicken-coup?"

"There's no radar on the island. That means there's a good chance to arrive unseen." Then her voice became excited. "I'll cut the Grumman's engines and lights. Then I'll do a long, low glide. It'll be rough hitting the waves without power. But, nothing I haven't done before. Then I'll taxi using only one engine to the far side of the island, where the empty hives are stored. I'll more the Grumman and head for the Big-House on foot." She cleared her throat as if suddenly uncertain. "Taking off is another matter. These Pratt & Whitney engines are big—nearly seven hundred horsepower each. The sound of their pipes carries a long ways on full-throttle. With the extra fuel, it takes lots of wave-butting to get airborne. That means we can't leave with Harris and Dyson in hot-pursuit. We'll have to tie them up or something."

"I'm afraid you won't like the 'or something.'"

"For my sister, I'll learn to live with it."

"Okay, you're hired. But no matter what happens when you drop me off, get away as quick as you can. Then get back there quietly. If Harris meets you because he heard the engines, tell him you're having problems with the plane. Don't try to take him out on your own. When you get a chance, come looking for me. I don't think Dyson will want to be anywhere near me without Harris to back his play. So the three of us should all be in one room. Make sure I see you before they do. I'll make my move. Then you come barging in. Don't plug anybody unless it's necessary. But if either of them try anything, make sure you drop Harris first."

She gave me a worried look. "Do you really think it will come to that?"

"Don't think before shooting. Just aim like they're so much plastic and squeeze the trigger. You mentioned a secretary... Denise?"

"Yeah. Silicone tits, young, blonde and no brains," Janine said. "I think somebody sent her to keep Dyson busy, at night. She's foreign. I don't know from where. Why did your wives leave you?"

"I've got an uncontrollable harem complex."

"At your age?" Janine scoffed. "What in hell are you trying to prove, Bishop?"

"Stop being judgmental and tell me about Denise."

"I don't think she's armed, if that's your interest. Her clothes are too tight to hide anything but what little God gave her to which man has made numerous additions."

"You're sure she's Dyson's playmate?"

Janine gave me a long lucid look. "How many secretaries have you met with fingernails an inch long?"

"Did you fly the secretary out to Dyson's island?"

She nodded. "The whole trip, Denise was all giggles and goop chattering about how much she was going to enjoy seeing her brother again."

"Brother? One of the disciples?"

"I don't know. She never said. I had no reason to ask."

"How often does Denise leave Dyson Island?"

"I can't say. Whenever she does, she must go with Dyson. I've never flown her back." There was a brief pause before Janine said, "You know, her accent's a lot like Harris's."

"Tell me about the cook."

"Name's Elsie," Janine replied. "About your age. A widow. Very sweet. I think she'd like to leave Dyson Island. But I don't think Dyson wants her to go. Too damn good in the kitchen. To keep her happy, he pays Elsie very well. I suspect she'll hang on until social security."

"Anything more I should know about Elsie?"

Janine laughed. "That old girl smiles if she likes you, let's you know if she doesn't," she replied. "Her pastries are to die for—my mouth waters just thinking about them."

"How do you know? Does Elsie pack you a lunch for the flight back to Austin?"

Her head wagged. "I had engine-trouble one trip. I had to stay there over a weekend while Dyson arranged for a mechanic to fly out. Elsie and I got acquainted in her kitchen over a fifth of Pinch, and caramel rolls. One bite of those sweet, sticky numbers and I was in heaven."

"If you love heaven, wait until you've had your chimes rung by me."

"You're beginning to sound like Romero." Janine's brow suddenly furrowed. "That weekend I spent on Dyson Island seems like ages ago. It was just after I flew Denise out."

"How close did Denise's arrival coincide with Lipton's disappearance?"

"She got there a couple of weeks after that."

"How do Elsie and Denise get along?"

"Well enough, as far as I can tell. The weekend I was stranded, the three of us huddled together in the kitchen like schoolgirls. Elsie supplied jam-busters and espresso while Denise shared Dyson's sexual preferences." Janine paused a moment before offering me a questioning smile. "Dyson's bedroom tastes run a bit on the kinky side. What about yours?"

"Nothing that a good set of handcuffs, warm oil and a video camera won't cure."

She rolled her eyes. "You're disgusting—in a kinkily fun sort of way."

"Speaking of disgusting, does your family know about your sister's involvement with Salvator Portello?"

"My mother is horrified that someone in our family would date a gangster. She's hoping it's just a fling. But from what Constance told mother, I'm not so sure."

I reached over and touched her leg. "Any chance of you, me and the autopilot getting together for a quick fumble?"

"Is that your best line?" she squawked, giving my hand a shove.

"You'd be amazed how successful the direct approach can be."

Her head wagged. "Not amazed, stunned—that it actually works for you." Then Janine tapped the windshield. "Too late for your idea of a good time, anyway. Those lights ahead mark Dyson Island. Anything serious going on with you in dating arena?"

"I've got you penciled in as a prospect."

"It would be my luck to end up with you," she murmured. With a kick to the pedals, Janine adjusted the Grumman's course. "Gird you loins, Bishop. Trouble is seconds away." She pulled back on the throttles and then nosed the Grumman into a shallow, rumbling descent. "The sea's a bit choppy. Better, tighten your seatbelt." She flicked on the Grumman's landing lights. "There's a floating dock just past the breakwater. I'll make a low pass over that end of the island and come back. My landing lights might spotlight Harris for you. Keep your eyes peeled on the ground."

"That won't make him suspicious?"

"No more than usual."

I took out the Berretta, checked its clip and made sure I had a round in the chamber. Then I set the safety and held it between my legs with both hands. If Harris was there, I would have to make the first round a kill. Anything less and he would return fire with no place for me to duck for cover.

"After I put the Grumman down, I'll make a wide sweep before taxiing up to the float," she instructed. "Sit tight until I tell you it's okay to get out. There are heavy currents surrounding the island. They make docking tough and swimming impossible." Janine managed a grin. "I'll drop you and leave. But I'll be back within twenty minutes. That gun looks older than you, Bishop."

I nodded. "My backup. A very tired Berretta with great jamming potential."

"You keep a gun that jams?" She flipped the lever to lower the Grumman's flaps. "Not only are you a little weird around the edges, Bishop, but you're not the brightest bulb on the Christmas tree. Watch the ground. Here we go."

SIXTEEN

There was no sign of Harris during the flyover. But that could mean he was simply late in arriving.

I waited until Janine gave me the word, then I unbuckled my seatbelt and threw open the plane's door.

Despite the darkness and the rolling waves, I managed to jump off the Grumman onto the dock without landing in the sea or loosing my grip on the Berretta. In so doing, I nearly knocked over a thin Hispanic woman. She quickly scrambled over to the plane while a wiry Latino grabbed onto one of the Grumman's wing-struts, trying to stabilize the flying boat. When the woman got aboard, he released his hold, raced over and jumped inside. I watched Janine and the couple argue for a few seconds. Then the pair headed toward the rear of the plane and the Grumman's engines roared. From the wave Janine gave me, it was apparent that I would have to take care of business on Dyson Island without her help. It was just as well. A woman like her can be a terrible distraction during a crisis.

As the spinning props kicked up a saltwater spray, the Flying Boat moved away from the dock. I retreated to the landside of the float, my eyes locked upon the receding plane as if it were the last chance of finding heaven while baking in the lowest level of Hell. The Grumman thumped across the black waves, its cumbersome airframe silhouetted by the bright moon. As the flaps dropped, it bounced higher and higher until the clumsy aircraft struggled clear of the clawing sea. Then it wobbled toward the stars, its engines droning like off-key singers struggling with a duet.

I glanced around, still expecting the less than amiable Harris. Surprisingly, I appeared to be completely alone. Somewhat confused as to why I would have such an easy arrival, I turned, stepped off the dock and moved across a patch of moonlit-sand and up a sharp incline.

At the top of the grade I came upon a gravel road and a white golf-cart. About a quarter of a mile past it, I could see the lights of a two-story building. I presumed that was the 'Big-House' of Janine's remark. From that same direction a buffeting breeze carried the scent of honey, flowers and the low sounds of sad music. Perhaps the wind had concealed the Grumman's engines from Dyson and company? Or, perhaps, they interpreted the sound as merely a passing aircraft? Or, perhaps, Janine's radio message about my pending arrival had not been brought to Harris' attention?

I tried to picture Jacob Dyson sitting in front of his CD-player listening to the music while weeping for the loss of wife, and son. The image did not play well.

I holstered the Berretta and then lit a cigarette. Why had neither Dyson nor Harris been at the dock when Janine landed? They must have known when she would arrive. Had they been too busy with other things to notice? Like an uncooperative redhead?

I crawled behind the cart's steering wheel and fumbled for the ignition-key. It was in place, so I turned it. Immediately, the red battery indicator lit.

I pressed the cart's accelerator and the electric motor jerked to life. A moment later I had the clumsy vehicle pointed toward the house with the motor humming and the wheels softly crunching on gravel.

There were two options open to me. Play the tough-guy and try to disarm

Harris and Dyson without killing them. I felt there would be little difficulty in persuading Dyson to cooperate. But considering Harris' alleged background, he would likely insist on shooting it out. If Constance Dyson had been abducted, I felt there would be no difficulty in justifying Harris' death. However, if she had come to Dyson Island of her own accord, then I would be considered an intruder and shooting Harris—despite provocation—could be viewed as murder. Alternatively, I could play it by ear until I knew her status, before taking any action with the potential for fatalities. Considering the unreliability of the gun I was carrying, I decided upon the latter.

When I was about thirty yards from the house I stopped the cart, got off, dropped my cigarette to the gravel, and crushed it under a heel. Then, keeping to the grass fringing the narrow roadway to silence my footfalls, I continued my journey with ears cocked and tippy-toes treading.

The music was louder and the scents on the breeze much stronger as I drew nearer the big house. As far as I knew, most flowers folded shut after dark. But that might not be a universal approach to pollination. It also did not mean that bees went beddy-bye when the flowers did. If they did not, would the fuzzy critters notice a newcomer? If so, would they take immediate dislike to P.I. type with a long history of honey-pilfering? I tried to put the images of Terrance and Rothfield out of my mind. But it was no-go.

When I reached the side of the house I crept along its brick exterior to the front. There, I peeked around the corner. The roadway I had followed terminated in a circle of gravel near the entrance. The door to the mansion was wide open. It allowed a rectangle of light to leave a yellow smear on a broad, concrete veranda. Standing at the concrete's edge, casually smoking a cigarette, was a big gray-haired man with a sour face. Even though I had never seen him before, I suspected that he was the inimitable Harris—swallow-tailed tuxedo, and all.

I toyed with the idea of attempting to blindside him. It would require a silent, forty-foot trek followed by some fun in the form of knuckles denting head. As tempting as it sounded, taking a shot at it came with a good chance that I would be spotted. That, in turn, could lead to gunfire unpleasantries. Nevertheless, with Harris out of the way I would only have Dyson to contend with. Well, Dyson plus whomever he'd hired to replace Little—plus the possibility of a scientist or five trying to get in on the action. Not exactly a cakewalk even if I was successful with Harris. But, the sight of the Berretta might be enough to intimidate the others. If so, all I would have to do is locate Constance, determining her desires in terms of staying or going, and waiting for Janine to return—without getting killed.

Of course if Constance Dyson did wish to stay on the island, I might have some apologies to make. But considering the oddball goings-on out here, I did not think Dyson would make too much of my gun-waving or Harris' headache. So with shoulders bunch, fists formed, feet on tippy-toes and eyes locked upon my quarry, I started in the big man's direction.

Despite my stealth and guile, a quick and successful takeover was not to be in my future. I was barely halfway to Harris when he suddenly tossed his cigarette to the breeze, turned and hurried inside, pulling the door closed.

I followed as far as the entrance and tried the doorknob. But it was locked.

I considered picking the lock in order to make a discrete entrance. But I felt there was too much risk in terms of discovery. With Harris inside and armed, it was better to sneak into the house through the back. Once within, I would locate Constance and then proceed as needed.

I turned and quickly headed back to the side of the house. There, I followed the brick wall toward the back.

The entire rear span of the mansion overlooked many moonlit acres of beehives, along with several outbuildings. The mansion's first floor was graced by a single, steel-covered door plus half a dozen windows running across the back. The windows would have been an easy entry except that they were protected against intruders by steel bars. On the second floor, were another half-dozen windows, each paired with a door that opened onto a deck. Because of their elevation, these windows were not girdled by steel.

I decided the door on the main floor offered the simplest access. So I strode over to it and tried the knob. It, however, was locked. Nevertheless, I was not likely to be observed while nefariously unlocking it. So, I dug out my lock-pick kit and selected the appropriate pick and pry tool. Then with the confidence of nearly forty years of experience in the burglar's art—from a criminal investigator's point of view—I squatted down, and set to work.

A few seconds later, the lock gave way. I stowed my burglary kit and then eased the door inward.

It moved merely an inch before stopping.

I peeked between the door and the jamb. Much to my disappointment a span of steel pipe secured the door from within.

I considered trying to unlatch the bar from its position, but I decided that would be too risky. Should I be successful, the bar falling from its supports would create a deafening rattle. This, in turn, would bring Harris running. I shut the door and stepped back to study the situation in greater detail.

Breaking into a home was easy. Doing so without being discovered was hard—possibly fatal—depending upon security, the owner's love of guns, not to mention pets with sharp teeth. In this case, guns were definitely an issue. As for toothy-critters with protective instincts, I was still in the dark—no pun intended.

Theoretically, I could bust my way in through a second floor window without making too much noise. Elbow-taps on glass-panes resulting in falling shards, offered a semi-subtle approach to infiltration. The noise generated would not likely be heard on the main floor. So I would probably get inside unnoticed. However, getting up there to put my elbow to work on a window had its own complexities. There were no ladders conveniently lying about.

This meant the only means at my disposal for reaching one of the overhead decks were hands and feet. It had been a long time since I had tried to scale the side of a house. Even longer since I had attempted to do it sober. I lit a cigarette and weighed options, again.

Considering my age and physical limitations, there was a strong probability that I would not be able to reach any second floor window in absolute silence. In fact, screams of pain and shrieks from falling would likely accompany my not-so subtle efforts. Regardless, that appeared to be my only option—other than facing-down Harris with a gun that was more lethal-looking than deadly.

After a few more minutes of smoking and considering, I came up with a plan. All I had to do was pull myself up the bars on a window directly below a deck. Once perched upon the bars at their highest point like a monkey in a fig tree who could not decide whether to go higher, or take a crap, I would lung upward and grab hold of the deck. Then I would merely have to swing up a leg, loop it over a deck- railing, and drag myself onto the deck. Nothing to it, really. I would just pretend I was Tarzan with eyeballs peeled on a very naked Jane.

I dropped my cigarette to the grass and grabbed bars.

After several failed attempts that conveyed some painful information about falling in the dark after clamoring up steel bars, I managed to lunge with sufficient force and accuracy. Not only did I catch hold of a railing with a leg, with not more than three or four muted wails of agony, I managed to clamor atop the deck. Admittedly, I had not yet breached the building's security. But I was close enough to reward myself with a few moments of breath-catching, hernia assessing and the usual testing for torn ligaments.

Not finding anything amiss, I crawled to my feet and staggered over to the door. I tried the handle. Much to my relief it was not locked. On tiptoes, I crept inside.

The milky moonlight filtering through the window gave me a shadowy view of the room. Its walls and ceiling were lightly colored, possibly in a pastel shade. The furnishings were meager. They amounted to a metal-framed bed, a highboy dresser and a chaise lounge. There were three doors in the room, not counting the one I used to gain entrance.

The door to my left was open, and I could see a bathtub past it. The door directly across from where I stood presumably led to another room or the second floor hallway. Beyond the bed was a sliding version of door-hood which, from its partially opened state, disclosed a closet.

A figure was silhouetted upon the bed. From the span of the hips, I guessed the occupant to be female. This assessment was confirmed when I heard a woman's voice groaning with delight. Whatever dream she was having, it was a good one. Not only did the groan repeat itself, I heard soft giggles as her hips began to undulate in a delightfully familiar rhythm.

Although the odds were against her being Constance Dyson, I tiptoed over to the bed to make certain the object of my search was not the one enjoying herself. Fortunately or unfortunately, depending on ones view of being awakened from a very satisfying dream, the sleeping Madonna was not Constance. She was a brunette with a teddy-bear snuggled to her bosom, her lips encircling one of its ears.

I left the woman to her fantasy and crept across the room. As I carefully opened the door, a flood of light announced that I had gained access to the second-floor hall.

I stepped out smiling and closed the door. I in the house and nobody was the wiser.

I did a quick assessment of the paneled hallway. Twelve doors were paired across from each other along a length of blue carpet. Janine had mentioned that six scientists resided with Jacob Dyson, less George Lipton, the one who had died. That suggested the remaining rooms were for employees and employer, plus a couple extra for securing uncooperative guests. Since I had already been through one of the rooms, there were only eleven more to investigate. By the time Janine returned, I should have accomplished my quest.

I decided the direct approach would be the best course of action. I would knock. If someone answered, I would identify myself as the new security officer. If no one answered, I would pick the lock and make my entrance. That plan had its drawbacks. Particularly, if the person answering the door was Harris or Dyson. Nevertheless, it was safer than a series of lock-picking intrusions.

A radio chirped Latin music from behind the door immediately to my right. Based on the music, I decided that it would be an unlikely harbor for Constance. So I moved past it intending to investigate the others first.

The next door was different from the others. It was equipped with a new handle and an expensive cylinder lock. That was no guaranty, but I suspected the added security indicated that Constance was probably shackled within.

I stopped and softly knocked. When I got no response, I tried the handle.

To my delight it turned.

Quickly, I pushed open the door and stepped into a darkened room. Then I closed the door behind me and held my breath.

For many seconds I waited while my eyes adjusted to the darkness, and I listened for the presence of someone else.

Not hearing anyone, I exhaled and fumbled along the wall for a light-control.

The room seemed to unfold in the glare resulting from the flicked switch, leaving me glancing around a dingy, plasterboard box. The light-source was a plastic-shaded bulb dangling from a chain attached to a ceiling hook. The lamp's wiring draped across the ceiling through eyehooks until it reached a wall. Then, it cascaded down to an electrical outlet. Not classy, but functional.

The furnishings were even less elaborate than the lighting. There was a small table covered by a square of vinyl, a sagging chest of drawers and a bed with tubular-steal headboard. The table's covering had dark crumbs upon it. At first I assumed these were the residues from a toasty snack recently enjoyed by the room's resident. But, then I noticed that some of the crumbs were moving.

The chest of drawers was clearly a hand-me-down item with decades of hard-use. One of the legs was missing. This necessitated leaning the bureau against the wall behind it. The wooden top was decorated by a myriad of cigarette-burns and more crumbs. Some of these, too, were moving. There was also a short-wave radio transceiver there. It was of a make I had not seen before. From the script used to identify the manufacturer, the transceiver was of Russian origin.

A wire stretched from a connection on the back of the radio up through the ceiling. Presumably, that attached to an antenna upon the roof. I went over to the bureau and opened the drawers.

Five minutes of rummaging later, I had examined several laundered shirts, numerous pairs of socks, several changes of underwear, and a cardboard box of business cards bearing the name 'Harris', along with an Austin address. Each item of clothing was American-made. The cards, however, had been printed in China.

After closing the drawers, I left the bureau to its woes and went over to the bed. It was covered with a green, wool blanket. I squatted down and reached beneath its iron frame. After batting my fingers through numerous spider-webs, I caught hold of a suitcase-handle. Seconds later, I had an old leather-number with scuffed corners resting upon the blanket. The case was locked. So I took out my pocketknife. Using the blade as a pry, I popped open the tinny clasps.

Within the case was a smelly tangle of well-used female underwear, beneath which was a disordered collection of Polaroid photographs. The latter were of the pornographic variety. Each of the snapshots strongly suggested that the photographer was in dire need of training. Nevertheless, most were of young women in a variety of naughty poses that tantalized my old eyes. All contained backgrounds suggesting a non-American location. After glomming through the pile, I decided that Harris might have some curious kinks as a collector of soiled panties. But I had to give him credit when it came to positioning the female form. Some of those photos were blood churning.

As I was deciding whether to keep the snap of a blonde with the biggest pair of lungs I had ever seen in my young life, a light breeze blew a cold chill up the back of my neck.

I dropped the snapshot, and quickly turned. The door stood ajar a few inches. Where a hallway light had shined before, there was only eerie blackness. I was no longer the only one who knew about my uninvited presence.

I rushed for the door. But as I reached it a hand came through the aperture, and switched off the light.

I grabbed for the Beretta. But before I could jerk it free, the door burst open and a huge figure lunged in.

I made a wild swing with my left hand and connected with something that felt like leather-covered granite. In response, a fist hit my chin with the force of a cannonball.

My knees buckled and red spots danced in my eyes. That was when a second hand closed on my throat.

I struggled with my fists swinging. But despite numerous knuckle-scraping connections my opponent forced me to the floor.

In choking desperation, I lashed out with my feet.

I caught my attacker somewhere sensitive, because I heard him groan. I took another swing with my fists. Again I connected. But from the tightening grip on my throat I was not making much of an impression.

Again, I kicked. This time, all I caught was air.

A split second later, the cannonball returned. This time, I went out like a candle-flame in a high wind. It was just as well. After my ordeal with barred window and patio deck, I was overdue for a nap.

SEVENTEEN

I regained consciousness sitting in a chair blinking into a pair of blue eyes decorated by caked-on mascara.

Soft leather covered the cushions of chair I was in. In fact, the leather was so compliant that it gripped my fanny with a tenderness I had not experienced since my last wedding-night.

My hands were behind my back. From the smooth, cool feel of what bound them I was wearing handcuffs. My suitcoat was off and my shirt's right sleeve had been torn away.

"He's coming around," the eyes said, in a soft sexy voice.

As she backed away, I got a look at a blonde coiffure, some skin-tight green silkiness that covered a svelte body, and caught the scent of *Soft Shoulders* perfume.

"You must be Denise," I said, groggily.

A moment later, feminine beauty was replaced by male ugliness as Harris crowded in from my left. Up close, his brows looked like gray lichens sprouting from the thick granite of his bruised face. Small eyes, like shiny black beetles, stared out from within the big man's stony features. What had been his nose looked more or less like a red granite outcrop with holes at the bottom. His lips were thick and purplish. His breath smelled of gin.

"What brings you here, Sweets?" Harris's growl had a Slavic ring.

"I'm the bad-news pixie," I told him. Then I jutted my chin toward his clothes. "Last time I saw a butler in a trick-suit like that it was in a movie. The dummy was dangling from a tree-branch while Charlie Chan looked through a telescope. As butlers went, he didn't have the brains God gave baby geese. From what I've heard about you, Harris, you're his twin in every respect."

He glared at me, a smile tugging at the corners of his chiseled mouth. The swallowtail coat was open. His arms seemed to bulge against its sleeves like ferrets trying to get out of a canvas bag. After a moment Harris tilted back and pointed a blunt, nail-chewed finger at me face.

"Cute," he said. "I hope you're this cute when I feed you to the sharks."

From the looks of him, Janine had been right. Harris was about my age but in a lot better shape. However my unique intellect and undaunted perseverance would not let a little thing like being out-muscled intimidate my unmitigated lack of tact.

"Sharks, hell!" I countered. "You wouldn't dare break up our sister-act. Audiences never pay to see the ugly one—the sister without the dowry."

"Cute," Harris said, again, as if he liked the way the word rolled off his tongue.

"Leave Mr. Bishop to me, Harris," another male voice declared. It was high with an almost childish tenor. "Why don't you finish arranging the logistics of our move? Your friends will arrive tomorrow morning to pick up the others. We don't want to delay them unnecessarily."

Harris turned and walked away, giving me a clear view of the room.

It was large and rounded, with a huge bay window at the back. I assumed the glass offered a view of the sea during the daytime. All I saw at the moment was a lot of blackness.

The walls were paneled in dark wood. The floor was hidden under an ugly, brown carpet. The ceiling glittered with embossed copper squares. Lighting was provided by gaudy, copper wall-sconces.

The furnishings were simple. One mahogany desk graced by a personal computer and printer. One credenza topped by a well-stocked liquor tray. One floral couch with cushions slightly disarrayed. Two leather Harvard chairs in front of a smoked-glass desk—one of which I occupied. One blonde with slightly smeared lipstick, mussed coiffure, blue eyes, headlights any Rolls-Royce would envy, and the perfume I had enjoyed earlier. After giving her figure another visual going over, I decided that Denise was the only furnishing worth keeping during the aforementioned move.

A middle-aged, chubby Mediterranean type sat behind the desk. His round head carried a thick growth of shiny black that was combed straight back in pomaded, Nazis fashion. His face was pockmarked. He had small pig-eyes and thick, purplish lips. Gold-rimmed glasses rested on the bridge of a long, drooping nose. He was thumbing through a sheaf of papers, pretending to be engrossed in looking for something. But from the red smear across his mouth, what his mind was really on was a lot farther down, and had probably been inside the blonde.

She sat coyly on the edge of the desk, eyeing me with a mix of surprise and curiosity. A diamond-studded bracelet decorated one of her thin wrists. A diamond pendant winked at me from within the warm nest offered by her ample cleavage. I winked back, in dirty-old-man fashion. The blonde stared demurely.

"Jacob Dyson?" I said, addressing the Mediterranean.

He looked up with a concerned start as if my question was intrusive. Then he spoke in a deferential manner. "I prefer my guests to receive invitations before coming, Mr. Bishop. It saves embarrassing rejections at my end. Unfortunately,..."

"Since I am here," I interjected, "where's Constance?"

Dyson wore a brown tweed sport coat. Between the lapels was a splash of gold silk with buttoned-down collars and a brown tie. He had a heavy gold watch nestled deeply in the black fur of his left wrist. A ruby ring in a gold setting decorated the fat, hairy pinky on his right hand.

"You're not much for foreplay, are you?" he smirked.

"Only because you're not my type," I countered.

The blonde laughed. Then she slid off the desk like a cat leaving a delightfully warm bed. Her eyes locked upon me as she slinked behind Dyson's chair. The diamond pendant seemed to be sending off a Morse-code signal with each of her movements. I assumed it was begging me to save her from Dyson's clutches. But when the blonde draped one arm casually across his drooping shoulders and purred like a Russian Blue in need of caressing, I sensed that I had misinterpreted the diamond's signals.

Dyson patted one of her hands. Then he asked me, "Where's the DVD?"

The blonde gave him a blank look as if being completely unaware of the requested item. Dyson's eyes narrowed as if he expected me to rise from my restraints and commit some form of atrocity.

"Safely back in Austin," I replied. "Get Constance. Then the three of us will fly there, and do a swap."

His hand, resting on the desk-edge closed into a tight fist. "From what I've been told, Mr. Bishop, you're not to be trusted."

"Only with other people's money," I declared.

"Mrs. Dyson is in one of the guest-cottages," intervened the blonde. Her voice oozed a sticky sweetness, amidst its Baltic heritage. "She's quite safe and unharmed. We spoke not many minutes, ago."

"That was completely unnecessary, Denise," the Mediterranean scolded. "Mr. Bishop has no business here. Therefore, he does not deserve an explanation."

"You must be the secretary I've heard so much about," I jabbed at the blonde. I had nothing against her. But I wanted to put the pair of them at odds over me. "From the lipstick on his mouth you must enjoy your job."

She flushed slightly.

"Love the long nails," I continued, sarcastically. "Take much dictation? Because with those ugly hooks you sure as hell can't type."

His face formed a smile but Dyson made no remark.

"I don't like you," Denise sneered. Her red lips twisted into a nasty snarl, looking like fat worms crawling over something rotten.

"I shall grieve over that for the rest of my days," I retorted. Then I returned my attention to her boss. "I don't care what your game is, Dyson. I didn't come here to make trouble. The DVD is of no value to me other than its bargaining power with you. My interest is in Constance. If she came here under her own steam and wishes to remain, so be it. I'll take you to the DVD and we'll part ways. If she didn't, then you and I and Constance will fly to Austin. She'll go her way while I hand the DVD over to you."

He tugged at one ear as if weighing my words. Then he shook his head. "The problem is, Constance must remain with me. To that end, I must have possession of that DVD."

"So you did abduct her?" I said.

He gave an obliging shrug. "One's needs must be met, Mr. Bishop."

"Indeed. The problem you've got is the help that's on its way here."

He laughed. "I doubt very much that anyone will bother to assist you." Then he tilted toward me, curiously. "Have you viewed the DVD, Mr. Bishop?"

I nodded, bluffing. "You should've been an actor, Dyson. Academy Award stuff, all the way."

Jacob Dyson flexed his fingers lightly. His nails were lacquered and short. From where I stood he looked like a man who loved to move his hands, when speaking. The type, who made neatly-planned inconspicuous motions to punctuate the importance of his words. Such pantomimes are always without meaning and done by the brainless. But for his personality type, they represented silent expressions of unchallenged superiority.

"Obviously, you have not seen it," he declared, with obvious satisfaction.

I grimaced. Not only I was still wading with alligators, the content of the DVD was not as previously described.

"Poor Mr. Bishop," snickered Denise. "You don't have a clue, do you?"

Dyson suddenly pressed the heel of on hand against the side of his head as if he was enduring a jarring pain.

"Are you not well, again, Dizey?" she cooed, leaning over Jacob Dyson like a worried mother. "Those nasty migraines."

He patted one of the blonde's paws as his hand fell away from his head. "Not to worry, my precious."

She laughed a little, almost under her breath, as if there was a joke I was missing. His face resumed its expressionless patina, like still water covered by brown pond scum.

"I think Denise has the right opinion of you, Mr. Bishop." Dyson glared at me as if I was a precocious child who had dared to open my mouth in the presence of my betters.

"I'm surprised she's got the brains to think one up," I countered.

Denise stuck her tongue out at me, trying to look contemptuous.

Dyson got to his feet, moving the blonde back with his bulk. Then he waddled around to the front of his desk, eyeing me with sudden interest as if he had seen me somewhere before. Surprisingly, Jacob Dyson stood barely five feet tall.

"The question is what to do with you until our departure?" he mused. "I do so dislike killing. But your reputation suggests that anything less could result in mayhem. You do understand my predicament?"

"You're betwixt a rock and a hard-place," I said, with an unsympathetic nod.

Dyson's eyes flickered in amusement. "Folksy, but accurate."

"Then why risk things getting out of hand?" I urged. "Bring Constance here."

He hesitated for the barest second. "I'm afraid that's out of the question, Mr. Bishop."

"Leave him to me, Dizey," Denise interjected. "I would so enjoy digging my nails into his eyes."

Dyson adjusted his tie. Then he self-consciously fumbled with the pockets in his sportcoat. Afterwards, his fingers dipped into the pockets of his brown slacks. I noticed with some envy that the tan slip-ons hooked to his large feet were new. Their glistening leather glinted like burnished bronze.

"How well do you know Constance?" he asked, cagily.

"Merely chit-chat and overheard conversations," I replied.

"If you have some misdirected idea about being on a hero's crusade to save her, think again. She murdered my wife and my son," Dyson said. "Did you know that? She also killed a man who worked for me—George Lipton. Constance is extremely beautiful, Mr. Bishop. No one can deny that. But she is so very deadly. The least provocation and she will react with a vengeance. The DVD proves her guilt. Should it fall into the hands of the authorities, she will be convicted and put to death. I am offering her life. All she has to do is help me complete my work. Afterward, I'll set her free."

Regardless of my situation, his voice sounded like he was telling the truth. "Risky business, keeping a cold-blooded killer around. Then, you're probably used to that—what with your Chechnyan pals keeping you on a leash."

His high voice edged toward a squeaky snarl. "You have a very irritating manner, Mr. Bishop."

"That's what my mother always said. Have your Chechnyan pals actually paid you in money?" I taunted. "Or was Denise the bait to keep you working?"

She started toward me, her hands forming claws. But he held out an arm to bar her path.

"Even if you are on the straight with the Chechnyans, they won't let you live to tell the tale of your success to the Russians," I warned. "Once the work is done they're going to kill you."

Jacob Dyson pulled an expensive, yellow handkerchief from his breast pocket and mopped at the sweat dotting his forehead. "My arrangement with them is none of your concern."

"Is that where you're moving to? To Chechnya?" I asked.

"Also not your concern," he snorted.

"Once you're there, you'll never be allowed to leave," I said. "A life without Chinese takeaway isn't worth living."

Dyson picked up some papers from his desk with shaking hands. "I'm afraid I have no more time for you, Mr. Bishop." He moved his shoulders as if to loosen the tension between them. "There is too much to do."

"If Janine Kirkland doesn't hear from me by radio within the next hour, she will notify Venezuelan authorities that her sister and I have been abducted by you," I warned. "Regardless of your lease arrangement with them, a small army of heavily armed men will come to investigate."

The papers fluttered back to the desk.

"Do yourself a favor," I suggested. "Get Constance. Then the three of us will settle our differences on the way to Austin."

His hands shook as he touched his slacks. His eyes were now wide and frightened. Then he reached into his suit and took out a small leather case. He opened its zipper and withdrew an old-fashioned, glass syringe. Afterward, he turned to the blonde, his voice suddenly impatient.

"Get the vial and rubber hose from my desk," he ordered. "I think we'd better send Mr. Bishop on a trip."

She went behind the desk and opened the center drawer. After rummaging around for a few seconds she said told him she could not find it.

"It's right there!" he snapped, impatiently.

"Oh, here it is." She came around the desk smiling and holding what looked like an insulin-dispensing vial in one hand and a length of rubber tubing in the other. "Let me do it, Dizey?"

"Tell Harris to contact Janine," ordered Dyson, as he snatched the vial from her hand. "Tell him to get her back at all costs."

"But I want to stick Bishop with the needle, Dizey. You heard how mean he's been to me."

"We don't have time for games, Denise!" he shouted. His cheeks shook like the jowls of a raging hound. "If Janine can't be stopped…"

"But only you can stop her, Dizey," cooed the blonde. "Janine hates Harris. You know that. He'll only make her angry like he always does. You must talk to her. Janine will listen to you, Dizey. She always does."

He filled the syringe from the vial. Then he eyed me for a moment as if, considering her words. Finally, Jacob Dyson nodded his head.

"Perhaps you're right," he muttered, pocketing the vial. "I'd better radio her." He pointed at my bare arm. "Tie the hose just above the elbow. Tightly."

"Then you'll let me stick him, Dizey?" she pleaded.

"Yes, yes, yes," he said impatiently. "But we need to hurry."

Denise adjusted the hem of her short skirt. Then she swayed over and did as instructed. I felt my right hand go numb as the blood flow slowed under the pressure from the stretched rubber.

He handed her the syringe. "All of it, now. And don't worry about hurting him."

She gave me a wink. "I'm going to enjoy hurting him, Dizey."

He watched as she inserted the needle. I winced in pain. I did not relish the idea of that fluid bringing about my death. But trying to keep her from the task would only prolong the inevitable.

"That's it," he said. "Now release the hose. There. Just let it fall to the floor. Very good, Denise. Now, press the syringe slowly. Not too fast. The blood stream must pick up the inflow. Too much pressure will force it back and out the hole made by the needle. That's it. Just so."

There was a burning along my arm the fluid in the syringe entered the vein.

"I'll get Janine on the radio," he remarked. "You keep on with it. Remember. All of it."

Dyson quickly moved off. As the door closed, Denise jerked the needle from my arm. Only a small amount of the fluid in the syringe had been injected. But I could feel a buzzing at the back of my head. Whatever she had pumped into me held extreme power over the human brain.

"Sorry," she said. "You'll drift off for a few hours. But you'll be okay. Just relax."

"What's your game?" I asked. "Russian? With the GRU? Generalnovo Shtaba?"

"He's got you shackled with your own handcuffs," she continued, ignoring my questions. "Do you have another key? Harris took the one he found on your key-ring."

"Tucked behind the lapel of my suitcoat. What did you give me?"

"A small dose of what Jacob's been experimenting with. The amount I injected won't kill you. But I can't promise anything else." She pressed the plunger on the syringe, spraying the remainder of the drug onto the carpeting. Then she set the device on the desk, went across the room and picked up my coat. "Listen carefully. He's moving his operation to Chechnya. The city of Grozny. Dyson purchased a café to front his operation there. It is called the Blue Train—The address is Str. Republicii number 56. Can you still hear me? The city of Grozny. The address is Str. Republicii number 56. He will be taking Mrs. Dyson there."

My eyes began to blur. "Why is he leaving?"

"Harris insisted. Those Portello people. They frightened Harris. He didn't realize until they arrived how vulnerable he was out here. Jacob has no choice but to comply."

"If Harris is a terrorist, Dyson doesn't know half of his problems."

"Harris convinced Jacob they will be answerable to no one in Chechnya."

"That's because Dyson will be dead. Harris killed Wolf?"

She shook her head. "He doesn't know how it happened. Dr. Wolf jumped on the supply plane and got to Austin. Harris and Dyson followed in the helicopter, but they couldn't find him."

"Wolf gone made Constance essential for Dyson's ongoing research?" I asked, my lips growing numb.

"Constance Dyson is his only hope, now. Dyson's collected a great deal of money from the Chechnyans. They are not about to let him live without getting what they paid for."

"You're taking a big chance helping me," I gurgled.

She hurried back to me with the key. "All you have to do is remember the address I told you. Where should I put the key so you can get at it?"

"My back pocket."

"I'll do what I can for your friend until you can get people there," Denise said, as she hurried behind me. She shoved the key into my right rear pocket and then came back to face me. "Mrs. Dyson will be safe as long as she cooperates. Dyson needs her alive and working. I will notify my people once we reach Chechnya. They will come here for you."

"Did Constance do what Dyson claimed?"

"You mean, kill her husband and the others?" She shrugged. "I doubt it. More likely it was Harris or Little."

"Was George Lipton another of your group?"

She nodded. "I was his handler. When George missed his transmissions three days running, I came here pretending to be George's sister. It wasn't hard to convince Dyson to take me on as his secretary."

"I'll bet not. I need to speak with Constance before she's taken away. How do I get to her?"

"That will only complicate matters."

"As may be, but I still have to see her."

"Very well. I'll convince Harris to bring you to her. I will tell him that her watching you die will instill a desire to do as she is expected. He is a sadistic bastard. He will see the pleasure in that. Now close your eyes. Harris will be back any time. Let him drag you wherever he wants. It's important that you convince him you are unconscious. Do you hear me? For both our sakes, he must believe you are unconscious."

My heart began to race. Then it became difficult to breath. "Did Jesus Romero kill Rodney Terrance?" I groaned.

She shrugged. "No. But Jesus contacted Jacob about finding Rodney's body. Jacob told Jesus to clear away any evidence that might point police-investigators here."

"Did Dyson order Albert Rothfield killed?"

Denise shook her head. "Albert worked for Jacob."

"Did Dyson order you to make an appointment with Peterson Barrows to meet Wolf at Ainslie Park?"

"Of course not. Jacob always dealt privately with Mr. Barrows. During those telephone conversation, I was always ordered out of the room."

"Where is Romero?"

She nodded. "He's dead. Harris gunned him down this morning."

"Why? Did Dyson order Harris to do it?"

"I don't think so. Romero and Harris did not get along. I don't think it helped that Jacob was forcing Mrs. Dyson to accompany him to Chechnya. Romero was in love with her."

"Why had Dyson tried to kill Constance?"

"That's ridiculous," she said. "Constance was no threat to Jacob. He is in love with her."

"In love? I thought *you* were his play-toy."

"I am as long as my job requires it," she explained. "But he does not love me. She and Jacob were lovers before I came to the island. Even while she was married to Jacob's son."

"How long is this stuff going to keep me down?" I asked, as the buzzing in my head grew louder.

"I don't know. But you must be silent, now."

"I can't seem to hold on..."

"Hush. I hear Harris coming."

Denise moved over to the desk and picked up the syringe, pretending to admire it closely.

My heart began to race. I closed my eyes and waited for what I was certain would be my end. But a moment later I felt myself disengage from sound, from smells, from feeling.

I opened my eyes. I was floating on my stomach just below the ceiling. Below, I could see my body slumped in the chair. Denise was leaning over me talking, warning me in whispers to go limp, and remain so. I had an urge to reach out and touch her shoulder to let her know I was not there anymore. But I could not float down to her. It was like I was a balloon filled with helium, completely lacking in motion-control.

Then I felt a sudden rush of delight as I realized how free I was. No more pain because of the beatings my body had endured during my life. No more physical limits because of my age. I felt so giddy I let go a laugh. Even when Harris strode into the room I continued my reverie, looking down at him and trying to spit into his hair.

He picked me up like a sack of grain, hefted me over one shoulder and strode out. Denise dropped the syringe back to the desk and followed. I, however, had no interested in where they were going or what they might do to my body. I was free of it with no intention of returning.

I tried to change my position. It took me several tries before I was able to successfully roll over onto my back.

I laughed again. I was like a pup learning new tricks. I reversed my actions and was delighted to find myself once more floating on my belly.

I extended my arms thinking I might soar off like Superman. But the action caused only a slight movement. Then I attempted a breaststroke action. That sent me forward, but only slightly. Then I began to think it, to concentrate on moving. Not just moving itself, but purposely going in a particular direction. Instantly, I was in motion, flying toward the window.

My flight was so abrupt that I was certain my body would shatter the glass.

Instead, I simply passed through it, leaving the glass unscathed and my sense of being unharmed.

For a moment I wondered how that could be? Then I realized that it was the way it only could be. I no longer had a body.

I looked at the moon. Again, there was a rush of movement and I was propelled upward like a rocket.

I looked down. My flight stopped leaving me floating high above the tiny island.

Suddenly I felt a terrible uneasiness. I wanted to run and hide. But I did not see any danger. Still, I sensed it. The terror was overwhelming. I began to fall. It was a slow feathery drop at first. Then it increased in speed like a car going from second gear into high with the accelerator rammed against the floor.

As I fell closer and closer to the ground, a shimmering light exploded in front of me. A split second later it enveloped me. Then there was the feeling of warmth. I closed my eyes and then everything went black.

EIGHTEEN

Deadly Sting

When I awoke, I was lying on a checkered linoleum floor in a room with one door, no furniture and one tiny window. The latter near the ceiling. I could see that the window's glass was gone and there was a large tear in the screen.

My hands were still cuffed behind my back. I was not sure how long I had been unconscious. But from the stiffness in my muscles and the agony in my skull, it had not been long enough.

From somewhere, I heard a buzzing sound. It was as if invisible people were whispering naughty secrets.

"Don't make any quick moves."

The female voice was faintly familiar.

With a groan I started to sit up. Immediately the buzzing became louder.

"Don't move!" she cried.

I dropped my torso back to the floor and strained my eyes to look peripherally. In one corner of the room I spotted the source of the warnings—Constance Dyson. She huddled on the floor like a frightened child; her back against a wall, her knees tucked to her chin, her arms wrapped about her shins.

Constance wore the same clothing as when she visited my flop. But one pocket on her windbreaker had been torn away.

"What gives?" I asked.

"Harris carried you in a few hours ago," she explained. The sunlight, cast through the window, danced her shadow on the wall behind whenever Constance made a movement. "He had the idea we were lovers. He said you'd be dead by sunrise. He told me to enjoy our last hours."

"That man is a real romantic," I muttered, dryly.

"What did he do to you?"

"Him? Just gave me a sore chin. But Denise fixed me up with a dose of Dyson's juice. That sent me on a trip like I'd nothing before. I'm almost sorry I came back. Where is Harris?"

"Probably crating equipment." She took a deep, ragged breath. "Dyson is moving his research location to points east."

"Chechnya, I'm reliably informed. How does he plan to get everything there?"

"A boat is expected today. It will carry the lab-stuff. A plane is supposed to fly the rest of us off the island."

"Where's Dyson?"

Constance made an impatient flick of one hand, sending a shadow dancing. "Probably trying to convince himself that going to Chechnya will be a positive career-move. You're certain that's his plan? Chechnya?"

I nodded. "He's bought a restaurant. When research is slow you'll probably have to wait tables."

"That lying bastard!" she gritted.

"Will the others buy Dyson's song and dance?"

"If they don't, he'll force them to accompany him. Harris will see to that." She fumbled her fingers nervously through her hair, giving the wall more shadow-dancers. "That may already have been done. I heard a plane land about three hours ago. It took off when the sun started to come up."

"That means Harris is gone," I mused. "Dyson's helicopter is a two-seater. So it follows that he intends to extend personal flight-service to you. Congratulations."

Constance hesitated. "I'm sure Harris didn't leave. I heard him yelling about something after the plane took off."

"That boat you're expecting… Will it take the hives to Chechnya?"

With a wag of her head Constance held out her arms as if she was trying to get the resulting shadow to embrace her. "Jacob will refit from local sources."

"Honeybees can be found everywhere?"

"They aren't at the poles," she replied. Her gaze in my direction was uncertain. "But elsewhere you will find one subspecies or another. Have you ever been to Chechnya?"

I gently shook my head. "But from what I've read, don't expect too much in the way of pizza-delivery."

I slowly shifted onto my left side. Again, the buzzing increased in volume. But after a few seconds the sound subsided to a low moan. I moved my shackled wrists so as to shove my fingers into my rear pocket and grope around. When I located the handcuff-key, I extracted it and managed to get the cuffs unlocked.

"When I get my hands on Dyson," I said, slowly easing into a sitting position. "I'm going to bust his head for the buzzing that damn drug keeps setting off in my head."

Constance jutted her chin toward me. "Slowly turn, look behind and up," she advised. "That buzzing is the swarm in the corner of the ceiling."

I did as instructed. What I saw looked like a writhing mass of yellow and black jelly, about six feet square. "What in hell are those bees doing in here?"

"I think Dyson ordered the hives burned." She bit her lower lip. "I've been smelling smoke for the last couple of hours. If so, those twenty or thirty-thousand lovelies are the unhappy survivors of millions."

I shoved cuffs and key into a pocket. Then I twisted slowly back toward her. "Is the door locked?"

Her brows arched in disbelief. "You think I'd be sitting here if it wasn't?"

"If I slide across the floor to where you are, will the bees attack?"

"I can't say with certainty. They're extremely agitated. What have you got in mind?"

"At some point, someone will come for you," I explained. "When that happens, I want to surprise whoever shows up."

Her forehead rippled in doubt. "How do you know it won't be more than one person?"

I scoured an itch on my bristly chin with the palm of one hand. "If that's the case, things will get interesting."

"You think you'll overcome whoever arrives?" she scoffed.

"I've been blessed with massive amounts of blind optimism."

She looked up at the bees for a few seconds and then nodded. "If you're coming this way, take it slow. One wrong move could get us both killed."

I eased onto my belly. Then, using the soles of my shoes and my forearms for traction, I squirmed across the linoleum in her direction.

The buzzing grew louder with each propelling motion. But I remained still in between until the bees fell back to their normal droning.

After what seemed like hours, I was leaning back against the wall between Constance Dyson and the door. My eyes were transfixed by the swarm. It seemed to implode on itself over and over, shimmering from gold to black to gold.

"What are they doing?" I asked.

"Somewhere in that mass is a queen," Constance explained, instructively. "The others are females. They're doing their best to protect the queen as well as provide whatever nourishment she may require. While you were unconscious, the queen convinced them to seek a place for a new hive. A few hundred left to look around. Those remaining will continue their vigil for as long as it takes, or until they die."

"Devoted souls."

"Unquestioningly." Constance reached over and lightly touched my wrist. "She is their Goddess. They serve her and no other."

"My first wife had that opinion of herself. She was very disappointed when it dawned on her that I was not the serving type. Will the bees survive with Dyson gone?"

Her response was flat. "There won't be enough pollen from the flowers on the island to support more than a few. Most of the food for the hives was flown in each week." Her eyes brightened with tears. "In the end, it will be just the Queen. For the first and last time in her life she will be alone. I can only imagine what she will feel, those final hours. I suspect she'll think she was abandoned."

Silence fell between us for many minutes, then. Both of us watching the swarm and its incessant shimmering.

"I remember part of what I experienced on Dyson's drug," I remarked, more to take my mind off the bees than hoping for a response from her. "I don't know whether it was hallucination or real or dream. But it was one hell of a ride."

I glanced over as Constance wiped the wet from the corners of her eyes.

"It was real," she said.

"Then, I understand its value. Wolf must've been a pretty smart guy."

She smirked. "Not half as smart as me. I created what you experienced, not him."

"You invented it?" I asked, unable to conceal my awe.

Constance shrugged. "Only the chemical formulation. The concept of drug-induced out-of-body travel started back in the 1970's. At that time there was a great deal of research done by both the United States, and the former Soviet Union. Currently the military is looking into a variation of the idea, but in a more benign way."

"You mean tax dollars will be spent to see if some joker can leave his body?

How would anybody know, either way?"

She laughed. "A question asked by many a member of the finance committee in decades past. Assuming you survive your present dilemma," Constance said, "next time you're near a computer, search the internet. It was called, *Remote Viewing*. Stanford Research Institute did the initial investigation into its potential. Later on, the task went to several other groups." She paused a moment before saying, "Think about it. Someone sitting safely at home could leave his or her body and travel anywhere, see and hear everything."

I nodded agreeably. "That idea is going to give a couple of women in my building a bad case of worries—once they hear I've done it."

"There would be no need for small countries to spend billions in military research," she continued. "They could simply inject one of their scientists and he or she could surreptitiously gather all that would be needed to keep pace with world-powers."

"Or a terrorist group like Chechnyan Islamists could use the same tactic to destroy established societies."

She gave me a narrow, probing look. "The process is not without its risks."

"What about murder? Could I inject myself, leave my body, kill someone and then return?"

"Theoretically, yes." Constance tilted closer. "But as far as I know it has not been done. What made you consider that?"

"I have perversity of mind."

She pursed her lips in thought, and eased back. "As you must have experienced, anything physical is difficult to control. So your method of killing would have to be subtle."

"This out-of-body stuff," I persisted. "You came to Dyson offering the Internet information?"

Her head shook. "Jacob already had it. In fact, he had revived that study for non-military purposes."

"Industrial spying? Or a casual float through a nudist colony?"

"I see what you mean about your jaded mind."

"Did Dyson have any potential customers for his out-of-body flying?"

"Several." Her voice rose slightly, as though the next words to cross her lips excited Constance. "We thought we would receive billions for it."

"Sounds like you find money very tantalizing."

"Scientists don't drink from gold goblets."

"What led Dyson toward the military end of the business, if there was all that money on the come?"

Constance smirked with one side of her mouth. "The risks to the traveler—the one injected—were far too great for civilian purposes."

"People died, I take it?"

"Several." She scratched her head, and then examined the fingernail. "Several more were left as vegetables until I modified the formulation. Companies frown on that sort of thing in the name of sneaking a peak."

"Only the reputable ones. Oil companies consider death as collateral damage necessary to ensure future profits. How did you get involved with Dyson?"

She gave me a bemused look. "Jacob read a treatise of mine on the uses of bee-venom extracts. He was very impressed."

"Sounds like you've got more than one fun hobby."

"I was teaching at the University of Minnesota at the time," she explained. "I had just completed my doctorate in medicine." A sudden smile lit her face. "That was where I met Phil. Jacob thought an alteration of the chemistry he was currently testing through the addition of one or more venom derivatives might resolve the problems he faced. So Jacob contacted me. We met. When he discovered that Phil and I were dating, Jacob gave me access to what his people had accomplished."

I snapped my fingers. "Just like that you bought into his scheme?"

Constance was silent for a time. "After examining his drug-formula, I told him that a venom derivation would only add to the risks. I did, however suggest that an extract of bee pheromone might be what he was looking for. The difficulty, of course, was in gathering it in sufficient quantities. The solution to that was synthesis. However that, on its own, offered even more complications. But Jacob was interested enough to offer me the job as head-chemist. I took it."

"How did Phil react?"

"By then Phil and I were engaged. So, he was thrilled." Her face underwent a change. Her mouth and jaw went slack. Her eyes became intent as if focused upon something evil creeping out of her memories. "Annie was not happy. Jealous, actually. My moving to Dyson Island meant her giving up the status as resident queen."

"From what I've seen of this rock it's not much of a queendom."

"Dyson Island isn't my idea of heaven, either." Constance fluttered her fingers making more shadow-dances, her eyes going back to the swarm. "But there was my work to consider. And, of course, the money-potential. A few months later, I proved that my pheromone suggestion had been correct."

"How did you test your work? By sending someone on a trip, like the one I took?"

She nodded. "In order to validate the process we needed many trips, taken by many different travelers."

"Which, I assume, is how Romero got in on it?"

Constance Dyson gave me a surprised look. "Yes. He and Rodney rounded up the volunteers."

"All I did was fly around during my out-of-body trip. The people you tested actually rummaged through files or drawers?"

"Something like that," she stated, with obvious reluctance.

"The family-Dyson must've been proud."

Constance went into deep thought, looking down at the floor between her legs. "Annie died shortly after my first real successful test. Phil was devastated. All I felt was relief. Shameful, I know. Unfortunately, a few weeks later, Phil was killed. I suspected Jacob of it and told him so. That's when things started going downhill for me."

"Meaning Dyson had you arrested for embezzlement?"

"Jacob knew damn well I hadn't taken a dime. He was just trying to scare me into keeping my theory about Phil's death quiet."

"Has Harris been on one of these drug-trips?"

She batted the idea away with one hand. "He's too stupid."

"How long after you moved here did Harris show up?"

"He was here when I arrived. Jacob introduced him as CIA." As she looked up, her eyes seemed to blur with the recollection of something or someone fearful. "I suspected Harris of being other than what was claimed. My suspicions were confirmed by one of the men he brought to the island in order to verify our success. The man—who was also introduced as CIA—was sent on a trip. But he had trouble coming out of the travel-state. The euphoria felt by the subject, once released from their physical body, is so fantastic that getting the person back can be a task."

"I can relate to that."

"When I finally got him back into his body, he began to speak in what sounded like Russian. I recorded part of what the man said." Her gaze wandered around the room. "I played it for Phil, who spoke Russian. He was horrified. He confronted Jacob about it. Jacob admitted doing business with the Chechnyans. Jacob claimed he had no choice because the Americans were not interested. When Phil relayed that to me, I went to the Feds. They began an investigation. Almost immediately, Phil was killed. I'm certain that Jacob blamed him and ordered Harris to arrange Phil's death."

"You didn't ask why Dyson would risk a business arrangement with the Chechnyans over a few million? After all if a guy truly has billions, why risk that type of camaraderie?"

Her cheeks pinked. "Annie's estate amounted to merely a few thousand, instead of the billions that I—we all—expected."

"Rumor has it that Phil was to blame for the shortfall."

Her chin dipped slightly, and she moaned, "All that money…"

More bees flew through the tear in the window-screen. They collected on top of the writhing mass of insects.

"The searchers couldn't find a good location so they came back?" I asked.

She spread her hands, her eyes concentrating on the swarm. "Not necessarily. Regardless, they're now making communication. It will take a few seconds for the information to reach the queen. At that point she will make the decision whether to go, or await further reports."

"This is pheromone communication at work?"

"No. Bees dance when relaying location data. The dance done by the searchers will be passed through the swarm to the queen."

I tapped the side of my head. "What's going to happen up her, because of Dyson's juice?"

Constance gave me a long contemplative look. "I wouldn't worry," she declared. "Considering the scars I'm seeing, I think you've done a great deal more damage through your choice of profession."

"Somehow that doesn't relieve my mind." I reached over and tugged her chin until she was looking directly at me. "What's really on the DVD?"

Twin lights of suspicion burned deep in her eyes. "It's as I told you. Jacob killing Annie."

I wagged my head. "I know it exists because Dyson asked if I'd seen it. I made a remark about his acting ability. At that point, he proclaimed that I had not seen it. Therefore he is not on the DVD."

She took a renewed interest in the swarm. "All I can tell you is what Wolf told me." Then she made an impatient face. "How would Dyson know what was on the DVD, anyway? He's never viewed it."

"I suspect Wolf gave him a quick peek."

"Why would Wolf do such a stupid thing? To do so would condemn Wolf to Harris' unpleasantness." She smirked. "Dyson would order Harris to force Wolf to give up the DVD followed by Wolf receiving a quick burial at a sea."

"Not if Dyson wasn't Annie's killer," I casually returned.

Constance made a dismissive movement. "Then it must've been Romero who killed her. He was with Annie just before she died."

"Maybe," I said, noncommittally. "But I don't think Wolf would have risked showing it to Dyson if money was not in the offing. Dyson wouldn't have been interested if the DVD merely linked Romero to Annie's death."

"Of course he would," she declared with irritation, "Jacob would want Annie's killer brought to justice."

"I agree with the substance of your justice-theory. But I don't think Romero was involved." I reached out and touched her chin, again. But Constance jerked away from my hand, resuming her study of the floor. "Wolf wanted out. I think he showed the DVD to Dyson figuring to collect a few bucks in addition to getting free of this rock. I think Dyson liked what he saw and agreed. Only you and Wolf were the brains behind Dyson's project. With Wolf intending to leave, you would've been the logical replacement—assuming Dyson could get you here. That is where the DVD came into play. He waved it and you submitted to his demand."

Her head twisted on her neck toward me, like a gate caught by a high wind. "You think I killed Annie?"

I nodded. "You killed them all. Annie, Phil, George Lipton, Terrance, Rothfield and Wolf."

Her fingers intertwined and then twisted, brutally. "That's ridiculous."

"I'm not saying you did it alone. I think Romero was invaluable to your murderous efforts."

She gave me a crooked smile. "Why would I kill any of them?"

"You killed Annie so Jacob Dyson would inherit. You were, by then, his lover."

She turned away, shivering. "That is disgusting."

"I'm not claiming you enjoyed it. When you realized those billions to be inherited were merely an empty promise, you went into a fury. Jacob Dyson placated your disappointment by telling you about the millions he was to be paid by the Chechnyans. That was a far cry from billions. But you were willing to continue your arrangement with him for a healthy cut of what he collected. That was when Phil got wind of the Chechnyan connection and threatened to go to the Feds. You saw those millions slipping from your grasp. Somehow Phil had to be stopped. That is why you got involved with Romero—not because Phil was having an affair with Janine. You needed Romero to help you get rid of Phil. It was Romero who delivered the hives to Ainslie Park. It was Romero who waited for Phil to arrive at your invitation. You met Phil and daubed him with the pheromone. You made a feeble effort at reconciliation, which you knew he would reject, and then left. As Phil headed back to his car, Romero released the bees. While the those fuzzy girls were busy stinging your husband, Romero set fire to the near-empty hives and drove away."

"I suppose I killed Rodney for mauling me?" she scoffed. "And Albert for being a poor companion?"

I shook my head. "It was the news-article that Rodney Terrance showed you," I explained. "He set it down in front of you at the café. Almost immediately, you became submissive. I couldn't understand its power after reading it. Then I remembered there was more to his interaction with you than just showing the clipping. Terrance leaned down and whispered not-so-sweet nothings in your ear. It was his words that changed your mind. Terrance told you that he knew how you and Romero had killed Phil. Further, that Terrance had a sample of the pheromone so he could prove everything he suspected to the police. At that point, you decided that Terrance had to die. So you agreed to go along, with him. En route to *Rancho Relajar*, you suggested that Terrance pull over. He was probably not very eager. Not after the beating I'd given him. So he refused. That's when you attacked, trying to get your hands on the gun he carried. But even in his debilitated condition, Terrance proved too much for you. I assumed he'd torn your shirt in a fit of passion as I watched you get out of his car. But the tear was actually the result of his defensive efforts."

"If that's true, why did Rodney drive me to *Rancho Relajar*?"

"Because that was where his boss expected Terrance to deliver you. Terrance knew that Romero would not be pleased to hear how he had tried to extort your favors by threat. Particularly, when his coercion included Romero's exposure to the police. Terrance felt he was safe from Romero's retribution by delivering you as agreed. Then he told Romero how you had attacked him en route without provocation. Terrance believed that anything you might say to Romero would be regarded as lies."

"So all by my lonesome I setup poor Rodney for a stinging?" she snorted. "Where did I get the hives? Where did I get the pheromone? I'd just gotten into town."

"You had the pheromone all along. As for the hives, you had already given Romero the task of approaching Dom with the idea of raising bees. Conning Dominic wasn't hard. Once Dom heard that millions could be made, he went running to Sal. After leaving me at *Rancho Relajar*, you made contact with

Romero. You convinced Romero that Terrance was a risk. The next day, you lured Terrance out of his apartment. Romero delivered the hives, cut the hole in the window and daubed on the pheromone. When Terrance returned, the bees were already in his apartment. They attacked him before he could escape."

"Nobody's going to believe you," she sneered.

"You rightfully figured the police would link the hives to Dominic. Since there was a link between he and Terrance, you were confident that Dom's criminal history would make him an easy patsy for Terrance's killing. You did, however, want to keep Phil's death from drawing suspicion. That's why you had Romero tell Dom that the best bees came from Greece. That was just hooey. But the distinctive characteristics of Greek bees, when compared to those that killed your husband, would keep the authorities from linking the deaths."

The muscles in her face began a spasmodic flexing.

"You killed Albert to get even for his betraying you to Jacob Dyson," I continued. "Again, Romero was called in to help. Again, the bees used were Dom's."

"Why would Romero help me? You were at the Hole in One. You saw what I did to him there."

"The hives had been dropped off at the motel earlier that evening. As with Terrance, Romero took care of providing the bees with access to Albert. Then he went to the Hole in One to meet you. The two of you were to celebrate getting rid of Albert. At the Hole in One you encouraged Romero's interest... to begin with. Then you turned on him. That's what got him so mad. You teased Romero into making a fool of himself in front of the whole place. You thought that Salvator Portello would come to your rescue and kill Romero. But that didn't work out quite as you'd hoped. Later, after Albert was dead, you met with Wolf in Ainslie Park. You thought you could scare him into handing over the DVD."

Constance Dyson looked over at me, her irritation growing. "If all you say is true, why would I shoot Wolf without getting my hands on the DVD first?"

"Accidents happen. Ask any music producer. A gun is brought out. A threat is made. The gun goes off. And if you didn't kill Wolf, what makes you so sure he didn't have the DVD?"

She looked away, her jaw muscles going back into flex-mode. "I can prove I didn't do it. My fingerprints aren't on the gun."

"You used latex gloves. I found bits of talcum from the gloves on the gun's clip. You came to me with it, hoping I would do just what I did—help you get rid of it after wiping away any prints you might've left behind."

"Clever, aren't you?"

"Not really. It was Romero who got me thinking about your homicidal leanings when he mentioned George Lipton. Romero suggested that you'd killed Lipton because Lipton had made a pass. I think that was the case. But along with Lipton's sexual interests came the threat of exposure."

Constance gave me an angry glare. "Exposure over what?"

"I think Lipton found the list you'd made as part your plans to kill your husband. Killers who are new at the business do love to make lists lest they overlook something that could reap them a death-sentence."

There was the sound of heavy, hurrying footsteps from beyond the wall behind me.

"It's show-time." I slid up the wall until I was standing erect. Then I sidestepped over next to the door-hinges so I would be shielded by the door as it opened.

A moment later a key grated in the lock. When the door flew wide, Harris strode into the room, gun in hand.

"Harris, he's behind you!" she shouted, in warning.

The big man jerked toward her voice.

I swung, putting all my weight and the strength of my legs behind the blow.

When my fist struck the side of his head, he dropped like a bag of meal. His gun clattered to the floor. But before I could get to it, Constance scrambled over and picked up the weapon.

"You outsmarted yourself, detective," she gloated.

"So it would seem," I muttered.

Harris regained consciousness and started to rise. I jerked the handcuffs from my pocket and threw them into the writhing swarm of bees.

Instantly, the buzzing became deafening as the insects flew from the mass, intent upon attacking. Constance fired the pistol.

The round missed me, and struck Harris in the side.

Before she could shoot again, the bees descended upon us. Constance turned and raced away. I started after her. But, despite his wound, Harris tackled me. The bees flew into the fray, stinging both of us.

I managed to get free of him, batted the attacking creatures from my face and charged the open door. As I passed it, I grabbed the knob and jerked it shut.

A split second later I heard Harris screaming. I quickly twisted the lock to secure the door and his brief future. My neck, face and hands were badly stung. It took several minutes to remove the stingers and their pulsing sacks of yellowish poison. Then I looked around.

The room I was in was furnished with a black, vinyl recliner and a table—upon which rested a portable television set and my Beretta. I hurried over and picked up the pistol, but when I checked its clip, I discovered that the bullets had been removed.

Disappointed, I thrust the pistol into my empty shoulder holster and hurried outside.

The early morning air was cool and crisp. So much so, I could see my own breath. The sun was rising above the ocean's horizon like a ball of fire floating on a pond. I looked around. I could not see Constance.

Thirty or so yards away I noticed a cabin. It looked like a good hiding place for a woman on the run. I headed there as fast as my old legs could carry me. I was not sure how I would confront her considering she was armed and I was not. But I thought that Constance might see reason if her only alternative to cooperating with me was joining Dyson in Chechnya.

When I reached the cabin's front door I tried the knob.

It was locked.

I considered calling to Constance through the door but decided against it. Odds were, she would just shoot through the wood. Instead, I gave it a hard kick.

As the door sprang open, I rushed inside.

From somewhere in the cottage I heard a vague buzzing. I stopped, perked my ears and rubbernecked.

The room was dimmed by the drawn shades across the two front windows. The air smelled faintly of Soft Shoulders perfume. There was a lot of white-painted furniture, including a Murphy bed. The latter was pulled down but the sheets and blanket looked like they had not been used. On the bedside table was a woman's fashion magazine, a plastic ashtray full of cigarette butts, an empty soft-drink bottle, and a glass. To the right of the bed was an armchair. A couple of pillows were in place as extra padding to the backrest. They were crumpled from recent use. Against the wall opposite the bed was a highboy bureau. On its top was an open overnight bag. To my right was a small kitchenette. To my left was a short hallway leading to the bathroom. The door to the latter was open. Beyond it I saw a closed shower curtain.

"Constance?" I said, not raising my voice. "Set down the gun. I'm the only thing between you and spending the rest of your life in Chechnya."

When I got no response, I started down the hall toward the bath. As I drew closer, the buzzing sounds became louder. I crept forward, a vision of the attacking swarm replaying in my head.

At the door to the bathroom I paused. The buzzing was coming from within. Above the shower curtain I saw a small, open window. Dozens of bees were flying out and in. I stepped inside the bathroom and slowly pulled aside the shower curtain. A swarm of bees had gathered against one corner of the tub.

I backed away and quickly returned to the front room. There my eyes focused upon the bed. Near the foot-railing, on the floor, I spotted half a dozen dead bees. A sick feeling suddenly filled my gut. I went over and lifted the bed slightly. More bee corpses came into view. Hundreds of them. I grabbed the bed-rail with both hands and lifted.

It was then that I saw Denise. She was lying on her side. Her long legs were scissored-out as she was running in place. One of her shoes was on. The other was off. Her skirt had hiked up offering a glimpse of garters, nylon tops and white flesh. She wore the same dress I had seen on her during our chat in Dyson's office, but she did not look the same. Instead of blushing skin her face was covered by bee corpses. Her open, staring eyes still had that vacant look. Perhaps even more so, now, because the pupils were blown wide. Denise's mouth was open so far it looked like she was still screaming out her last breath. There were dead bees inside it. Thousands of others clung to her dress, and limbs. In one of her hands was a torn piece of black cloth.

I squatted and took the cloth from her stiff hand. It was a good match to Constance Dyson's windbreaker.

I stuffed it into my suit, stood, and hurried over to the front door. From there, I looked out at the mansion in the distance. Columns of smoke rose from behind it—presumably the result of burning hives. My only hope of getting help to the island was by short-wave radio transceiver. The only one I knew about was in Harris' room.

I set off in that direction wondering how many of Harris' terrorist pals were on the island and what Russian would be for: "My gun just looks unloaded."

When I reached the mansion I hurried directly up the stairs to Harris' room.

The radio was gone, along with his personal items.

I then did a quick search of the place from top to basement, hoping there might be another transceiver. But the house was deserted of occupants as well as communication equipment.

Upon returning to the main floor I heard raised voices coming from outside. A man and a woman were arguing. From the direction of the sound, they were in back of the mansion.

I hurried down the hallway from the foyer toward the rear of the building. At the back door, I stopped and listened.

Constance was doing the shouting. I opened the door, and stepped outside.

She had her back to me. Beyond her, stood Jacob Dyson. He had one hand on the bloody patch of shirt covering his big belly. Constance held a pistol. Its hammer was cocked. Her finger was coiled on the trigger. The barrel was pointed at Dyson.

"I *had* to kill Annie!" Constance screamed. "It was the only way to get the money."

"I didn't want her killed," he croaked.

"Sure you did," she snorted. "You wanted the money as much as me."

She squeezed the trigger twice.

Dyson opened his mouth wide, as if he was going to scream out his last breath. But no sound came. Corrugated lines formed across his forehead. He closed his mouth. The muscles along the line of his jaw dimpled. Then he crumpled to the ground, in silence.

"Are you keeping count?" I asked, moving toward her.

She whirled, pointing the pistol at me. "He was going to kill me."

"With what?" I asked, still moving towards her. "His bad breath? You shot him in cold blood."

"No!" Her voice became dull with the after-boredom of having killed. "It was self-defense."

Constance Dyson was hedging for time. Time to build a rational story filled with rational justifications. Time to dig an escape route from the truth. Time to tunnel deeply to a place where she could bury her murderous shame.

I stopped about ten feet from her and held out my hand. "Give me the gun."

She took a deep breath. "It's just your word against mine."

"You made a mistake turning the bees loose on Denise. She didn't know anything about your involvement in killing Phil. She was doing her best to help you."

Constance lowered his head, taking on the posture of the martyr. "She knew. George told her."

"Stop it."

Constance flared. There were red fiery points in the centers of her eyes. Death-points. "Once *you're* dead there will only be my word."

"You're forgetting the DVD."

She blinked her burning eyes. They seemed to smoke, as if her brains were on fire. Her hand flexed on the pistol as she weighed options.

"Peterson Barrows has it," I told her. "If I don't come back from here, he's going to give it to Austin P.D."

Her face changed like fog caught on a breeze. Then her mug set in a smiling mask. "Then I'll have to kill him before he does." Constance raised the pistol to fire. "But before that…"

"Put the gun down, Constance," a painfully familiar male voice declared.

I glanced over to see Salvator Portello, the Sicilian Brothers and Janine Kirkland approaching.

Constance Dyson dropped the pistol, and ran over to the Mafia Don. "Thank God you're here, Salvator! He shot Jacob. I thought he was going to kill me, too."

The gangster pulled her into his arms. "You have nothing to fear, my darling."

Her shoulders slumped as Constance wrapped her arms about his waist, and clung to him. She hid her face against his chest. "If you still want to marry me, I'm willing," Constance told him.

His hands busied themselves with her back, his eyes upon me. She stood quiescent, keeping her face away from mine. I glanced over at the Sicilian Brothers. They looked on trying to remain unemotional. But I saw Thomaso's face flicker with regret. He knew his boss was cutting a bad deal. But there was nothing he could do about it.

"Of course I want to marry you," Salvator declared, without emotion.

He eased her back as if to let go. But with a small cry, Constance flung her arms about his neck.

He let her have his mouth.

She seemed to devour it. Then with a satisfied sigh, she twisted her head away, and hung limp against him.

"Thomaso and Pietro will take you to the plane," said the gangster, as he eased away from her. "I will deal with Mr. Bishop."

Constance straightened up jerkily and gave me a smug look. Her eyes still burned with a fierce, threatening light. For the first time in my life I felt compassion toward Salvator Portello. He was in love with her. But all she felt was blind arrogance. He was her protector. She would be dutiful as long as that suited her needs. But that was all he would get from Constance Dyson—duty.

She smiled at me, then—a victor's smile. I do not know if Sal saw it, or not. But to me it meant she had other things in the works, bitter vindictive things.

The Sicilian brothers fell in on either side of her. Then Constance moved off, with them trailing. The trio moved in unison like two guards escorting a prisoner to her death-cell.

Salvator watched until they were out of sight. Then he came over to me. "If you think I stopped her out of some wave of moralistic enthusiasm, think again."

"I'd never accuse you of that, Sal," I said.

He came close and thumped my chest. "What you saw here. What you heard here. You forget. Understood?"

"What about Dom?" I asked. "She tried to frame him for two murders. Should he forget, too?"

"You leave my brother to me, Bishop." Then Salvator Portello turned and walked away.

Janine hurried over to me, looking pale. "I thought he was going to kill you."

"Sal doesn't dare," I told her. "Not until he and your sister take their wedding vows. I'm the reason she's willing to marry Sal. He knows that. If I'm dead, she no longer needs him."

"But we all heard what she said." Janine wet her dry lips with the tip of her pink tongue. "We saw her kill Jacob in cold blood."

"Sal would never betray her to the authorities, even if your sister leaves him after they are married. In Sal's line of work, that would be akin to suicide. Constance knows that. You won't talk because she's family. Constance knows that, too. But without Sal lurking in my shadow as her protector, I don't have those limitations. I suspect at some point she will want reassurances from my end—fatal ones. But I'll deal with that when the time comes."

Janine's dark brows formed a dark arch. "You're not going to tell the police about this?"

I shrugged. "Sal meant what he said. Besides, other than Dyson's body, I can't prove any of it. Every authority on bees in the world claims that what your sister did is impossible. As for Dyson, he abducted her. Using deadly force to escape is permitted under those circumstances by every country. Wolf will remain an open issue. But Salvator has the gun. Without the weapon there will be little movement in that investigation."

"What about the DVD that Peterson Barrows has?"

"I suspect that Salvator will quietly retrieve that. In fact, I would not be surprised if he was on the Grumman's radio right now giving instructions along those lines."

"We'd better get going," said Janine quietly. "There was a lot of radio-traffic on the flight here. Sounded like Russians." Then she glanced around. "Anybody else for the flight to Austin?"

I wagged my head. "I went through the house and didn't see anyone. Dyson must've shipped the good guys to Chechnya. That probably didn't do too much for his popularity. But I guess they'll return home once they find out he's dead. Harris had a run-in with a very cranky bunch of bees. That sent him on an earlier flight—to his maker." I reached out and pulled her into my arms. "What prompted you to bring Sal here?"

"I knew damn well you were in over your head," she replied, squeezing me tightly. "I figured he was my best shot at getting some help to save your bacon."

I slid my hand down to her bottom and squeezed. "What about you, me and the autopilot on the way home?"

"With my sister and her gangster pals in the back watching? What kind of sexual pervert do you think I am?"

"I'm getting the feeling you have less sense of adventure than I've been giving you credit for."

"If you don't move your hand you won't have any need for adventure—ever."

NINETEEN

When I entered Peterson Barrows's office the next afternoon, it looked as though elephants had held a sock-hop there. The floor was littered with books, papers, bookends and other items usually associated with shelving. His filing cabinets had been toppled and their drawers pulled out, emptied and crushed. And his wall-safe was open, its door ripped from the hinges. Barrows was there, looking only slightly unruffled by whatever had transpired. He was filling boxes with the contents of his desk, like a man late for everything.

"No time to talk, Bishop," the lawyer declared, as I approached his desk. "That crazy bastard Portello went too far this time. His goons came in and tore this place apart. They held me at gunpoint, for Christ's sake. They threatened to kill me unless I gave them the combination to the safe."

"I take it they got the DVD?" I said.

He stood up and nodded grimly. "As a result, I demanded out of my lease. Portello agreed."

"Lucky you," I said, dryly. "I just came from my bank. The not-so-nice lady who handles my account said you stopped payment on your check for my services."

"You can't expect me to bear the entire loss," he protested, resuming his box-filling efforts. "With the DVD gone, I have nothing further to liquidate on behalf of my deceased client. Therefore his estate is unable to pay me and I am unable to pay you."

I stopped in front of his desk. "As you reminded me during the Wolf fiasco, we have a contract."

The lawyer stopped his packing, stood erect and laughed rudely. "So, sue me." Then he pulled back his lips and talked through his teeth. "The amount you were advanced sufficiently covered your expenses."

I stuck a cigarette in my mouth but did not light it. I was trying to decide if

I should have a smoke prior to or after I punched out his lights. But before I reached a decision, Janine Kirkland waltzed in.

She was wearing white cotton slacks, white open-toed sandals over bare feet, and a white silk blouse. Resting on the bridge of her delicate nose was a pair of white-framed sunglasses with black lenses the size of golf balls. From what I could tell, there was absolutely nothing on her beneath all that white.

I drooled. Janine blew me a kiss and then turned to face Barrows.

"Here's the bill for flying your private flatfoot to Dyson Island and back, Mr. Barrows," she announced, setting a detailed listing on his desk. "I would appreciate payment, now."

I decided to have the cigarette, first. So, I dragged out the Zippo and gave the weed some flame.

Peterson Barrows ground his teeth. "I did not authorize that expenditure, Miss Kirkland." He snapped his eyes shut, popped them back open and then grinned at her. "Therefore you will have to make your demand to Mr. Bishop."

Janine glanced over at me and laughed. It was a nervous ripple of laughter that disclosed her very nervous surprise, and shocked disbelief.

"I'm not joking," he declared.

The tip of her tongue brushed along her lower lip. I returned the lighter to its keep and waited for the forthcoming explosion.

"We had an agreement," she eventually told him. Then she jabbed a thumb at me. "Bishop acted as your agent in engaging my services."

He shook his head. "Not so. Therefore I am under no obligation to pay."

Her shoulders trembled and she bit into her lower lip. I could not tell whether Janine was simply at a loss for words, annoyed to the point of homicide, or just indecisive as to how she was going to kill him.

"He stiffed me, too," I chimed.

Peterson Barrows pointed a finger at me. "Any business arrangement you made with Bishop is his financial responsibility."

Janine glared over at me and then back at him. Her voice raised several notches toward hysteria as she declared, "I'm out nearly two grand in fuel-costs." Breathing heavily because of growing anger she continued with, "Somebody's going to pay, or so help me…"

Barrows coughed, fumbled out a handkerchief, and blew his nose in dramatic, trumpeter style thus interrupting her threat.

"You could sue him," I told her. "I'd be happy to act as a witness in your action."

Janine reached down and picked up a bookend from the floor. She hefted it in one hand as her eyes darted back and forth between me, and the attorney. "I get paid here and now," she vowed, "or I bust heads."

I liked her style. Confronted by two stubborn males who outweighed and outgunned her, Janine Kirkland was ready to do battle for what was rightfully hers.

Barrows pushed his jaw out at her, causing the muscles in his neck to twist into hard lumps. "Tough cheese." Then he pointed to the door, "I suggest that the two of you leave before I telephone the police."

Janine looked over at me. Her eyes had become as hard as flint. I shrugged, gave a wink to Barrows, turned and then left his office.

Out in the hall I could hear Janine renewing her threats and Barrows arguing a faltering case of non-responsibility. As far as I was concerned, suing the bastard would take more time and effort than it was worth to collect the few hundred I was out. So I decided on a slightly different course of reaction, to his crooked behavior. Something that would give me more than my money's worth in terms of retribution, along with a great deal of entertainment. I took out my cell-phone and dialed Salvator Portello.

"Sal? This is Bishop. Wait! Don't hang up. This is about Rita and her problem. Are you in your office at the Hampton Building? Good. Send somebody up to the fourth floor. I've found the man responsible. Yeah. Peterson Barrows. Yeah I'll hold." I heard Salvator's muffled voice screaming orders. Then he came back on the connection demanding to know Barrows's intentions toward Rita. "I was just talking to him about that, Sal. I did my best to get the man to do the right thing. But he flatly refused. Normally I'm against violence in such matters. But after hearing him brag about how Rita had fallen to her knees and begged him to save her family from shame... How he actually got Rita so intoxicated that she could not resist his unwelcome advances..." I let my voice crack as if I were overwhelmed with emotion. "I'm sorry, Sal. I did my best." For the next fifteen seconds I heard Sicilian words that ran the gamut between dip-tank swimming lessons to neutering with a rusty chainsaw. Then he told me to hold Barrows there. I sniffed loudly as if fighting back tears. "No problem, Sal. Barrows isn't going anywhere."

As I rang off, I heard choking sounds coming from Barrows's office. Then I heard Janine vowing to emasculate the lawyer if he didn't cough up some cash. After which, he screamed for help as if she truly had his balls in hand. I put my phone away and rushed back into to his office.

It took me a second to two to locate the pair. Janine had him pinned to the carpet between one filing cabinet and the desk. He was bug-eyed and red-faced, clawing at her hair. She had both hands at his fat throat, and squeezing for all she was worth.

"I'll kill you, you bastard!" she screamed.

As fun as it was to watch, I was concerned that he might just get in a lucky punch. So I ran over and jerked Janine off him.

"Shyster, I'm gonna' shove that desk up your fat ass so far you'll be spitting splinters!" she yelled, and tried to charge past me to get at him.

I gave her a shove, sending her tumbling to the floor as the lawyer crawled to his feet bellowing, "She's an animal. I'll have that woman arrested."

"Not a chance, Barrows," I warned. "I witnessed the whole thing. This poor terrified girl was acting in self-defense against your disgusting sexual advances. If anybody's going to jail, it's you. So I'd come to some arrangement with her, before things get worse."

The lawyer flushed all the way to his scalp. "Why you lousy, no good..." he began.

"Stay out of this Bishop," she yelled, clamoring to her feet. Janine shook a threatening finger in my direction. "Because if he doesn't come across, you'd damn well better!"

I blew Janine a kiss. "I fully intend to."

"I'll have both of you locked up," Barrows bellowed as he staggered back against his desk.

I started to explain the futility of his threat when the office door banged open and the Sicilian Brothers stormed in.

The two thugs rushed past me over to Barrows and each grabbed one of his arms. Then they sprawled the lawyer backside-down, upon the desktop.

"What in hell is this?" squealed Barrows.

"Mr. Salvator sent us," declared Thomaso, the eldest of the brothers. "*Lei ha preso due scelte. Il matrimonio o ho tagliato i suoi testicoli.*"

Barrows looked over at me in terror. "What in hell did he just say?"

"Either you agree to get married or he cuts your balls off," I translated."

"That's what I want to see," cheered Janine. "And I hope they use a rusty knife."

The lawyer started to get purple again. "Marry who, for Christ's sake? One of them? It isn't legal."

"Miss Rita," said Pietro. "As if you didn't know."

"Rita? Rita who? I don't know any Rita," the lawyer bellowed, looking from one angry brother to the other.

"You keep lyin' and I'll cut more off than our balls," growled Pietro.

"Yeah," chimed Thomaso. "We'll fix it so you have to pee like a girl."

"You're both crazy!" cried the lawyer, trying to struggle free. "Bishop for the love of God, help me."

I let go a disappointed sound with my lips. "Sorry, Barrows. But I'm not about to risk my neck—considering you'd never pay the bill for saving your sorry ass."

A fat sneer made deep lines around Pietro's nose, and mouth. He unzipped Barrows pants with one hand while holding the attorney's left arm with the other. Then Thomaso, using his free hand, took out a straight razor and flipped it open with practiced expertise. The sharp blade gleamed like a diamond under the room-lights.

"Dear God," whispered Janine, in horror. "They're actually going to do it?"

"The Sicilian Brothers are known for their dedication to duty and defense of feminine virtue," I told her. "Cover your ears. In about thirty seconds Barrows will be singing soprano."

"I swear on all that's holy, I don't know any Rita!" Barrows screamed, as he renewed his struggles. "Bishop! Don't just stand there!"

"One last time, Shyster," growled Thomaso. "Do you marry, or not?"

I took Janine's arm and escorted her back several paces. "Have you ever eaten Rocky Mountain Oysters? Battered and deep-fried, or sliced and seared in butter? Very tasty."

Deadly Sting

"Help!" shrieked Barrows. "Bishop! Tell these lunatics I don't know any Rita."

"Sure you do, Barrows," I proclaimed. "Rita Portello. Salvator's sister."

"Dear God, no!" Barrows whimpered, suddenly falling limp against the desktop. "They think I impregnated *that* Rita?"

"Any man stupid enough to do that deserves to lose his balls," declared Janine.

"I warned you to stay clear of her, Barrows," I scolded in my best imitation of a sympathetic friend. "But you wouldn't listen. You got Rita drunk and then took advantage of her. After she realized she was pregnant, you refused to her pleas of marriage. It was disgraceful."

"It's a conspiracy!" the lawyer shrieked. Then his eyes widened in terror as Pietro reached into Barrow's pants and grabbed. "No! Wait! Bishop! Look! I'll pay you. I'll pay Janine. Anything your want! Just help me." As Pietro exposed the lawyer's testicles, Barrows screamed, "I'll marry her, for the love of God!"

"He might change his mind, Thomaso," I warned. "Maybe you should remove one just so there's no doubt that you guys mean business?"

"Bishop, you lowlife scum, I'll get you for this!" wailed the lawyer, as he kicked and squirmed.

Pietro released his grip. Then Thomaso jerked the lawyer to his feet.

The younger brother warned Barrows as Thomaso put away the razor, "You change your mind when we get to Sicily and we'll cut off your head."

"Sicily?" Barrows croaked, looking from brother to brother. "What in hell's in Sicily?"

"Rita Portello," I chimed. "You'll love it there, Barrows. Hills. Valleys. Cemeteries. And Sal has a private airstrip so you won't have to deal with customs. And wait until you see his vineyard. The wine is to die for. I think it's because Sal keeps the ground so well-fertilized—with fresh meat."

"This way, shyster." Pietro dragged Barrows toward the office door.

The lawyer gave me a terrified look, as he stumbled past. "What if Rita won't marry me?"

I made the sign of the cross.

Barrows's knees buckled as he nearly fainted.

The Sicilian Brothers wrested him back upright and dragged the semi-conscious man out into the hall.

"Can you believe it? Getting a gangster's sister pregnant and then refusing to marry her?" Janine chuckled. "You'd think a lawyer like Barrows would have more sense."

I jabbed a thumb toward the door. "Barrows didn't get Rita pregnant."

Janine gave me a confused, blinking stare. "Rita lied to her brother about Barrows being the father?"

As the lawyer's staggering footfalls faded down the hallway his whimpering voice echoed, "Rita Portello doesn't look like either of you guys, does she? Not that it matters. I'm just not too keen on a mono-brow."

"Of course not," I told Janine. "I doubt that Rita's ever met Barrows."

"Then how did Salvator get the idea that Barrows got Rita pregnant?"

I tapped the center of my chest. "I told him Barrows was responsible."

Janine gaped.

"There's no way we'll collect from him," I explained. "So, I figure the guy deserves whatever trouble I can make."

"But if her brother intends to force Rita into a marriage with that—that louse…" she began, leaning forward with earnest. "Do you hate Rita Portello that much?"

"It won't come to that."

She hesitated before asking, "So what you're saying is, Rita isn't really pregnant?"

"According to Salvator, Rita is definitely pregnant," I said. "Both Rita and Momma know who the father is. But neither are talking."

"So Rita doesn't want to get married?" Janine asked, smiling faintly in confusion.

"No," I replied authoritatively, "trying to get married has been a tradition with Rita pretty much since she was old enough to notice boys. Unfortunately, Rita hasn't had any willing takers. There have been a few reluctant acceptors who made a run for it at the eleventh hour. Some are still alive." I stretched with pride. "The trouble is she's in love with me."

One hand went to her mouth as Janine burst into laughter. "You've got to be kidding!"

"What's wrong with me? I'll have you know that Rita's asked me to marry her half a dozen times—maybe, more."

Her hands went akimbo at her hips. "And you turned her down? Just how ugly is this woman, Bishop?"

"Rita's absolutely beautiful. Wait until you see her at Salvator and your sister's wedding."

Janine frowned. "Then why did you turn her down?"

"Because marriage inevitably ruins any good relationship. Rita and I have this terrific understanding. We get together every so often and ring each other's chimes."

Janine touched the side of her face, as if she'd been slapped by the words. "No offense, Bishop. But you've got more miles on you than a Gypsy cab. At your time of life you should grab any offer made."

I shook my head. "Marriage is just a bad joke."

Janine snorted, "Speaking of jokes… That one on Barrows is going to haunt you." One hand flitted through the air in the direction of the door. "What's going to happen when those goons drag Barrows in front of Rita? Huh? And she says she doesn't know him? Did you think of that?"

"Stop worrying," I told her. "I'll get a phone call from Rita that will start with, 'Bishop, you bastard.' After which, Rita will make a lot of vile threats in several languages about my prank. When she gets tired of that she'll hang up and start in on Sal for believing me about Barrows."

"And you don't think that will send Salvator back to you?"

"Why should it?" I said. "Sal will assume that Rita's lying. He'll view it as her effort to protect Barrows from family-retribution."

"But over there a forced marriage is possible, isn't it?"

I nodded. "But it won't happen. Should Sal press the issue, Rita will simply call-in Momma Portello. Momma will tell Salvator to back off—or else."

"That gangster's afraid of his mother?" she scoffed.

"Nobody messes with Momma Portello."

"But what happens to Barrows when Rita won't marry him?"

"Sal will either butcher the bastard and bury him in Sicily, or send Barrows home. Personally, I don't have a preference."

"I don't like the Barrows," she declared. "But I don't want him killed or—or altered."

"My assessment of you is dropping as we speak."

"When was the last time you and Rita rang chimes?" she asked.

"Why?"

"Is there a chance that Rita is pregnant by you?"

"Of course not. I mean at my age... What with my high cholesterol... And there's my bad back... Not to mention my trick knee... What makes you ask a fool question like that?"

"In your own words, she loves you. So who better than you to father her child?"

I felt the color drain from my cheeks. "Janine, I know Rita like a book. She wouldn't get pregnant unless it was something she wanted. Further, she sure as hell wouldn't do such a thing without consulting me."

"How old is Rita?"

"Forties. Why?"

"Ah. That means Rita's clock is about to run down."

"Come, again?"

"At her point in life Rita might be desperate enough to get pregnant without consultation. Especially, if she's been under a great deal of pressure. Like from her mother. Wasn't she expected to marry?"

I swallowed thickly as Rita's words about Momma wanting a grandchild echoed between my ears.

"You look a little green around the gills, Bishop. Worried about possible parenthood?"

"What say you and me go play with my jewelry collection?" I said, changing the subject. "Have you ever worn nothing but fine gold and exquisite gems? All you have to do is lay back on the bed. I'll do all the decorating. I'm told the bundle is worth half a million."

"Where in hell would you get half a million worth of..." Janine Kirkland's jaw dropped with a jerk. Then she gave me a light tap on the cheek. "You stole back Annie's jewelry from Romero, didn't you?"

"Of course not," I said, heading for the door. "Those tidbits are a bequest from a maiden aunt who adored me."

Janine's head wagged fervently as she blocked my path. "Constance sent

Salvator to Romero's apartment looking for those jewels. When Salvator came back empty-handed, my sister nearly blew a gasket."

"You mean the wedding's off?"

"Nope." She leaned toward me. "But you can bet Constance will nag Salvator to the grave about those trinkets."

I smiled. "That's something to look forward to. Him in a grave."

Her face closed up on me. Then she demanded, "Where are they, Bishop?"

"Not that I'm admitting anything, but…"

"I want half."

"A third."

She gave me a hard jab in the chest with a forefinger. "Half. Otherwise, I'll point my soon-to-be brother-in-law in your direction over the jewelry and Barrows."

"I'm thinking about dropping my playtime offer due to your greedy lack of cooperation," I warned.

Her chin lurched toward me as if her neck had been jerked by a rope. She narrowed her eyes. They watched me with a greedy kind of guile. "Do we deal?" She thumped my chest, again. "Or do you join Barrows under a grapevine, in Sicily?"

"How do you know those jewels *are* real?" I protested. "They could be fakes. Junk that Phil Dyson had made as he disposed of his mother's goodies trying to recoup all those stock-losses?"

Janine's dark eyes looked into mine from under a corrugated forehead as she said, "Why don't you and me go to where you've got them and I'll find out?"

I pulled her into my arms. "They're at my office." I kissed her mouth lightly. "While we're there, I'll show you my etching."

"Etching?" Her face flushed with amusement. "You have one lousy etching?"

"Actually, I don't have any. But I do have a pair of handcuffs once owned by Houdini." I let one hand slip down her back.

She grabbed my wandering mitt and nudged me toward the door. "I'm very fond of old handcuffs."

"How about old detectives who like to play with them?"

She winked at me. "Only if his jewels aren't disappointing."

"I'm not sure how to take that."

"Don't worry, Bishop. I'll show you."

The End

www.ingramcontent.com/pod-product-compliance
Lightning Source LLC
Chambersburg PA
CBHW060116260626
47160CB00005B/1904

* 9 7 8 1 6 0 2 1 5 1 0 0 0 *